THE CAVE OF
THE DARK MOON

Other Books in the
Dark Moon Trilogy:

The Iron Labyrinth

THE CAVE OF
THE DARK MOON

Merrilee Beckman

*To my husband, Robert,
for your constant support of this book.
And to my daughter, Mari,
for your steadfast editing and
deep insight into every chapter.*

My intention is to tell
of bodies changed
to different forms.

The heavens and all below them,
Earth and her creatures,
All change,
And we, part of creation,
Also must suffer change.

—OVID, *The Metamorphoses*

CHAPTER ONE

Colum gripped the hilt of his sword hard enough to turn his knuckles white as he swung his broadsword violently at Sig-noff, striking right, then left. It was an unnerving sensation to handle a double-edged sword after being away for so long. He hadn't lost his effortless reflexes, but living on the surface of the world had weakened his body. Sig-noff sliced through Colum's chainmail into his left bicep, deep enough to draw blood but not cause serious injury.

"Keep your guard up, Colum!" yelled their instructor, watching from the side.

Another flurry of clashing swords, the sound swelling into a percussive cacophony. Colum lunged close enough to nick his opponent's ribs, then sprang back. For a few half-frozen heartbeats, the men clanged back and forth, each searching for an opening. Lurching forward, Sig-noff crashed his sword down on Colum's helmet. Colum staggered backward, blood running from his nose. He managed to keep a grip on his sword but was barely able to deflect Sig-noff's next blow. Sig-noff slashed across the supple mesh mail on Colum's chest. Colum lifted his sword halfway up, attempting a last uncontrolled swing, but the effort was too much. He swayed sideways and fell. His sword clattered on the floor.

"This match is over!" declared Sendai, their instructor.

Sig-noff slid his sweaty fingers over the pommel of his sword. "Good fight," he said in a hoarse, rasping voice.

The taste of blood and sweat mingled in Colum's mouth as he staggered out of the training room and into a blue-lit corridor. The corridor was part of a twisting, forking maze of other hallways that formed an iron labyrinth deep underground. Unlit by sunlight or electricity, the labyrinth was illuminated by a blue light, the origin of which was a mystery. Colum had arrived here years ago along with 111 other men, brought as slaves by an omnipotent king known only as "Uncle." His life in the labyrinth was fractured when, in a rage, he broke Uncle's back. As a result, he found himself returned to the Earth's surface with his memories of the labyrinth erased. Now he was back, having been given a rare second chance to finish his training and become the person Uncle intended him to be.

Now he walked exhausted through the iron corridors to a room with a row of showers. After washing off, he picked up a pot of gruel from the "kitchen" and hauled it to his small iron cell.

At last he sat down, famished. As he was about to eat the gruel in front of him, the cell door grated open. A large man with ebony skin and amber eyes stooped slightly to get through, an iron pot of gruel identical to Colum's dangling from his hands.

When the man saw Colum, the heavy pot clanged down on the floor as he flung out his arms. "Colum!" he bellowed.

"Bambara!" Colum jumped up to embrace his cellmate.

"I can't believe you're here! None of us ever thought we'd see you again!" Bambara frowned down at his gruel. "You must have had some fine food while you were gone. Now you're back to eating this *offal*." Bambara squatted, scooped a spoonful of steaming gruel into his mouth, and swallowed with a grimace. "Welcome to another meal of horse hoof porridge," he said.

Then he rubbed his eyes with the heels of his hands. "I still can't believe I'm looking at you."

Colum laughed. "Neither can I."

Both men dove into the disgusting gruel, eating it as fast as possible. Then they nudged their pots away and leaned back against the iron wall. Filaments of blue dust drifted in the air.

"How long were you gone?" Bambara asked with a belch.

"A full year. What happened after I left, Bambara? Sig-noff and I fought with the broadsword just now, and it seems like his skills have gotten much better."

Bambara guffawed. "It doesn't take a lot of technique to cut a man's head off with a broadsword. But it's true, Uncle has been driving us harder than ever. Even the instructors are learning new striking techniques in karate."

"What kind of techniques?"

"How to work with pressure points and nerves. You thought the adrenaline surged in you before? All I can say is, be careful in your next session. Not only are the men better at karate; they've become more unflinching all around."

Colum regarded his cellmate. Bambara had been a mercenary fighter on his home planet, Illinee, before coming to the labyrinth. "I can't imagine you ever flinching in battle, Bambara."

The warrior's amber eyes glittered. "Quite the opposite. I inspired terror. Uncle told me once it's not my expertise he wants me to impart, it's my ferocity. But the only way I can teach ferocity is by example. And I'd hate to think of all the men the blue light would have to resurrect then."

"I'm glad we're on the same side, my friend," said Colum.

Bambara filled his cup with water from a spigot on the wall. "I wish to salute you, Colum! I heard about the savage beating you took for breaking Uncle's back." He held the cup up to his cellmate and drank. "I'll never understand why you returned when you were free. Not even I possess that kind of ferocity."

Colum looked at his cellmate. "You seem bothered by something, Bambara."

The large man nodded, drenched in the blue light of Uncle's

kingdom. "It's a dream I keep having." The big man lowered his voice. "I'm standing in front of an open door. Beyond the door looms dark, empty space. It feels like the innermost marrow of something."

"What kind of 'something'?"

"I have no idea, except that in my dream, it draws me to it like a powerful magnet. I want to slam the door shut." His eyes locked on Colum's. "*But I can't.*"

Colum blanched. "I had a similar dream."

Bambara raised an eyebrow. "Don't tease me, Colum."

"I'm not! In my dream, I was going down a spiraling staircase. Below was a dense darkness that held something menacing . . . menacing yet *vital.*"

"To me, our dreams are like a lodestone, Colum, pulling us toward what lies in the darkness," said Bambara solemnly.

"You're right. It carries a certain . . ." Colum began to pace their small cell, searching for the right word. ". . . *necessity.*"

"That you had a similar dream must be why I told you mine." The seasoned warrior shivered. "Before I came here, I had another dream. In it I roll a sheet of golden sunlight into a ball. I remember wondering why I can stare at the light and not go blind. I told the dream to an elder who has known me since childhood. He cried when he heard it. I'd never seen him cry before. The elder told me it was my destiny to roll the sheet of gold into a ball. He said I didn't go blind because I'm part of the light." Bambara paused. "Soon after, he told me I was being sent to Uncle *because of my dream.*"

"Do you think your people sent you to Uncle because the darkness of the labyrinth is lit with a blue light?"

"You mean because there's no sun here?"

"Yes, exactly. Maybe they did it for your own good, thinking you'd be safe here." Colum looked solemnly at his cellmate. "Have you told Uncle your dreams?"

An artery pulsed at Bambara's temple. "No, have you?"

"Since Uncle has never shown any interest in our dreams, it didn't occur to me."

Colum entered a training room. He needed someone to challenge to a karate match and soon caught sight of Simt. The man had been a classics professor in his former life and wore a pair of iron-rimmed glasses, which set him apart from everyone else in the labyrinth. The blue light had healed the other men. It had healed Simt, too, except for his faulty vision.

"Colum, I'm so glad to see you!" exclaimed Simt. "I've missed you."

"And I have missed you, professor!"

The two men embraced, then sat together on a bench.

Simt clapped Colum on the shoulder. "Do you remember the karate moves?" asked the professor. "It's been a long time."

"I'm about to find out." Colum smiled at the professor. "You're looking fit, Simt." In the early days of their servitude, the bookish professor had been wary of physical contact and injury. Now he possessed a body corded with muscle and an aura that radiated power.

The two men watched a sweating pair of Uncle's slaves on a nearby mat punching, kicking, and blocking one another. To Colum, they seemed an equal match.

"I can't believe how much everyone has improved since I've been gone," he said with a sigh.

"Uncle is upping the ante for our training. The time when we'll be sent out on missions is getting closer." Simt looked away from the mat at Colum. "Why did you risk Uncle's wrath to come back here?"

"I felt adrift in London."

"Adrift?"

"Untethered from my real purpose." Colum laughed. "The truth is, Simt, I missed all of you."

Simt laughed with him, then resettled the wire frame of his glasses on his ears. "I wonder how I'd feel if I were suddenly back in England as the person I am now."

"And who is that, Simt?"

"Someone who has been pulled into the depths and no longer looks for superficial answers. Someone who can endure the grueling labor, the sword fights and karate matches, the nauseating gruel, and most of all the intensity of our audiences with Uncle. Someone who no longer lives on the surface of himself. Someone no longer afraid of the darkness."

Simt's last answer gave Colum a chill. "You've certainly been purified and transformed in Uncle's furnaces, my friend. It sounds to me you're ready for the king's missions."

CHAPTER TWO

A cascade of cold water engulfed Colum, jolting him out of the fatigue he felt from his last work shift. He stepped from the shower, grabbed a clean shirt and pants from a pile of grey woolen clothes, and pulled them on. He walked to the "kitchen" next door, where he picked up a pot of warm gruel, and from there he returned with it to his cell.

Belly full, Colum fell asleep on his straw pallet to dream of a tawny lion loping toward him across a yellow savanna. The feline stopped in front of him and spoke. *"Soon you will be given a new way of seeing."*

He awoke to find Bambara watching him. "Were you dreaming?" asked the warrior.

"I was."

"The people in my village believe that dreams, if they're powerful enough, can spill over into our lives out here," said Bambara. "When the elders told my mother I was being sent away because of my dream, she threw her arms around me and cried and cried. But finally, she kissed me and turned away." His voice thickened. "After that, the elders, too, turned away. My name will never be spoken again. My glory as a warrior never sung. Because of my dream, I am dead to them now."

"Every man in the labyrinth is dead to those who once knew and loved us."

"No, Colum. Your people remember you. They mourn your loss and continue to speak of you. I am too dangerous to remember."

"Too dangerous? But why?"

"My people fear I am a portal for the darkness in my dream." He sighed. "A warrior is always ready to face death, but this is different. Dying in battle is not like being sucked into a black void and forgotten by everyone."

Colum picked out a bow and some arrows in an exercise room. He took aim at a target on the far wall, thinking of his conversation with Bambara.

Is the darkness Bambara and I saw in our dreams real?
Zoom. Whack. Bull's-eye.
Can Uncle help us? Does his power extend to our dreams?
Zoom. Clatter. Miss.
Is what lurks in the darkness beyond Uncle's control?
He was about to release another arrow when Rast, a younger slave, came running in his direction.

"Colum, come quick! It's Bambara!" cried Rast.

Colum sprinted down the corridor after him.

They turned into another practice room where Bambara, his face a livid purple, was holding the slave Gish by his heels and spinning him around. Blood spurted from Gish's sword arm to spray across the room. Bambara's deadly speed, maintained with an iron steadiness, had turned Gish into a blur. If he let him go now, the man's head would squash against the wall like a gourd.

"Bambara, slow down!" shouted Colum. "*Slow down! NOW!*"

Bambara seemed to recognize his cellmate's voice. With a full-body shudder, he lessened his speed. The whirl of Gish's circling body slowed. Finally, Bambara released the man's feet, sending Gish skidding across the floor. When his head hit the wall with a thud, two men quickly ran over to lift him up and carry him away.

Uncle's chief guard, Hugo, over seven feet tall, strode through the doorway. Bambara swayed and nearly fell, but Hugo caught him and held him steady.

"Can you hear me?" asked Hugo, but there was no response. "Colum, take him to Uncle."

Colum placed an arm around a limp and dizzy Bambara and slowly led him through the iron corridors. When they entered the oldest part of the labyrinth, the one that surrounded Uncle's throne room, the passageways began to broaden and the ceilings sloped higher. At last the two men came to a place filled with a billowing mist. There was nothing below their feet here, yet some unknown force kept them from falling. They traversed the mist with light steps and soon arrived at an arched entranceway. On the other side of it lay an iron room filled with iron benches. This was where Uncle's slaves waited for audiences with their master.

"Bambara! Colum! You may enter now!" called Meath, the man standing guard at the door to the king's chamber.

The two slaves walked past several other men waiting on iron benches.

Uncle's throne room was made out of rock, not iron, and formed the center of the labyrinth. The king's large, muscular body rested on a straight-backed iron chair. He dressed in the same grey wool outfit as his slaves, but instead of bare feet, he wore sandals. Colum and Bambara knelt on cold flagstones in front of their king. Colum noticed Hugo enter after them to stand quietly behind the king's throne.

The king stared at Bambara. "You attacked Gish. Why?"

Bambara's jaw hardened slightly. "He provoked me, Master."

"And just how did he do that?"

"He turned his back on me while I was giving him instructions."

"For that you disobey your king's orders?"

"You wouldn't like it if I turned my back on *you*, Master," said Bambara in a defiant tone.

It was an audacious reply. Uncle closed his eyes silently. Colum knew from experience that the king was penetrating Bambara's mind, seeking out his slave's most vulnerable thoughts and memories.

Finally, the king's eyes reopened. "There is a darkness within you that is not yours. It seems I was *deceived* about why you were sent here." Uncle leaned back in his iron chair with a measured breath to stare at his warrior-slave. "What do you think lurks behind the door in your dream?"

Bambara's eyes smarted. "A *presence*, Master."

"Go on."

"I felt it might grab me and yank me through the door, and I'd disappear forever." Bambara's forehead furrowed. "Only it couldn't locate me. Not *exactly*."

Colum thought he saw Uncle tremble.

"It will though," the king announced, "and when it does, you can't be here."

Bambara shuddered. "What are you saying, Master? This labyrinth is my only protection. The blue light holds the darkness at bay. That's why my people sent me to you."

"Not even the blue light can keep *that* darkness out."

"I don't understand, Master. Nothing enters the labyrinth without your consent. You hold all the power here."

"I'm sorry, Bambara, but you must leave."

"And go where, Master?" asked the tall, ebony man, his voice quaking.

"Through the door in your dream."

Bambara recoiled. "*I cannot!*"

"The presence behind the door searches for you even now." The king's voice held deep sympathy. "You, of all people, know what absolute courage and absolute sacrifice are. To do this is your duty as a great warrior."

Bambara looked shaken to his marrow. "Am I nothing to you?" He sprang to his feet, his face flushed with heat. "I won't be sacrificed. *Not this way!*"

"You are far from nothing to me, Bambara," replied the king. "This is your destiny. Your greatest feat as a warrior will be to make that sacrifice. You will burn like a star dispelling the darkness!"

The ebony man's throat clenched so hard he could barely answer. "I *won't* go through that door, Master."

"There is no blame in that," said Uncle in a kind voice.

Bambara looked relieved.

"Yet, willing or not, *go through it you must.*" Before Bambara could protest, Uncle froze him with a single glance. "*BEETLE!*" boomed the king's voice, sending shock waves throughout the labyrinth.

Bambara let out an earsplitting cry, his eyes rolling back in his head. He flickered briefly in and out of visibility . . . then vanished.

His disappearance was so intense it seemed to suck the air out of the room. Throughout the labyrinth, iron floors vibrated in swelling, rippling waves. Men lost their footing. Work on shifts and matches in the exercise rooms ceased. The blue light dimmed, went out momentarily, then slowly returned, as if the labyrinth's natural order had been disturbed. The hearts of everyone in the kingdom beat dangerously fast.

Colum stared open-mouthed at the king. Had Uncle really thrown his friend into the horror of his dream's darkness? "Where is he?" he asked.

"With the Beetle . . . in the Void," replied Uncle. His voice was flat, as if all his energy were spent.

Colum felt an existential dread. "Beetle? What in God's name is that?"

Uncle stood and placed his hand on Colum's forehead. Immediately, Colum found himself approaching a space that was the negation of all color and form. Slowly, a luminous, oval-shaped form appeared in the space. On its head, a pair of slender, sensory tendrils waved back and forth and sideways. The sensitive, coiling, ever-reaching tendrils glowed with light. Under them, two eyes flamed with an alien splendor. Uncle's hand jolted away from Colum's head as if it might be burned, and the scene vanished.

"The presence behind the door!" gasped Colum.

"One powerful enough to birth new worlds."

Colum swallowed, his mouth too dry to speak. "Then you should know, Master, that I had a dream, too."

Uncle looked rattled and closed his eyes. After a long silence, he reopened them. "How did I miss these dreams? Did someone in the cave mask them from me?" The king returned his attention to Colum. "There is no door in your dream. No presence. Only a darkness you have not yet reached."

"Does that mean you're *not* sending me to the Beetle, Master?"

"I forged you to be my column. The last thing I want to do is put that column in jeopardy." He paused. "But then, you're already moving toward the darkness. Perhaps the labyrinth was never your destiny."

"Bloody hell, Master, you can read our minds, paralyze our bodies, and erase our memories. There must be some way you can stop a dream from coming true!"

"It would be a great calamity to lose you, Colum, but the universe is deep, and this labyrinth teeters on a shaky platform over it." He stared deeply into Colum's eyes. "My duty is first and foremost to the labyrinth, a duty inscribed in iron."

"Lose me, Master?" It felt to him as if a cataclysm were approaching. "You're not going to exile me again, are you?"

"I thought I was the one drawing you back from London." The king sighed deeply. "But now I wonder if it was the Beetle who drew you back, and not me at all."

At that moment, Dervor stepped into the throne room. She was the only woman in Uncle's realm of iron, and Colum was deeply in love with her. To be with Dervor again was the reason he decided to return to servitude in the labyrinth. "You summoned me, Master?"

"Yes. Stand over there by Colum."

She walked swiftly to Colum's side, fear in her eyes.

"Do you know what just happened?" asked Uncle.

"I felt the kingdom shake," she said. "We all did."

"I spoke the *word* and sent Bambara to the Beetle."

Dervor blanched.

Colum thought of the creature creeping up on his friend. "Can you bring him back, Master?" he asked.

Uncle's voice deepened. "Once the *word* is spoken, it cannot be unspoken."

"And what will happen if the Beetle finds him?"

"It will use Bambara as fuel because his warrior spirit is fierce, fiery, and strong. It would spit out lesser men." The king sat back down. "The Beetle dwells in the immense, mysterious underbelly of *everything*. When an old world is about to end, the Beetle stirs into action to launch a new one. For that, its fire must reach nuclear critical mass."

"It wants me for fuel too, doesn't it?" said Colum, fear in his voice.

"*I don't know!*" The king pounded his fists on the arms of the iron chair in a rare expression of anger. "Your dream wasn't as specific as Bambara's. But such a spiraling staircase does exist at the edge of this labyrinth."

"Where does it lead, Master?"

"To the cave beneath us."

"The one Sny came from? That wild, half-human creature who crawled around in my brain and drove me mad?"

Uncle nodded. "You must seek help from Lillake, Queen of the Cave. She has knowledge and powers I don't possess, as well as access to the abyss where the Beetle dwells."

Colum fought off a fresh surge of panic. "But that will bring me closer to the creature, Master!"

"I'm sorry. We're out of options. The Beetle won't be able to detect you in Lillake's cave, but you'll have to convince her to help you. Only be careful. The presence of a man is likely to shake her women up like hornets in a nest." Uncle frowned. "Which is why I'm sending Dervor with you. She can act as your buffer."

Colum felt as if he were getting on a roller coaster with no tracks.

"When you arrive, inform Lillake that if she helps you, I'll relinquish all claims to the lake. She and her women have always wanted sole access to it." Uncle's voice intensified. "Beyond that, I won't be able to help you. My own powers don't work in the cave, so you'll be on your own there."

The king stood and clasped Colum and Dervor to him. "My fervent hope is that you both survive. *Now go.*"

CHAPTER THREE

Colum followed Dervor in silence through the iron corridors that angled their way through the earth.

No matter how deep we go, she never hesitates to take the correct turn, and not just because the blue light is showing her the way. It's as if she's being drawn by another force.

In the deepest layers of the labyrinth, the whiff of something overwhelmingly sweet froze Colum in his tracks. *The Lake!* His heart pounded at the visceral memory of those icy waters rushing into his body and battering him into its depths, when, as Uncle's slave, he was forced to confront the Lake as a living entity and nearly drowned.

He gasped. "I'm not sure I can do this."

"There is no other way," said Dervor in a low, calm voice.

Colum took several deep breaths to control his fear. Then, with a nod at Dervor, he braved a tentative first step onto the cave's ledge. As he started to walk across the wet, slippery rock, waves began to shoot up, spilling over onto his bare feet. The lick of the cold, cloying wetness made Colum's flesh contract. He knew the lake was alive. Any second, a roiling whirlpool might rise up to sweep away his precarious footing and suck him under forever.

Dervor inched along the ledge. Now and then, she turned her head to check on Colum, who continued to take one timorous step after another.

The lake splashed harder and higher against the rocky basin. Each step was a check and balance that required total concentration. His toes clung to the damp ledge with a will of their own until at last they made it across. Uncle's former slaves left the cave to enter a hall carved out of granite. The silence was abrupt after the splashing waves of the lake. There was no blue light here. Instead, torches soaked in coal oil flickered in iron brackets mounted on rock walls. Dervor lifted one out and handed it to Colum, taking another for herself.

Colum remembered being lured to this very hall by a cat-faced woman named Sny. He remembered her saying, "The blade of time is thin here, but it still exists."

At the end of the hallway, the pair entered another small cave. Embedded in the middle of the floor was a circular stone, the size of a manhole cover, with two iron handles fastened on each side. Dervor placed her torch in an empty bracket on the cave's wall. She removed the leather water bag she had slung over her shoulder, drank deeply from it, and passed it to Colum.

"Well, at least the lake is behind us," she said.

Colum exhaled. "What now?"

Dervor pointed to the stone in the floor. "Under there is a staircase that leads to the entrance of their cave."

"Where are we?"

She returned the bag of water to her shoulder. "I'm not sure. We're in some kind of liminal space between the cave and the labyrinth."

"What a place to be," he said with a shudder. "Do you think this Queen of theirs will help us?"

Her eyes met his. "As long as we don't go in guileless."

"Guileless?"

"To enter the Queen's cave is to crawl back *in utero*, which, as you can imagine, is highly dangerous. With no blue light to save us, the danger is twofold: reabsorption or abortion. We need a stratagem. Some tricks of our own."

"Why do I suspect you have a few in mind?" asked Colum, feeling like a complete amateur.

Her large, grey eyes shone in the torchlight like two silver moons, giving her an alien appearance. She looked androgynous in her nondescript loose wool clothes and close-cropped hair matted with sweat.

"We aren't in the labyrinth anymore," she said, her face softening. "No one is watching us."

He gave her a baffled look. Slowly, her words sank in, and he looked at her all over again. *After years of laboring in the labyrinth, separated not only from her people but from her planet, she still has this radiant glow in her eyes.*

"I've never met a woman like you, Dervor. I came back to the labyrinth for Uncle, but even more, I came back for you."

"I hoped against hope you'd return."

Colum startled at her confession.

"After you left, I realized my love for you wasn't a flaw, and it wasn't some disobedient act against Uncle that I could conquer. If anything, my longing for you only grew stronger."

Colum reached out to stroke her cheek. "I love you, Dervor."

She trembled at his touch. "For the first time, we have the freedom to be with each other."

He saw her looking at him in a new way, one that gave him an odd feeling. Still, his ingrained resistance to being physical with her made him hesitate. "I nearly lost you once for defying Uncle. I can't let that happen again."

"But Uncle isn't here, my love. We're on our own now." She kissed him on the mouth.

A shaft of joy swept up and down his spine, and he gathered her in his arms. "Dervor . . ."

"See," she said, laughing, "we kissed and nothing bad happened."

He laughed with her. "Are you saying there are no rules to break?"

"I'm saying we belong to ourselves now." She began to untie

the drawstring on her pants, and he pulled off his rough wool shirt. For the first time, they stood naked together.

Tears welled in Colum's eyes. "You're *beautiful!*"

Colum lay down on top of their discarded clothes on the floor and Dervor joined him. Unswerving love and desire filled them. Her breasts brushed his bare chest. He felt the smooth hardness of her belly against his and ran his hands over her waist and hips. They kissed long and fervently. Perspiration glistened on their skin. Soon cries of passion resounded in the cave. At last they shuddered into orgasm.

"I can't ever lose you again," rasped Colum, quivering with the power of his feelings for her.

Dervor nestled closer into his arms. "No matter what happens, my love, I belong with you now."

They slept briefly together. When Colum awakened, Dervor was already up and pulling on her shirt and pants. She looked at Colum somberly. "We have to figure out a strategy for how to act when we reach the cave."

Colum noticed how the torchlight accentuated her high-boned cheeks and lit up her large, grey eyes. "I don't want to end our time alone together."

"I'm afraid we don't have much time before the women become aware of us."

"You're right." He stood and dressed hastily.

"They're tricksters, so we must stay constantly vigilant."

"You don't have to tell me that. They were in my head, remember?"

"How could I forget? I still don't know how you withstood *that* siege." She pulled him close and kissed him.

"What do *you* think our strategy should be?"

"First, don't judge these women, no matter what happens. We're the intruders this time, and judgment will only enrage them. Second, try to let go of any preconceptions about them. Third, no rash displays. Keep a low profile. And fourth, they may surprise us. Who knows? So keep an open mind."

He stared at her. "You almost seem excited to go there."

"I have a strange feeling I may learn the truth about myself in that cave."

"What truth?"

"I don't know." Dervor looked at the ground. "I've felt for a long time as if an important part of my life is missing. I think Uncle erased some of my memories."

"How can someone like Sny help with that?"

Dervor shrugged. "It's just a feeling I have." She pointed to the round stone lid in the cavern floor. "Ready to lift it?"

"Aren't you afraid?"

"Yes, but I've had glimpses of these women during my time in the labyrinth. I admire how elemental, *ecstatic* even, their lives are." Her grey eyes widened. "And after all these years of being hidden away as Uncle's slave, I'm hungry to experience a little elemental joy myself."

She returned her clear gaze to the circular lid on the floor. "Ready? There's no turning back once we start down those stairs. As soon as we enter the cave, we'll be like moths rushing to the light of their fires."

Dervor took hold of a handle in the circular lid with both hands, while Colum grasped the other one. They lifted it up and, with a loud scraping noise, pulled it to one side. Underneath the lid loomed a rock staircase that spiraled into darkness. Its stairs had been worn into a slick smoothness through aeons of use.

Dervor took a deep breath. "These women are completely unpredictable, my love. We mean nothing to them. Still, Uncle wouldn't have let us come if he thought we had no chance at all."

"Let's do this," he said.

Torch in hand, Dervor lowered herself first into the stairwell. The stairs wrapped around a central limestone column, and the two of them clutched its cracks and crevices with their right hands to keep their balance. Round and round they went in tight descending circles. Colum's heart was pounding.

This is like a dream, but who is the dreamer? Am I asleep in bed in my London flat dreaming it all—from my first entry into the labyrinth until now? And if that's true, when I awaken, will my presence on these stairs fade away without a trace? Will Dervor, too, fade into oblivion?

The flames of their torches, flickering in the stale air of the stairwell, did nothing to boost his courage. Colum groped each step with his toes, testing for the forward edge before he dared step onto the next one. His torch dimly lit the center pole, barely illuminating the stair he was on, let alone the one that came after.

How long will the torches last? If these flames flicker out, we'll be in total darkness with no way to navigate the stairs. I could easily miss a step and plunge off! How far would I fall? Is there even a bottom below us? Do the stairs end midair in all this darkness? So far we haven't come across a single landing.

"Where are the landings?" he cried down to Dervor.

"I think there's only one," Dervor called back. "The one that connects to their cave."

"What if we miss it?"

"Let's not!"

Colum found traction in the roughness at the edges of the rock steps. The dangerously worn middle of each stair gave no grip. His head began to whirl with the never-ending circularity of the downward climb. He felt dizzy and tired and his steps were starting to fumble.

"I have to rest!" he called.

Dervor's voice rose from the darkness. "Stay where you are! I'm coming up!"

Colum sat down on a step and froze in place. It was easy to imagine himself plunging in a wild forward arc off the staircase, his feet scissoring as he fell through an infinity of space.

Suddenly, Dervor's face emerged out of the darkness below. She handed him her water bag. "Breathe, my love," she commanded in a gentle but firm voice.

The mere sight of her calmed him, and he made a conscious effort to slow his breathing. "We *must* be close to the landing," he said and took a long swallow of water.

She gave his hand a squeeze. "There's no way of telling."

Colum thought of the endless years Dervor had labored in the labyrinth. It showed in her fortitude now. He handed back the water bag and, gripping the rock pillar with hot, sweaty hands, pulled himself to his feet again.

"You're unsteady," she said.

"I'll be careful. Just promise to stay close."

"I will."

Dervor continued on, her torch popping in and out of visibility as she wound ever downward around the pole. Whenever her light disappeared completely, Colum would call out. She'd wait then until he was close enough to see her burning torch again. They descended the staircase until there was no water left in Dervor's bag and Colum's calf and thigh muscles were so spent he couldn't control their trembling.

At last she called up to him. "Sing with me!"

"Sing?"

"One of your English songs."

Colum swayed. "I can't sing, Dervor. I'm too dry." The thought of going any farther made him vertiginous. "I can barely concentrate on going from one step to another."

"I think we're close, my love. If we sing, they'll know we're coming." Her voice rang out in a lusty English song she must have learned from other slaves in the labyrinth. "*And the next thing I'll pray for, I'll pray for the Queen, that she have peace and plenty all the days of her reign.*"

Colum tried to follow, although his own voice was shaky and tentative. "*And where she had one ship, I wish she had ten.*"

"Louder!"

"*And never want for a NAAAAVY!*"

Dervor's voice sailed up to him. "*SAID THE SAILOR, AMEN!*" She paused briefly to catch her breath. "*Now the next thing I'll pray for is a pot of good beer,*" sang Dervor, "*for good liquor was sent us our spirits to cheer.*"

"*And where we got one pot I wish we had ten!*" Colum felt a rush of blood course through him, and his exhaustion began to lift.

"And never want for some liquor. Said the sailor . . ."

A shrill, brazen voice joined their chorus, *"Amen! Amen!"*

Colum and Dervor jumped at the sound of the unexpected singer. They looked down and spotted the flare of another torch. Relief flooded Colum. They reached the level of the torch to find themselves standing on a rock ledge in front of an older woman. She was hunched over and not more than four feet high. The strands of her wildly skewed hair twisted and tangled together in an unruly mess. The woman wore a black wool robe with a hood. Inside the folds of the hood was a face with dark red skin and two peering eyes. One eye was a healthy brown. The other eye seemed to be putrefying.

The woman held her torch close to the strangers' faces with an impudent stare. "Come down to gawk at the savages, have you? Come to civilize our wilds?"

Dervor spoke with utmost politeness. "No, ma'am. We're here to speak with your Queen."

"Is that so? And just who might you fine young singers be, coming all this way on the off chance our Mistress will see you?"

"We are messengers sent by Uncle, ma'am," replied Dervor.

"Uncle, is it?" The hag's good left eye started to bag out, losing its original shape. Soon it turned into a yellow sac of thick pus, which trailed down her face in sludge-like lines, giving off a foul odor. The hag shoved her face in front of Colum, who winced slightly. "Don't like my smell?" she taunted. "A bit rancid for your sensitive nostrils?"

"Your mastery over the composition of your face is most impressive," said Dervor without a hint of irony or aversion.

The hag grinned at Dervor, and her suddenly rotting eye resumed its natural shape. "I am Strix."

"I am Dervor, ma'am."

Strix shook her hand as if they were meeting as two respectable women. The hag turned then to Colum. "And what shall I call you?"

"Colum," he nearly stuttered.

Strix's brown eyes narrowed into slits. "Ah, we know you. We've been watching you." The crone held out her hand to shake his, but as soon as their hands contacted, Strix's fingers began to swell and change color, going from a fleshy pink to a sickly purple. The swollen fingers started to crack open in spots, oozing pus.

Taking a deep breath, Colum shook the woman's gangrenous hand.

Strix turned her attention back to Dervor, staring into her grey eyes as if looking for something. "Your defenses are strong, child. I can't probe your mind," said the hag with admiration.

"We are under orders to speak only with your mistress," explained Dervor.

"Then allow me to escort you to our cave." The old woman motioned them to follow her as she shuffled off the ledge into a tunnel opening. Once inside the tunnel, she picked up her pace. Colum had to scramble to keep up with her. *The hag's changing eye trick is one thing, but where does she get her boundless energy?*

The tunnel narrowed, forcing all three onto their hands and knees. They crawled like moles along the damp, uneven floor of the subterranean passage, squeezing through a few sections on their stomachs. Colum's torch flickered out first, then Dervor's. Strix continued on unfazed, while her two followers scurried to keep up with her, afraid to get lost in the darkness. At last the tunnel widened back out so they could walk upright again, and then finally it opened onto a huge underground chamber many stories high.

Colum gasped at the vastness of the cathedral-like space seething with women. He never imagined the cave to be this immense. Wherever he looked, he saw one form transforming into another: woman into tiger, lizard into woman, woman into falcon. Some forms were oddities he had never seen before. The intensity of the scene made his heart beat faster.

Scattered fires covered the floor, each with a three-legged, cast-iron cauldron over it. The cauldrons were of various sizes, some holding only a gallon or two, others large enough to accommodate a goat. Water dripped down from the rock dome far above and sputtered into steam on the floor. Colum noticed that the tunnel they stood in was only one entrance to this cave among many.

Most of the women in human form wore brown and black cowled robes. In the distance flowed a subterranean river. Women laughed and splashed in its waters like shimmering undines. The violent charm of all those transmogrifying forms made him dizzy. The mood of the cave was festive, a free-floating miasma of sounds, smells, and shapes that made Colum anxious and giddy at the same time. Two squealing bats fluttered over his head, their squeals part of a cacophony of howls, hisses, screeches, and innumerable other sounds. The vocalizations of mammals mingled with the tones of flutes, lyres, rattles, and drums to create a variegated dissonance, all playing together like some strange, uncanny, orchestral piece.

The onslaught of sound on his ears was accompanied by the assault of strong smells wafting up his nostrils. Colum detected a distinctive, personal aroma on each woman who came near him. One smelled like pine cones, another of goat manure. A third woman's smell was like a warm, overripe mixture of strawberries and oranges. Colum's olfactory receptors began to go wild, swamped by the multitude of odors. He realized how devoid of smells the labyrinth was, aside from sweat and iron.

A cheetah seemed to appear out of nowhere, pawing at his waist. Startled, Colum jumped backward, causing Strix to laugh. A woman with legs longer than her torso, whose nose was a vulpine variant of a wolf's, stared briefly into his eyes. No sooner did she leave than a blue-haired girl with green eyes rose out of the river and sprinted over to him, dripping wet and naked. She reminded him of a nereid from some ancient world. Without warning she straddled his thigh with her legs and rubbed up and down, emitting a series of short cries, then leaped off smiling and zigzagged away skirting the fires. Colum watched her disappear, wondering what just happened.

Strix leaned over to croon in his ear, "Poor little lamb who has lost his way. Baaa. Baaa. Baaa." She shoved him, and the three of them moved farther into the cave.

Sounds bounced off the high rock walls making the whole

chamber hum. Here and there, smoke from the fires obscured the air. Colum smelled foods simmering in the women's cauldrons and roasting over their fires. Some of the odors were appetizing enough, while others caused him to physically contract with varying degrees of disgust.

He startled when a large scorpion went by, holding her tail and stinger proudly upright. "Greetings, Neringa," Strix said to the creature.

They passed a woman whacking a log with a splitting maul next to a toddler with a beatific face and shock of red hair sitting on a pile of furs. When he smiled at her, the child's mother frowned. Strix gave him a push to move on. The women in the cave seemed to be of all ages. Most were middle-aged or older, but there were youthful faces, too. Skin, eye, and hair colors varied, and not all variations were within the human range.

At last they came to an unattended fire.

"Wait here," said Strix.

"Where exactly *is* here?" Colum asked.

"Where indeed?" Strix jabbed her elbow in Colum's ribs with a rasping laugh, and he couldn't tell if it was a friendly gesture or meant to hurt. "Some call our cave 'The Realm of the End of Day.'" Her brown eye transmogrified into a lemony yellow as she shuffled away, calling over her shoulder, "Others call it 'The End of All Flesh.'"

After Strix passed out of sight, a strident voice sounded behind him. "We meet again."

Colum's heart slowed when he turned to face its owner. "Sny!"

The Cat Woman's rapacious eyes held no warmth. "And this time we meet in *my* world."

Memories flooded Colum. He was transported back to the passageway by the lake where Sny once transformed herself into a clammy cat and bit his arm with vicious, spite-filled fangs. He remembered writhing in the king's throne room as she tried to control his brain in an act of malicious fury, forcing him to speak words that weren't his own.

The woman's sharp fingers grabbed his jaw like pincers, and her hot fetid breath spewed over him. "Stroking your manly stubble in our cave, are you, Colum?" Her words made him queasy. "What are you doing *here?*"

Colum gripped her wrist and yanked it away. It took fierce control not to strike her, but he knew that at this juncture, to do so could be an irrevocable mistake. "I've come to speak with your Queen."

Sny's cheeks turned crimson, but she, too, managed to control herself. "You must be hungry after your long journey." She took his hand and pulled him over to a woman who tended a cauldron a few feet away. Dervor followed them.

"Greetings, K'lifah," said Sny with a friendly nod. "I wonder if you'd share some of your stew with our visitors. They've come a long way, and I'm sure they must be hungry."

K'lifah was slender and exceptionally tall with a nose that seemed to be perpetually running. "Of course, sister."

Steam rose out of the woman's cauldron. While K'lifah filled two stone bowls with her stew, Colum noticed pieces of decaying carcasses scattered around her fire. The woman licked at the mucous strands that dripped from her nose into the bowl she now handed him.

At the first taste, Colum's stomach turned over. With an iron will he managed to eat a few more spoonfuls and keep the contents down.

Sny grinned at his discomfort. "Not fond of this particular dish?"

"Have you forgotten?" he retorted. "We eat gruel in Uncle's kingdom."

"Are you calling K'lifah's stew *gruel?* I fear your only way out of here may be as the shit out of our bodies," she sneered.

Dervor ate the full contents of her bowl without complaint. "Thank you, K'lifah," she said, handing her bowl back with a smile.

The tall woman wiped her dripping nose with a glance at Colum. "Such a pity you're burdened with this puny fellow."

K'lifah's predatory air made Colum's flesh contract. The whole cave was beyond disorienting to him.

Sny turned her attention to Dervor. "You possess a tenacious spirit. How did I miss that?"

A new figure strolled over to K'lifah's hearth, her eyes hidden in the shadows of a cowl. There were deep cracks and lines on her lower cheeks and around her mouth. "Follow me," she said with a curt nod to Colum and Dervor.

Colum put his bowl on a rock, glad to be rid of it, and Sny stepped aside. Their new guide led them once more through a sea of perambulating women.

"What's your name, ma'am?" queried Dervor.

"I am called Yaga."

Dervor raised her eyebrows. "I've heard of you."

"You've heard of me? How is that possible?"

"I've been in the labyrinth a long time, ma'am. Once in a while, news of your cave gets through."

"What exactly did you hear?"

"That you are one of the oldest and wisest women here."

Although Yaga's voice was somber, her lips formed a smile at Dervor's compliment. "Not nearly as old or as wise as our Queen."

"Are you taking us to see her now?" asked Colum. The sooner they saw the Queen and stated their mission, the sooner they could leave. At least that was his fervent hope.

"Our Mistress is not in the cave now. I'm taking you to my hearth as my guests until her arrival."

Yaga's hearth was situated near the center of the cave. Like all the others, it had an iron cauldron suspended over a pile of glowing red embers surrounded by animal furs. The crone threw off her hood. Her hair, the color of stone, straggled in disorder over her shoulders. Yaga's cheeks were creviced hollows, and her white eyebrows bushed out wildly over watery blue eyes. Her lips were so thin that Colum had to look twice to make sure they weren't simply a horizontal line drawn beneath her nose.

"You are welcome to stay at my hearth as long as necessary."

"Thank you, Yaga," said Dervor with sincere gratitude.

Yaga peered at Colum. "So you are the column Nirah has been forging." Before he could answer, she pointed a long, bony finger at her pile of furs. "Rest now. You both must be exhausted after such a long climb down our stairs."

Colum longed to get off his feet and stretch his aching back and legs. "Thank you, Yaga."

"It is quite novel to have two visitors of your caliber in our cave," said the crone. With that, she pulled her hood over her head, spit into the embers, and shuffled away.

Colum collapsed on the furs and stared at the women buzzing around him like bees in a hive. "I had no idea this place was so huge," he said in a low voice. "And you were right, there's no privacy here. At least in the labyrinth we had our own rooms."

Dervor's eyes shone luminous in the firelight. "They prefer a communal life." She smiled gently at him. "Let's sleep while we can, my love. I'll stand guard first, though I doubt anyone will act against us before our audience with the Queen. Still, it's better to stay vigilant."

He was asleep before his head hit the furs.

CHAPTER FOUR

It was Colum's turn to keep watch over Dervor, asleep at his side. The strain of being in Sny's cave made the back of his neck cramp, yet Dervor looked so peaceful and warm lying near the soft flames of Yaga's fire. Colum frowned. He hadn't expected his whole life to change again so radically.

I thought Uncle was in control of his world and that I finally knew where I belonged. Now it seems he isn't, and I don't. What is Uncle's relationship to this Queen Lillake, anyway? He seems to respect her. Is she from Illinee? Not likely.

A woman slowly approached him. She wore a light tunic that only partially covered the swell of her breasts. Auburn hair rolled over her shoulders in waves, and her green eyes glowed like two shining emeralds. She entered Yaga's hearth in a single flow of graceful motion and lowered herself onto the spread of furs.

"Welcome to our cave, Colum," said the woman, smiling.

Even the embers seemed to glow brighter at her arrival. A slight scent of musk wafted up his nostrils, igniting a nervous exhilaration in him. Colum gazed at his reflection in her eyes. It was like peering into a flawless green mirror with every detail of his face sharp and clear.

"You know my name?" he asked.

"Oh, yes, the whole cave knows who you are."

"May I ask what your name is?" The nearness of the woman raised the hairs on his arms.

"I am Ayylo, the Queen's daughter." Her fingers gently caressed the back of his hand. "You're not like most men."

He suddenly felt lightheaded. "What makes you say that?"

"For one thing, no outsider has ever spiraled down those ancient stairs before. We are most impressed. Several of my sisters expected you to descend past the cave's landing into the darkness below."

Both the praise and the implied threat infused Colum's cheeks with a hot flush. "I don't think I would do it again."

Ayylo laughed a soprano laugh of pure delight. "And what propelled you to such a rash act? The desire to visit our world? Or have you always known you were meant to go deeper?" She gave him a serious look, sliding her hand off of his. "You are either mad to visit us, Colum, or forged of true iron."

"May I ask you a question?"

"Of course."

"Does the staircase lead beyond your cave to anywhere else?"

"Those stairs are a dimensional gateway built only to connect Uncle's labyrinth with our cave." Ayylo looked at Dervor sleeping next to Colum. "She touches something deep and powerful in you. I feel it."

Dervor awoke and, upon seeing their visitor, sat up.

Ayylo turned an alluring smile on her. "Greetings. I am the daughter of the Mistress of this cave."

"And I am a slave of the king of the labyrinth."

Ayylo smiled. "You are not a slave to us, Kasi."

Colum was surprised that Ayylo knew Dervor's Illian name.

Ayylo pointed to a small group of robed figures all casting looks in their direction. "Several of my sisters desire to meet with you."

A glimmer of misgiving crossed Dervor's face. "Colum and I wish to stay together."

"Ah, but men do have a way of upsetting some of my sisters. Don't worry. I'll stay with Colum to make sure he's safe." The woman looked sincere. "I promise he won't be out of your line of sight."

"All right," Dervor said, nodding. She looked reluctant but stood to join the waiting figures.

Colum glimpsed a woman in the group who seemed to fade in and out of visibility like a ghost. "Are you sure Dervor is safe?" he asked Ayylo with a shiver.

"Oh, yes, Kasi is highly regarded by many of us," purred the Queen's daughter.

Dervor glanced back as Ayylo's perfectly formed hand draped over Colum's arm to pull him down on the furs close to her.

A woman with ten eyes positioned across her face, in two horizontal rows of five each, watched Dervor watching Colum. "Are you concerned about the man-boy?" she queried.

A slender woman with a sinewy head and neck that undulated like a snake stuck out her tongue and licked Dervor's face. A cold, reptilian breath swept over Dervor. "Ah, yes, Abruta," said the Snake Woman, "she is concerned about the man. I detect a whiff of rank sex in her sweat. The two of them have most certainly *tasted* one another."

A large woman, whose round brown eyes were set so wide apart Dervor wondered if she could focus on what was in front of her, introduced herself. "I am Amorpho."

"What a great, wild cow you are, Amorpho!" Dervor exclaimed, her voice full of admiration.

The woman placed her hands on the swell of her huge hips with an appreciative grin. "So I am. You and I must drink beer together."

"I would like that."

Amorpho's brown eyes followed Dervor's back to Yaga's hearth. "Are you jealous, child?"

Dervor's whole body went taut. "Wouldn't you be?"

The bovine woman laughed out loud. "Ayylo is quite capable of spinning your man out in bliss." Amorpho's look turned sympathetic. "Don't worry, though. None of us will touch a hair on his head before your audience with our Mistress."

Abruta, the ten-eyed woman, slipped an arm around Dervor's waist and led her a few steps away for a more private conversation. Five of her eyes studied Dervor, three watched Colum and Ayylo, and the last two observed her sisters hovering close by.

"Ayylo's powers are irresistible," said Abruta, "but it is you Colum loves." The woman's multiple eyes pierced through Dervor's protective mind barriers. "Your heart, not any loyalty to Uncle, has brought you to this cave." She seemed to look deeper. "You need sisters after such a long time in the labyrinth, don't you, dear?"

Dervor's strong chin trembled. "Yes."

"When Uncle spoke the *word*, our whole cave vibrated. We knew at once that one of your own was being offered to the Self-Existent One." Her ten eyes glowed brighter in the firelight. "Your master plays a risky game sending you here. But what game is it exactly?" mused Abruta. "Is it simply to save the life of a slave?" All ten of the woman's eyes riveted on Dervor. "And just whom did he sacrifice?"

"A slave named Bambara."

The woman closed two eyes. "Ah, a most worthy sacrifice. He was a great warrior on Illinee." Her eyes reopened. "Now tell me why you are here. The Beetle does not seek you."

"I came to assist Colum." Dervor glanced again at Yaga's hearth as Ayylo stroked Colum's thigh.

"You are angry, child," said Abruta, watching Dervor's face. "Don't be. That is simply Ayylo's way of being friendly."

"So you say."

Abruta ignored her comment. "Tell me, Kasi, did you have a choice in coming here?"

"Uncle sent me. But even if he hadn't, I wanted to come." She stared at two eyes in the bottom row of the woman's face. "What is the Beetle, Abruta?"

"It is a sacred scarab, one that self-generates in the darkness. It carries within itself a boundless luminosity strong enough to bring whole worlds into form."

Dervor looked shaken. "Uncle said Colum would be safe from the Beetle in the cave."

"I have been watching him for a long time, even before he entered the labyrinth, and am quite aware of his courage, tenacity, and iron will." A perplexed expression crossed Abruta's face. "But those qualities aren't enough to save him from the white heat of the Beetle's blast furnace. It has been five hundred generations since anyone has merged with the Self-Existent One. But the time for another merger is now . . ." Abruta was silent a moment, then changed the subject. "At least you are both safely down the spiraling staircase and settled in the warmth of our cave." Her ten eyes widened. "Others have fallen or been shaken off those stairs."

"I can imagine."

"You were never in danger of falling, Kasi. The darkness has a far greater pull on Colum." Abruta sighed, and several of her eyes migrated to him. "I know you're impatient to be with your companion. Go to him."

Colum looked up to see Dervor return to Yaga's hearth, where she joined him and Ayylo on the soft animal pelts.

Ayylo gave her a sympathetic look. "Life in the labyrinth is grim, Kasi. All that cold iron, full of sharp angles everywhere. All your sensual pleasures suppressed. I don't know how you survived this long."

"It is meant to be hard," replied Dervor. "That's what makes us strong."

Colum looked around the cave. "Where do all the tunnels lead, Ayylo?"

"They go this way and that. Some go in circles. Others dead-end. A few lead to our forest."

Colum raised his eyebrows in surprise. "Forest?"

"Yes," she replied with a toss of her glorious hair. "Men in your world stray into it at times."

"What happens if they do?" asked Colum.

Ayylo idly twisted a few strands of her auburn hair around her forefinger. "It depends on which one of us comes upon them. If I meet a man in the forest and find him desirable, I make love to him."

"And afterward?"

"If he survives our passion together, I restore him to his world, but first, I wipe out his memory." Her green eyes glimmered in the firelight. "When I unite with a man, no part of him is ever free again. He may recall me in his dreams or experience in waking life a longing to reunite with the force of life I carry . . . a longing no human woman can satisfy." She stood with a casualness that was pure flow, flashed them a parting smile, and departed.

Dervor and Colum found themselves in a state of sudden arousal.

"Hold me, my love," whispered Dervor.

He pulled her into his arms and kissed her passionately. At once his awareness of the other women in the cave faded into the background.

A thought flitted through his mind. *Is this Ayylo's doing? Has she aroused both of us? Does she have that kind of power?*

Smoke from Yaga's fire rose into the air as her two guests discarded their clothes. To Colum's surprise, no one seemed interested in what they were doing. He pulled the pelts over them to stroke Dervor's smooth, honed body, barely aware of the cacophony of forms and sounds all around them. Before long, cries of pleasure rose from their furs. Colum held her tighter and laughed, crazy with joy. "I can't believe we're naked together under a bunch of animal furs in Sny's cave. It's so improbable, *impossible* even, and yet . . ."

"Inevitable?" she asked, throwing off her covers.

His eyes glowed with love. "Why is it so easy to be with you this way?"

"Because we have no king to determine our every breath. And because we belong to each other."

He kissed her. "I've never known such contentment, Dervor. Not as a child. Not as a man. All I want is to lie in your arms forever."

Orange and red flames flickered under Yaga's cauldron. Colum brushed aside a few strands of loose hair on Dervor's face. Her gaze held such deep love he had to turn away.

Just then, a cry of distress sounded through the cave. The two lovers sat up with a start and hurried to dress. The cry had come from one of the tunnel entrances, but there were too many women milling around to make anything out. Unbidden, the robed women shuffled into a makeshift aisle. Colum and Dervor scrambled to get close enough to see what was happening.

A tall figure with disheveled, coppery hair that reached to the back of her knees prodded a man through the newly formed aisle using the blunt end of a spear. He wore a camouflaged hat, jacket, pants, and leather boots. Directly behind the copper-haired huntress appeared Sny with another hunter in tow. Colum could only imagine how terrified the men must have been making their way through the dark, cramped passageways, only to emerge into this immense cave filled with wild-looking women. Sny pulled her balding and somewhat overweight captive by a rope tied around his wrists. Blood streamed down his face from a long gash on his head.

The man in camouflage looked disoriented as he stopped to blink in the light of the unexpected fires. The copper-haired woman struck him in his lower back with the butt of her javelin, and he staggered forward.

Ayylo emerged out of the crowd to stand next to Colum and Dervor. "Stay close to me," she said.

Colum wondered if she'd come to guard them. In a quiet voice, he asked, "Ayylo, who's the woman with Sny?"

"Kle-Ptuza," replied Ayylo. "She and Sny are lovers. They often hunt together. You'd both do well to stay away from those two."

"What's happening?"

"The two men with them entered our forest."

"You mean they were trespassing?" he asked.

"That's right."

Sny suddenly kicked her captive behind a knee. He sprawled backward, landing heavily on the cave floor. The Cat Woman yanked him back to his feet with her rope. Colum was close enough now to see the man's eyes roll back with fear and hear his small gasps of breath. He started to take a step toward the man.

At once Dervor clasped his arm to stop him, whispering, "Remember, Colum, we can't interfere with what happens here."

While everyone watched Sny tie her captive to a tethering post for animals, the man in camouflage made a mad dash toward the tunnels.

The women moved aside like waves in an ocean to give Kle-Ptuza a clear view of the runaway. The copper-haired huntress turned toward the racing figure with a vicious laugh, then pointed the four fingers on her left hand at his fleeing form and released a blast of energy from them. The energy slammed into the man's back with enough force to knock him to the ground. Once the man was on his knees, Kle-Ptuza flung her rope at him like a lasso. It wrapped around the man's neck, and she slowly reeled him back to her.

Colum noticed for the first time that Kle-Ptuza's fingers weren't actually fingers but hard-nailed, curved talons.

The man seemed to notice too. *"What are you?!"*

"WHAT am I?" sneered the huntress and gave the hapless man a sharp push backward. "A *what*? Not a *who*?" After another hard push, he stumbled and fell. Kle-Ptuza dropped with her knees on top of his chest and Colum heard a rib crack, along with air being dispelled from the man's lungs.

The man's mouth twitched in nervous gasps. *"Ple-ase. I di— did—n't mean . . ."*

His friend, still tied up at the post, spoke in a nasal-sounding voice, as if he had a cold or a broken nose. "We didn't know it was your forest! Let us go! I swear we'll never come back!"

Drenched in sweat, he darted his eyes from one angry face to another. "What do you want from us?"

"Want?" Her expression was beyond menacing. "I suppose we could make a meal of you, but men are such foul-tasting creatures. Still, you may be digestible with enough spice."

A vein stood out on Colum's forehead. His heart raced dangerously in an effort not to interfere. Dervor pulled on his arm. Together they retreated several steps back into the crowd.

Sny looked at her captive with sneering contempt. She pulled her dagger from the sheath on her waist and, with blurring speed, whipped it across the balding man's throat. Bright red blood splattered outward, spraying her face and chest. His head slumped forward. She yanked it up with one hand. Another woman held a bowl out to her, and Sny took the bowl and placed it under the man's neck to collect the spurting blood.

Kle-Ptuza dipped her hand in the bowl, scooping out the contents and smearing them over the face of her captive. The thick, gooey substance darkened his skin. The man lost his nerve at that point and started to sob.

Sny fetched a bristly boar's hide and draped it over his body. "Behold, sister, the boar you hunted in the forest!"

Kle-Ptuza's voice rang throughout the cave. "MAN TO BOAR!"

Women everywhere burst into a turbulent uproar, a chorus of voices repeating her cry. "MAN TO BOAR! MAN TO BOAR!"

All eyes were on the man, who twisted and turned violently under the boarskin. Finally, his movement ceased, and a boar with tusks stood in his place. Colum was stunned in disbelief. In some inexplicable way, the hunter had merged with the boar's hide to *become* the wild peccary that now stood in front of him. A powerful whiff of its musky breath entered Colum's nostrils.

Kle-Ptuza stripped off her tunic to leap naked onto the boar's back, her heels digging into its sides. The creature lurched and raced off, gathering speed as it stampeded through the cave. Beast and huntress circled around the fires, whipping up flames as they went, knocking over cauldrons and pouring out their steaming-hot contents. Robed women scattered in all directions to get out of the way.

Colum caught a glimpse of Kle-Ptuza's copper eyes glittering with excitement as she rushed past him on her crazed steed. The sight made his stomach knot, but he couldn't break his own fascination with the whole macabre scene.

What's happening? Am I hallucinating? Is there anything left of the hunter? Did Kle-Ptuza actually turn that man and the boar's hairy pelt into a single living form? I do know one thing: the poor bastard will never get out of here alive.

The tumultuous path of rider and charging boar now took them both to the river that flowed along one side of the cave. The pair splashed into the water and swam together, only to emerge soaking wet not far from the tunnel entrance they first came through. With rapid thuds of its hooves, the boar stampeded into the tunnel with Kle-Ptuza still on his back.

"She'll release him in the forest," said Ayylo, standing next to Colum.

"As a boar?" he asked, confused.

"Boar? Man? None of us are determinate forms forever, Colum. Either way, he shall roam freely through our forest, satisfying his unslakable lust to live."

"What about his mind?"

"His human mind is most certainly plunged into darkness. Not that the boar will miss it." She gave him a sympathetic look. "These are matters of deep earth, Colum. And why are you here if not to learn of them?"

Some women were already pulling their overturned cauldrons into upright positions and rekindling their fires. Wood smoke from the fires wafted out in drafts through openings in the cave's rock walls and domed ceiling high above. Colum, his eyes dry and burning, wished he were back in the barren, iron corridors of Uncle's labyrinth, far away from this place. He knew he was no safer from these women than the two hunters.

"We couldn't save them," said Dervor, her face smudged with flying ash. "Let's go back to Yaga's hearth. We're under her protection there."

"Did you see Kle-Ptuza turn that hunter into a bloody animal?" he asked, his breath trembling.

"Is Uncle any different?" countered Dervor. "Would you rather be turned into a boar or eaten alive by ants? We don't know these women, Colum. We can't judge them."

"You call them *women*?" He shook his head, frustrated. "At the very least, they're capricious and untrustworthy. To me, they're wild animals in human form and not the other way around. You're right. We don't know them and we never will. We made a terrible mistake coming here. Why did Uncle ever think they'd help us?"

A nearby elfin woman sang liltingly to the accompaniment of a lyre. Her bluish-purple hair rippled over her chest like glistening ribbons in the firelight. Her song held a deep sadness, undergirded with great strength, and filled Colum with strange, conflicting emotions.

"We couldn't stay in the labyrinth," he said, sobered by the woman's song. "The only thing that matters to me now is being with you . . . wherever we are." He sighed. "I'll try harder to fit in."

"Don't despair, my love. The Queen may yet agree to help us."

Colum blinked repeatedly from the smoke produced by Yaga's fire. He looked at Dervor and noticed how clear and shining her eyes were, as if the smoke had no effect on her.

"You're remarkable," he said softly. "It's almost as if you belong here."

"Uh-oh, here comes Sny. She's still excited by the kill."

He stood up to face the Cat Woman, who glared back at him defiantly.

"You're drifting, Colum," sneered Sny. "You've always been drifting. You're like a piece of hollowed-out wood carried along in a river, only now you've landed in our cave." Her tone turned acrid. "And we *burn* driftwood."

"We are here to see your Queen. We don't plan to stay long," he replied.

"Do you really think you can control this little escapade of yours?" She spit into the fire and strode off.

CHAPTER FIVE

Dervor and Colum knelt at Yaga's grinding stone, busily milling grass seeds into flour for bread. The crone kneaded salt and water into their freshly ground flour, patting the dough into round shapes with her hands. She dampened her fire and buried the dough in its ashes. Once the biscuits had baked, she plucked them from under the hot coals and placed them on a wooden platter before passing them to her guests.

Brushing off the ashes, Colum drizzled honey on his wattle-seed biscuit and bit into it. The warm, flavorful goodness surprised him. "Delicious," he announced.

While he ate, Colum heard someone call his name from a nearby hearth.

"Ah," said Yaga, "that is Hursag calling. She is quite close to our Queen. Go on and see what she wants."

Colum was unsure, but Dervor leaned over and whispered, "You'd better go. I promise to keep my eyes on you."

Colum walked over with hesitant steps. Hursag, looking at least as old as Yaga, sat on a large rock next to her fire.

"Come closer," she urged and patted the rock on which she sat. Delicate blue veins crisscrossed the thin skin on her hand.

Colum sat down, wondering what was expected of him. The old woman's stiffened hood covered her head like a giant insect shell. Inside the hood, her face was as cragged and creviced as the cave's granite rock.

"I have something for you," crooned the hag, opening her hooded cloak to reveal two breasts that sagged to her navel.

The sight nearly made Colum retch Yaga's biscuits.

Hursag lifted up a breast. "Come, taste my milk. You'll find it quite sweet and warm."

Colum looked at her in disbelief but managed to compose himself. "Thank you, ma'am, but my stomach is still full of Yaga's bread."

The crone's amber eyes shone in the firelight. "I don't offer my milk to just anyone."

Colum glanced desperately at Dervor, who stared back. He didn't need a reminder that his refusal could jeopardize their safety in the cave. He fought to conceal his disgust. "These days I take my milk in tea, ma'am."

"Come now, child, I can see you're in need of a mother's milk." The crone resettled herself on the wide, smooth rock, her black robe open to the waist. "Now sit on Na-na's lap like the good, hungry boy you are."

A searing alarm went off in Colum's chest, and it took all he had not to leave. Uncle's training hadn't prepared him for this kind of debilitating humiliation. With flaming cheeks, Colum positioned himself on her thighs. He assumed her legs would be thin and fragile at such a great age and tried to be careful. Instead, her limbs were as strong and hard as iron.

"Curl up just a bit more, *little one*," she prompted.

Colum drew his long arms and legs toward his chest in a fetal position in order to fit in the crone's arms. His sense of mortification had him so rattled he couldn't think.

"That's the way. See how adaptable you are?" murmured Hursag. "Now drink some of Na-na's special milk."

With an iron will, he pushed down the self-loathing that

swept through him and, reaching out, lifted the crone's heavy breast to his mouth. Nearby, a few murmured twitters could be heard.

"Good, good," said the hag, grinning. She squeezed her breast vigorously and warm milk spurted into his mouth.

Colum couldn't swallow fast enough. Her milk overflowed, nearly choking him, spilling down his chin and neck. Gradually, the stream slowed to accommodate his swallowing. He glanced at Hursag's face and saw it aglow with maternal satisfaction. Colum sucked her milk in streams and spurts while she ran her scrawny fingers through his hair. Just when he thought his bloated stomach couldn't take anymore, she shooed him off her lap.

He stumbled back to Dervor, warm milk sloshing in his belly like something rancid. Yaga was nowhere in sight. Nausea gripped him. "I feel sick," he said, doubling over and clutching his stomach.

"If she's watching us, you vomit at your peril," warned Dervor.

Colum rinsed his mouth with water several times. "How can that hag still produce milk?" he rasped and roughly wiped his lips with the back of his arm. "She's obscene! This whole place is a hell realm!"

Ayylo approached their fire. "I saw you with Hursag just now, Colum."

His face turned crimson.

The Queen's daughter lowered herself onto the furs, luscious and languid like a cat. Her musky scent wafted up Colum's nostrils, making him slightly faint. "You should know that Hursag never gives her milk to anyone."

"Is that a compliment?" he asked.

"A very high one. But then, you're not like other men. You came to us from the labyrinth, not the forest. Down the spiraling staircase, not over the bridge." The Queen's daughter stared at him. "None of Uncle's slaves have ever risked such a journey."

"We need the Queen's help."

"Then know this: no one is closer to my mother than Hursag. And despite that Hursag is a fountain of fertility at such a great age, she has never nursed anyone in our cave before. How strange that she bestowed such a great honor on you."

Before Colum could respond, the clarion blossoming of flute tones echoed through the cave, pulsing excitement and a sense of expectancy into him.

"What's happening?" asked Colum.

"My mother arrives!" cried Ayylo with a radiant smile. "She is in our forest and will soon be among us! Wait here by Yaga's fire until I return." With that, the Queen's daughter rose, brushing her hip nonchalantly against Colum's thigh as she left. A hot flush suffused his cheeks.

"You're blushing," said Dervor. "Does Ayylo's fire burn too hot for you?"

Red flames from Yaga's fire sailed into the air, morphing into blues and violets the higher they went. "It must be the fire," he replied lamely.

Dervor changed the subject. "Are you ready to meet the Queen?"

"No, but it helps to have you with me. These women seem to like you."

"I wonder." She looked into his blue eyes. "I've always wanted to know how deep existence goes, and it's obvious this cave goes deeper than the labyrinth."

"There's no doubt about that."

"It offers such a different view of life. And as bizarre and chaotic as it is, I'm willing to do what I can to fit in. We're here for a reason, Colum."

"You mean besides getting the Queen to help us?"

"Yes. Don't you wonder where this place will lead us?"

"If it leads *anywhere*."

Dervor nodded in the direction of another hearth. "See the women over there?"

Colum noticed three figures in dark brown robes eating and chatting by a nearby fire. "What about them?"

"The big one is Bruha. I saw her change into a hippo not long ago. Imagine if *she* accidentally knocked into you!" She laughed and Colum's mood lifted slightly.

In my world, people would call her one of nature's mistakes. But here, she's simply who she is.

The three women from the adjoining hearth suddenly rose and hurried off. All over the cave, women began to scurry in the direction of the tunnels. An ongoing stream of women swept through Yaga's hearth, pushing and buffeting Colum and Dervor along with them. Colum grabbed Dervor's hand and gripped it tightly to keep from being separated. The swarming figures moved forward, circling around all the fires in a graceful, organic oneness without upsetting a single cauldron. Some retained their human forms. Others shape-shifted into an entire range of animals, birds, and insects from the grotesque to the liltingly beautiful.

A small tan snake with bright green markings slithered around Colum's ankles, nearly knocking him off balance. Only the press of women held him upright. He saw a giant spider walking among the women. The arachnid held her eight long legs and articulations close to her body's center of gravity. A bull and ram proceeded side by side, like old friends. Colum held tighter and tighter to Dervor's hand. An owl flew overhead, close enough for the breeze of its flapping wings to muss his hair. He caught sight of a passing jaguar with the face of a young woman. The Jaguar Woman gave him a half-quizzical glance as if he were the odd one, not she.

He looked in time to catch a fleeting glimpse of a tiny woman with bee wings continuously rising into the air to see what was happening above her sisters' heads. A very tall woman with a muddy green complexion and a small tree branch growing out of the middle of her forehead strode by. Her mossy hair swung so wildly from side to side it slapped Colum's cheek as she passed. Shivers of excitement collected in his gut. Firelit sheens of tails, feathers, claws, tusks, horns, shells, scales, and wings, along with a cacophony of excited screeches, hoots, croaks, hisses, growls, chirps, and screams, assaulted him on every side and made him reel. He felt part of some mad illusion and was sure the cave would burst under the onslaught of all this rich, exuberant life.

"The Dark Moon comes!" shouted someone.

"She is among us!"

Cries of unfeigned delight filled the cave.

"Mistress! Welcome to our Mistress!'"

"Our Queen has come!"

"She is here!"

The women's heartfelt joy and adulation—the uncanny dissonance and passion in their chorus of voices—created a charge in Colum so primal it threatened to undo his civilized self. He glanced at Dervor and saw her whole body quivering.

She's transported too! My own heart is racing! Perhaps this Queen is some kind of living goddess, and I don't belong here any more than those two hunters who messed around in her forest.

"Praise to the Mistress of our cave!"

"Here it is sung!"

"Song of our Holy Mistress!"

"Sing it here!"

Ayylo appeared out of the crowd to stand next to Colum and Dervor. "I'll introduce you to my mother now," she said. The thought of meeting Lillake made Colum feel a little faint.

Lillake sat regally on a simple stone chair with snake carvings wearing a robe of blue-black raven feathers. Her hair parted in the middle to fall in crinkly, tight, blue-black waves over her shoulders. A pair of rippling limestone stalactites like two long icicles hung down from the cave's ceiling to form a pillar on either side of her throne. The Queen stared at the women, her emerald-green eyes glittering in the torchlight. The whole cave quieted as smoke from the fires rose in think swirls toward the dome.

Ayylo came forward. "Mistress, two emissaries from Nirah wish to speak with you."

Lillake beckoned for Colum and Dervor to approach. The women parted to make way for them.

"Welcome to my house," greeted the Queen.

"Thank you, Majesty," replied Colum, thinking he had never heard a more melodious voice.

"We are grateful for your reception, Majesty," said Dervor.

The Queen looked at her. "How strange for Nirah to send two of his favored slaves at a time when the cord between our realms hangs by a mere thread." She gave Dervor a brief nod. "State your request, child."

"A friend of ours was sent to the Beetle, Majesty," Dervor said, her voice wavering slightly.

"We know." The Queen sat tall and erect on her throne. "Your own king spoke the *word* that sent him there. Our river splashed against its banks, our fires dimmed, and the walls of our cave shook at the sound of Nirah's voice."

"A dream sent our friend there," said Dervor, glancing at Colum.

He cleared his throat. "And I had a similar dream, Majesty."

Lillake gazed intently at Colum. "Not quite similar." She paused for a moment. "Since it is impossible to undo the *word* your master has spoken, what is it you desire of me?"

Colum blurted out his burning question. "What does it mean to go to the Beetle, Majesty?"

"It means to become one with the Holy Scarab."

He looked at her blankly.

A solemn look crossed Lillake's face. "By vanishing into the flaming furnace that is the Beetle, your friend has become fuel for the scarab's self-originating luminosity." She paused. "In the flaming furnace of the Beetle, Bambara's flesh was burnished brighter than gold. He is one with the Beetle now, which is a most glorious destiny."

Dervor interjected quickly. "If you help Colum avoid such a 'glorious destiny,' Majesty, our king offers you access to the lake."

The women close enough to hear their conversation murmured angrily.

"What kind of mockery is this?" asked Lillake, raising her eyebrows. "Nirah asks us to stop the sun from rising, and for *what*? Access to a lake that has never been his to control or possess! Everyone knows the lake is its own sovereign entity."

"Yes, Majesty, of course it is. What I meant to say is that in return for your help, Uncle will renounce his jurisdiction over the cave that harbors the lake. As you know, the cave is part of the labyrinth."

"How clever of your king to present something so tempting," said the Queen without a trace of sarcasm. "The scarab evokes a terrifying awe for all of us, but it is not malign, and it is not to be interfered with. In the darkest depths, the sacred scarab creates rays of dazzling light powerful enough to ignite *a new dawn for a new world*."

Colum and Dervor stood speechless in front of her.

The Queen's name suddenly filled his consciousness: Lil . . . *LAKE*. He had forgotten how profound her connection to the lake was. Did she possess the same destructive forces as those terrifying waters?

Lillake turned to Colum. "Come closer."

Colum steeled himself to step forward.

As he looked into her eyes, the Queen's black pupils expanded within the semi-liquid spheres of her green irises. Suddenly, it was as if he were sucked into her eye. Everything disappeared. Adrift in the darkness of Lillake's eyeball, the fires, smoke, sounds, smells, and shape-shifting women, even the cave itself, were nowhere to be seen. The space in her eye felt devoid of life, cold, claustrophobic, exactly the way the lake had so long ago. On impulse, Colum stuck out his tongue, stretching it into the dark, moist, gelatinous substance. It tasted sweet to the point of nausea, but before his stomach could react, he began to spin. Soon the lightning-fast centrifugal force of the spin propelled him through the Queen's dark pupil into the space of her emerald-green iris, and he found himself looking out into the cave.

There he saw the fires and shape-shifting women. The scene in front of him rolled gently in place like swells of the sea. The cave had become irresistibly beautiful. And he knew without a doubt that its beauty, along with the women, river, stalagmites, and stalactites, were all contained *within* the Queen. The realization jolted him into another spin. This one catapulted him out of Lillake's eye and back into the cave.

Everyone around him flickered in and out of existence like

flames. No form held steady for long. He swayed dizzily on his feet and fought not to fall.

"You are the column," announced Lillake, telepathically, *"and now you are forever imprinted on my retina. What you see, Colum, is LIFE AS IT IS, constantly shifting, illusive, evasive, here and not here."*

As she stood up to address the multitude of women, the raven feathers in her robe flared out. "Colum and Dervor are here as our honored guests!" exhorted the Queen in a voice all could hear. "I extend to them our hospitality. Treat them with respect!"

Not a single dissenting murmur could be heard anywhere. The Queen waved her arm and the women dispersed. Lillake addressed Colum and Dervor once more, her magnetism charging the space around them. "You may stay at Yaga's hearth and are free to go where you will."

CHAPTER SIX

Yaga shuffled over to her cooking pot and tasted it. She was stewing a goat with some root vegetables. Appearing satisfied with the results, she dished the warm slurry into bowls. Colum studied the woman as she bustled about. The crone's weathered face had the patina of old age, yet he was sure her energy easily equaled any man in Uncle's labyrinth.

"Try this," said the crone, handing him a bowl of her stew.

Its raunchy odor nearly overpowered him, but he was hungry and ate. After a few spoonfuls, Colum gave the woman a surprised look. "Delicious, Yaga."

She laughed. "That's not saying much after a diet of Nirah's gruel!"

Dervor laughed too. It was a little unsettling for Colum to see how relaxed and open she was with these women. Their volatile, mercurial impulses seemed to intrigue her. He, on the other hand, found their alien nature dangerously reckless, if not outright threatening. Yaga wandered off before they finished their meal.

Dervor peered at her companion. Colum's face was tight, and

he kept scanning the area around them. "Are you all right?" she asked.

"I just wonder how long we'll have to stay here. It feels as if we're stepping deeper into a trap." He looked back at her. "A very dangerous trap."

"We're safe enough now. Even Sny wouldn't dare to go against the Queen's will."

"Lillake has her own agenda, Dervor. Who knows how long she'll host us?" He took a deep breath. "Host me, that is."

"We aren't exactly trapped if we're here as Lillake's guests." She paused. "Why are you in such a hurry to go?"

He stared at her ash-stained face and searched for the right words. "It's easy to be a guest when you're a woman, but I'm a man, and I feel their resentment all the time." Colum remembered peering through Lillake's emerald eye and seeing the whole cave filled with beauty and mystery. "I'm sorry, Dervor. I don't want to force you to leave this place if you're not ready. It's obvious some of these women want to know you better." His eyes glazed over, giving him a faraway look. "All I'm saying is that in their cave, men will always be seen as intruders."

"But where else can you avoid Bambara's fate? Nowhere," she reminded him. "And we aren't here as truants, Colum. Uncle freed us to come, which means nothing is fixed. You of all people know that. Just think of the demanding situations you've navigated."

He nodded. "Uncle did tell me once that nothing is final."

"He's right. Remember how lost and confused you were when you first came to Uncle? In the labyrinth, everything was repetition and conformity. Every aspect of our lives was proscribed. We worked, trained, and had audiences. We're free of all of that now. Nothing in the cave is planned. Life is constantly in flux. To me, their changing forms and wild, raw existence are exhilarating!" Her face glowed in the firelight. "We are on an unplotted course, my darling. Which means we must begin all over again. Let's not be daunted by what comes."

Colum winced when an owl let out a piercing screech. "And what about the Beetle? Shall we be daunted by it? After all, according to Lillake, it's a living blast furnace. I can just see it coming at us like a comet to torch the earth's surface and burn us all to ashes."

She stared at him with shining grey eyes. "The only thing I care about is that we're together and that whatever happens, we'll meet it together."

"I thought you wanted to stay here."

"Not without you," she replied tenderly.

"These women realize how special you are, Dervor. You're not some clueless woman snatched off the surface of the earth. You're from another planet and have survived countless years in Uncle's maze." Colum hesitated. "What I wonder is, why is the Queen letting *me* stay?"

Dervor fixed her eyes on him again. "What do you mean? She knows you swam with the pyrite in the earth's core and that you returned to the labyrinth *voluntarily*. You're hardly any man, my love."

"Touché," he sighed.

"I say we stay in the cave for now. I think we're safer here than anywhere else." Dervor leaned forward to kiss him, and soon they were under Yaga's furs making love again.

Women walked past their wriggling forms with barely a downward glance, until at last Strix stepped brazenly into their hearth space. Greasy pores pockmarked the crone's nose. Her hair was gathered in a loose knot on top of her head with frayed ends sticking out, and her robe was stained and nubby.

"Can't keep you two apart," she said.

The two of them scurried to dress. "Greetings, Strix," said a breathless Dervor, coming out from under the covers.

The crone grinned. "Some of my sisters wish to get to know you better, my dear." When Colum made a motion to follow her, Strix put up her hand to stop him. "Oh, look who's coming to keep you company!"

Colum and Dervor turned to see Ayylo headed their way. When Dervor frowned, he whispered, "It's all right. I love you."

Dervor and Strix left, and the Queen's daughter entered Yaga's circular hearth. She lifted her arms overhead in a long, lazy stretch, releasing a scent of hot musk from her pits. The odor, somewhere between rot and sex, was so potent it deranged Colum's senses and made him feel drunk. He slumped onto Yaga's furs.

Weakly, he said, "I was wondering . . ."

Ayylo arranged herself close to him on the furs. "Yes?"

Colum's nostrils flared at her musk. "Are you a cat who turns into a woman or a woman who turns into a cat?"

Green and gold fire leaped from her eyes, and she purred exactly the way a cat would. "For us, the two are never wholly separate. Right now I'm a cat-*woman* lolling by a warm fire with a man of iron from the labyrinth." She laughed lightly. "I'm curious, Iron Man—what animal would you shape-shift into if you could?"

Fires crackled around them in the vast, dark chamber, and the eerie notes of a nearby conch-shell trumpet tore at his heart. "I don't think I know myself well enough to say."

The fiery-haired daughter of the Queen smiled. "It's your animal nature you don't know."

He gave her a long look. "You're different from the others, Ayylo."

"In what way?"

"For one thing, you don't treat your men like prey."

"Oh, but I do, though they're a different kind of prey for me than for most of my sisters." Ayylo lifted her hand as if it were a lazy paw and stroked his cheek. "You aren't like other men either. I've never seen a man suck at Hursag's breast before." She drew a breath. "It's not an accident that you're here, Colum."

Without warning, Sny stepped inside the parameters of Yaga's hearth. The Panther Woman gave Ayylo a brief nod of recognition before fastening her gaze on Colum. Her hand rested on the hilt of her blade, and a low growl sounded in her throat.

"One day you *will* catch my blade, slave-of-Nirah," said Sny menacingly. Before he could reply, she strode off.

"It's not wise to antagonize that one," warned Ayylo.

He frowned. "Sny considered me fair game when I was still in the labyrinth. I think your warning is a little late."

"There *is* a way to go undetected among us."

"I find that hard to believe."

"Right now, Colum, you're somewhere between visitor and intruder. Take on the smell of our nest and my sisters will ignore you."

"How do I do that?"

"Let me be the orchard in which you dwell."

He let out a shuddering breath. "You mean as one of the *many* fruits waiting there to be plucked?"

She flashed him a brilliant smile. "You might enjoy a new experience."

"I don't think changing my scent will stop Sny," he said.

"Is she the reason you hesitate? Or is it Dervor?" An erotic aliveness charged the air between them. "Dervor is more than welcome to join us in the orchard. My taste flows to men *and* women."

He blushed. "I'm not ready for that."

"Not yet, perhaps. But ah, the thrills we three could have." Ayylo stood up to the bleating of a nearby goat and departed.

Colum was relieved when Dervor stepped onto Yaga's hearth. "Every woman here is trouble. This cave would swallow me whole if I let it."

"Does your attitude have anything to do with Ayylo?"

"She suggested we become a threesome."

Dervor's breasts rose and fell under her wool shirt. "She did?"

"I don't trust any of them, and that includes her."

"Wouldn't you like to feel things you've never felt before?"

"With you, Dervor, not Ayylo. I have no desire to become her plaything."

"She's inviting us to play the games with her, not to become her plaything. And what if we are playthings to each other for a little while? In the labyrinth, all we do is work. This is our chance to learn what it's like to play."

A spiky porcupine plodded across the edge of Yaga's hearth close enough to stare into Colum's eyes. Its look was more curious than threatening. When it moved on, Colum and Dervor sat down together, each watching the other's face soften and blur in the haze of Yaga's fire.

"Of the women you've met, do you have a favorite?" asked Colum. "Someone you'd like to know better?"

"Oh, yes," she said, nodding. "Abruta."

"The one with all the eyes?"

"Uh-huh. I trust her. Don't ask me why." Dervor rested her head on Colum's shoulder. "What about you?"

"They frighten me too much to have a favorite."

"I asked Strix whether all panther women have panther daughters and all falcon women have falcon daughters."

"What did she say?"

"Apparently, there's a certain arbitrariness to it. Though all the women give birth to daughters, no one shape-shifts until puberty, so sometimes their animal will surprise them."

He laughed curtly. "Like a butterfly giving birth to an elephant?"

"Now that *is* a stretch of the imagination!"

Dervor nodded.

"To me they're dangerous, and not just because of their powers. I'm afraid if we stay too long our discipline will erode." He stroked her hair. "It's obvious they want you to stay. And if you did, I'd have to stay too. I couldn't survive losing you, Dervor. Not again."

She pulled his face toward her and kissed him hard. "You won't lose me. We're in this adventure together."

He kissed her back. "Do you know how much I love you?"

"And what if I turn into a groundhog and can't turn back?" she laughed. "Will you still love me?"

"That's not funny."

Her grey eyes turned somber. "We'd better sleep while we have the chance. I'll keep first watch."

Colum lay down and pulled the furs over him. He dreamed of the cave's fires merging with the night stars to become a single field, and in the middle of the field was a luminous beetle. He could see every shining thorn and hair on its legs, the junctions of its golden shell, the flash of intelligence in its eyes. Colum watched the scarab fly off on crimson wings pushing a flaring ball of starlight through the heavens, then awoke with a racing heart to find himself still in the crepuscular light of the cave.

"Bad dream?" asked Dervor gently.

He stared at her, unable to answer. The dream had left him keenly aware of some kind of profound relationship between the beetle and himself, one for which he had no words.

Later, while Colum watched over Dervor asleep, Yaga hobbled back to their hearth. "Our Mistress wishes to see you both," the crone announced.

Lillake sat on her throne when they arrived, blue-black raven feathers glistening in her hair. A string of lapis lazuli beads adorned her neck, and a cluster of silver beetle wings dangled from each earlobe. They all glittered in the light of several torches secured on iron rods. The rods were set up in a semi-circle behind the Queen's throne. She was attended by several women who stood on either side of her.

Dervor and Colum bowed when they arrived.

"I have looked for your friend, Bambara," announced Lillake with a shake of her hair. "It seems he is now wax and wick for the beetle's flame and will not be returning." She stared at them with her emerald-green eyes. "I have decided, Colum, that for the time being, you are welcome to stay and live among us."

"Thank you, Majesty," said Colum.

"I allowed you both to come here," continued the Queen. "No one enters this cave without my knowledge or consent." She focused on Dervor. "It is our hope, Kasi, that you will become one of us. You are a free spirit. As such, you belong with your sisters."

Colum somehow knew the Queen's invitation held no trickery.

"Remember the time before you were wife or slave, Kasi?"

asked Lillake in a soothing voice. "When you walked your own path, sang your own songs? When you saw the world through *your* eyes and no other's?"

Dervor's voice lowered to a whisper. "When I was a child."

"Yes, Kasi. Join us and that path will be yours again."

Strix gave Dervor a look of encouragement. "Get the flies out of your ears, woman. Hear what it is our Mistress offers."

"Sniff the breezes of our cave, Kasi!" cried Yaga, giving her own vigorous nod of encouragement. "Smell true freedom!"

"Dance with us, sister!" called a tall, willowy woman named Huluppu. "Sing with us!"

"This is the place of beginnings," cried another. "Here you may begin your life anew!"

Sny stepped forward. "You've padded the Iron Dragon's twisted maze for far too long. Nirah has hammered and tempered you into something you're not," she said earnestly. "You never belonged there, sister. We offer you a hearth and a fire and sisters who will love you always. Stay with us."

"The rose in the labyrinth turns blue, Kasi. Passions grow cold and wither under all that iron," snorted the Bull Woman, Amorpho. "Your soul is a winged bird meant to fly free!"

"Amorpho sees correctly, child." The Queen nodded. "Take off your shirt."

Dervor pulled off her wool shirt to reveal a muscular, toned upper body.

"*LET YOUR WINGS EMERGE!*" commanded the Queen.

The women watched in hushed silence as Dervor's scapulae shimmered and reddened. The muscle, tissue, and skin stretched, then tore open, leaving only the smallest smearing of blood. A nascent pair of wet, folded wings pushed their way up and out through her shoulder blades. The wings dried quickly in the cave's warm breezes and unfolded gently. With a sideways glance at herself, Dervor watched the bright crimson feathers fluffing out into a complex pattern of bold gold lines that crisscrossed through the red. The sumptuous plumage reached down to her heels, tapering at the tips. Colum noticed more and more women assemble to witness Dervor's marvelous transformation. He heard whistles, hoots, and cries of approval all around.

The Queen beamed. "More than wings await you, Kasi. We've never had a *phoenix* before."

The women began to chant, their voices producing a sensation of lightness in Colum's body.

When Dervor floated a few inches off the floor, Huluppu reached out to steady her. "Take small jumps, sister, and see what happens," coaxed the graceful, slender woman.

Instinctively, Dervor used her scapulae, supported by a whole new combination of muscles, to flex her red-and-white wings. Soon she began beating them like a fan, slowly at first, then faster and faster. The wings glittered like flames in the torchlight, lifting her several feet into the air. The sight elicited a chorus of surprise and delight from those who watched.

"Fly like the phoenix you are, Kasi! Soar round the dome of our cave!" urged the Queen.

With sweeping motions of her wings, Dervor flew up to the dome and circled the entire cave while the women below let out wild ululations.

Colum stared up at her in awe. *The Queen is right. Why wouldn't she join them? To soar on those amazing wings! Now that is freedom! Yet there's no way I can become one of them. If she decides to stay, what will I do?* The thought of losing her burned in him like an inflamed nerve. *Is any of this real? Is it possible we're under some kind of mass hallucination induced by the Queen? But Lillake is as entranced as anyone.*

"Wings like yours, Kasi, aren't meant for the cave alone," proclaimed Huluppu. "They are meant for flying to the stars!"

Bull-like Amorpho spoke to the Queen, "Mistress, she carries great power. She is *more* than worthy of being our sister."

Dervor landed not far from the Queen, spraying ash and sparks into the air.

Keket laughed. "Such a graceful landing. She handles her new power well."

Dervor looked at the sea of faces that surrounded her. "I rejoice in my wings!" she called out as her fluttering feathers slowly settled. "My deepest desire is to join with you, my sisters!"

The women sounded a collective roar of approval. "Welcome, sister!" cried multiple voices at once. "Bask in the warmth of our fires!"

Colum watched, terrified. *Has she forgotten me already?*

"Before I do," said Dervor, "there is something I must tell you. I was sent to the labyrinth for an act of treason."

"You tell us nothing we don't know, Kasi," said Yaga sympathetically. "It is common knowledge that the King of All Illinee ordered your son to be hung and you to be imprisoned in the labyrinth."

Dervor's face expressed shock. "No, you're mistaken. My son was only a child at the time. He was returned to his father and lives on Illinee, a free man."

Colum knew that Dervor had fled Illinee to follow the charismatic traitor, Ulli, taking her three-year-old son with her.

A woman whose face was covered with feathers responded, "Sny speaks the truth, Kasi! Your son was hanged!"

Only long-practiced discipline kept Dervor on her feet.

"Like all men," called out Kle-Ptuza, "Nirah and the King of All Illinee are treacherous deceivers. Nirah told you half-truths to keep you his docile slave."

"No! I did betray the King, as well as my husband, but the Lord of Illinee would never punish an innocent child for my treason."

Abruta's ten eyes glistened in the torchlight. "Oh, but he would, Kasi, and he did. Your son was given a black fate indeed."

"It's the truth, Kasi," said Bruha. "Which means you owe Nirah and the king nothing." She laid a large, comforting hand on Dervor's shoulder. "Your wings herald your newfound freedom from them."

Sny raised a clenched fist in the air. "Uncle's tyranny over our sister is ended!"

The women shouted in jubilant agreement.

Lillake's eyes shimmered with a heatless flame. "Your soul is a winged bird that rises from the ashes! Stay with us and FLY!"

Instead of looking happy, Dervor seemed to crumple as if under a huge weight.

"The source of your deep unrest in the labyrinth has always been the death of your son, Kasi," said the Queen quietly, "and the fact that Nirah erased your memory of it."

"You lie!" shouted Dervor. "Uncle would never do such a thing!"

Colum looked at her in horror. *Did she just call the Queen a liar?*

It was like shaking a hornet's nest. The watching women stirred angrily, but Lillake raised her hand to quiet them. "We are not the liars, child," she said, her voice gentle but firm.

Abruta spoke in a compassionate voice. "I *saw* your son's hanging with my own eyes, Kasi."

Dervor's face turned suddenly haggard as if she had aged years in only a few moments. "I don't believe it. I won't believe it. To be hanged is to be suspended in darkness with no end in sight. Only those who betray the King of All Illinee are hanged."

"He forbids you to lie yet hides the truth himself," said Kle-Ptuza with a glare. "No man can be trusted."

Dervor clutched at her belly, crying, "Oh, my *sweet, sweet boy. Where are you now?*"

Huluppu's voice held urgency. "All that iron has crushed your heart's song, Kasi. Stay with us and you will learn to sing again."

"Swallow Nirah's bitter herb no longer, sister," urged Strix. "Take no more blows from him or his tyrant king."

"You have a place with us!" urged Sny.

"Join with us, Kasi!" cried several voices at once, their faces radiant with welcome once more.

Kle-Ptuza walked over to Colum, and her lips curled back in a snarl. "Is it he who stops you, sister? He hovers over you like a disease, clouding your senses. His very presence sullies us all." The huntress drew her knife. "I will return his carcass to Nirah as a warning to keep his slaves in their proper place!"

She lunged, but Colum leaped clear. He tried to run, but the women started to close in on him, leaving him without a path to escape. Someone pushed him from behind and he stumbled, falling at the feet of Keket.

"Vile man!" yelled Keket, pulling out her dagger.

The uproar broke through Dervor's grief, and she looked up just as Keket raised her dagger while several women held Colum down.

"No!" Dervor yelled. She grabbed a knife from the belt of a woman next to her and flung it at Keket, striking her in the chest. Keket slumped forward, red blood staining her dark robe. The faces in the crowd blanched, and a single collective gasp of disbelief filled the cave.

The Queen rose from her throne, calling out in a thunderous voice, "*SEIZE HER!*"

Several robed women threw themselves at Dervor, who was soon subdued. Panic swept through Colum as he looked on, helpless. He breathed in the smoky air of the cave as he listened to the women's screaming, howling voices. To him, the cave had become a hellscape.

Why did I bring her here? What was I thinking?

"Hold her!" commanded Lillake.

Amorpho and Bruha grabbed Dervor, and the Queen pointed her fingers at the woman's back. Streams of energy shot through them, targeting Dervor's red-gold wings. Her feathers fell off in ugly clumps and left bleeding sores on her skin.

Shouts of outrage resounded in the cave over Dervor's attack on Keket.

Lillake turned toward the rock wall, raised her arms in a high arc, and pointed her fingers at the wall. A windlike force swept through her hands, blasting the rock apart. Clouds of dust filled the area. When it cleared, three-quarters of a rectangular box made of solid granite hovered in the air. The Queen directed another stream of energy at the rock in the box's center, disintegrating it into powder. Then she blew on the fine powder to send it flying in every direction. Women close to the vault coughed and choked in the swirling dust. The rectangular chunk of hollowed-out granite now boasted a hollow interior big enough for a body.

The Queen's emerald eyes turned to Dervor. "Your wings are wasted, but one way or another, you *will* stay with us." Her next words reverberated throughout the cave. "*Place her in the rock!*"

The furor of the women subsided and a hush filled the cave.

Dervor recoiled, realizing the newly made stone coffin was meant for her. "Kill me first," she pleaded.

Colum watched, stunned, as the Queen lifted Dervor high and deposited her in the rock vault.

"Let Uncle retrieve you now!" shouted Sny.

"Kill a *sister*, will you?" shrieked Kle-Ptuza. "To save the drag-on's bloodless slave?!"

"Your thirst shall never be quenched!" shouted another.

A chorus of voices followed.

"Your hunger shall never be satisfied!"

"The power of seeing is taken from you!"

"The power of hearing is taken from you!"

"The warmth of our fires is taken from you!"

"The light of our fires is taken from you!"

"*Move away!*" commanded the Queen, and with a wave of her arm, the vault slid back into the rock wall. Within moments, the last trace of its outline vanished.

"The deed is done!" shrilled a woman. "Keket, our sister, is avenged!"

Colum watched Dervor disappear, a wrenching pain twisting his heart. His mind raced to find a way out of this fever dream. He glanced wildly around the cave in a desperate search for a single friendly face. Any second now, the women's vengeful malice could turn on him. He must find an ally, and fast.

At last his gaze fell on Hursag. If he hoped to save Dervor, there could not be the smallest hesitation. He bolted toward the crone.

"Nana, I'm frightened!" he cried out as he got closer. "Nana, I need milk."

The crone settled on a pile of furs, beckoning for him to join her. Colum sank down breathless beside her. This time when Hursag opened the front of her robe, Colum's need to save Dervor was too stark and urgent for any self-indulgent embarrassment. He nestled as close as possible into Hursag's body and let her bony arms fold around him.

"Drink," she said. The crone's face turned soft as she regarded the supplicant, but this time she made no effort to lift her saggy breast to his lips.

Colum used one hand to raise her breast to his mouth and attempted to suck. Nothing happened.

"A *true* son knows," replied Hursag.

The very air vibrated with danger. With his need to save Dervor first and foremost, Colum cried out in his mind for help . . . to what or to whom he hadn't a clue. His cry carried the whole of himself, stripped, transparent, with nothing held back.

Suddenly, his cheeks took on a life of their own, and he found himself sucking on the hag's nipple in vigorous, rhythmic waves. To his surprise and relief, fresh, sweet milk spurted into his mouth. Colum sucked until his cheeks were sore and his ears popped. He sucked until he felt he would burst if he drank one more drop. It was then that the crone's steady flow of milk stopped.

With a deep sigh of contentment, Hursag smiled at him. "Don't be frightened, sweet babe." Her voice had turned soft and intimate. "Nana won't let anything bad happen to you."

Sny, who had watched from a distance with fury on her face, making no attempt to interfere, now approached Hursag. "He'll betray you, Mammi. He only uses you to save his wretched neck."

The crone smiled sublimely. "Leave us, Sny. This little one is tired and needs to sleep. I won't have you disturb him."

Warring emotions showed on the Cat Woman's face. She squeezed the knife handle on her belt so tight her knuckles whitened, then walked away without another word.

The women's vengeful energy had made them hungry, and they slowly dispersed to eat and talk idly around their cauldrons.

Abruta sauntered over to Hursag's hearth. Five of her eyes stared at Colum, who still had milk dribbling from his lips. Five fastened on her friend.

"It seems you have what you've longed for at last, sister," said Abruta.

Hursag hummed as she stroked Colum's hair, producing a powerful desire in him to sleep. He tried to fight it. The last thing he wanted was to lose his vigilance, not with Dervor buried alive in the rock.

"You resist sleep, my sweets?" asked the crone.

"I feel so sad, Nana."

"Because of your friend, *I know*. We'll speak of her later."

Colum's heart constricted at the thought of Dervor sealed off in claustrophobic darkness. *I'll play at being Hursag's child until I find a way to free you, my love! I'm still here. I won't leave you alone in this place. Use that iron will of yours, my darling. Please don't give up hope.*

"Close your eyes, little one," crooned Hursag. "It's time to sleep."

He slumped unconscious in her lap.

CHAPTER SEVEN

Colum woke up lying on a pile of animal furs close to a fire. He looked up at the vaulted ceiling and realized he was in a cave. A swift hawk flew overhead. Since hawks don't fly in caves, he wondered if he were still dreaming. Then, as if someone had pulled a giant plug inside him, it all came back in a huge sickening rush. Dervor was buried alive inside the rock wall. *Is she conscious? Can she breathe?* He felt a desperate, panicked need to save her.

The smell of burning wood stung his nostrils and throat, and he became aware of Hursag sitting next to him. Strands of smoke from the fire wavered in the air like thin ropes between them. The crone was talking in a low voice to another cowled figure, and he tried to make out what she was saying.

"Colum is no longer welcome in Uncle's world," said Hursag.

"He has shown great courage in coming here," replied her visitor.

"Brave or not, Abruta, he can't stay with us, not as he is. Sny and Kle-Ptuza aren't the only ones who want him dead."

"We must watch over him that much closer then. At least for

the time being." She tossed her head and her hood fell backward, revealing ten multicolored eyes. Two of them turned and focused on him. "He's awake."

At a loss for what to say or do, Colum sat up.

"Greetings, Colum," said Abruta. Three of her eyes turned to the rock wall that held Dervor, two remained on him, and five looked out into the cave.

Colum stared at the fire with a sinking feeling. "Is Keket alive?"

Abruta nodded. "She is. We intervened in time to save her."

A sigh of relief escaped him. "Does that mean the Queen will let Dervor go?"

"No, for it was Kasi's intention to kill Keket," replied the woman.

"She acted because Keket was going to kill me."

"I shall try to explain," continued Abruta gently. "Kasi came here to become one of us, whether she knew it or not. She never belonged to Nirah. A woman with her spirit wasn't meant to live in a world of men. We all knew it, which is why we welcomed her as a sister." Sadness filled all ten of Abruta's eyes. "Though in the end, her love for you proved too strong. She couldn't let you die."

Hursag spoke. "She made her choice."

Colum thought of Dervor utterly isolated and lost in the wall of rock. He looked at Abruta with torment in his eyes. "You care about her. I know you do. Please, Abruta, help me free her. She doesn't deserve this."

Abruta directed all ten eyes at the limestone cliff that held Dervor. "At the moment, she is hardly breathing. Her mind is silent. She is like a fawn frozen in fear and poised for flight."

"Can you really see her, Abruta?"

She nodded. "Understand this, Colum. Aroused by her treachery, our sisters would have torn her apart. The Queen placed her in there for her own safety."

He drew in a sharp breath. "Even so, she can't stay there. The Queen has to let her out. Do you think she's just waiting for things to settle down?"

"I am not privy to our Mistress's plans, Colum. All I know is that Kasi is being pulled into the darkness of herself."

He shuddered. "I feel so helpless."

"Is her experience really so foreign to you? Didn't you crawl into the pyrite's narrow crack of rock, barely able to move and full of fear? And what happened? You were taken on a joyous, wild ride through the earth's fiery depths."

"But Abruta, don't you understand? I crawled into that rock on my own. This isn't a choice for her."

"Kasi came to our cave voluntarily, did she not? She knew the risks. She also knew your presence as a man among us would be fiercely resented." Abruta paused to let her words sink in. "You, Colum, are the one who doesn't understand. Kasi chose you *over* her new sisters. Because of her actions, we learned where her true loyalty lay."

A grim expression settled on Colum's face. "This is not how we hoped things would turn out. She should have let Keket kill me."

Abruta gave him a sympathetic look. "Kasi acted on instinct. She loves you."

The pressure he felt to free Dervor nearly crushed him. "Help me get her out of that rock, Abruta," he pleaded. "Please, before she loses her mind!"

The woman's unnerving eyes returned to him. "I can no more go against our Mistress than you could go against Nirah."

Hursag spoke. "I cannot facilitate Kasi's release, but I can offer you a way to stay close to her."

"What do you mean?"

"Become my child and you won't have to leave our cave."

"You want to adopt me?" asked Colum, taken aback.

She shook her head. "What I offer you is a chance to be reborn."

"Reborn how?" The crone's words made no sense.

"You already know that in our cave, all forms are malleable. You even felt the truth of that in the labyrinth. Nirah himself heated and beat your iron, folding and refolding it into the form you are now. He shattered your surface self in the fires of his furnace and, with the blows of his hammer, strengthened and reshaped your rarefied mettle to make you the man of iron you are today."

Colum watched the smoldering ashes from Hursag's fire settle gently on the rock floor. "I don't care about myself," he said. "The only thing I care about is getting Dervor out of that bloody rock in one piece. She loved being with the women here. She should never have been forced to make the decision she did."

"Her fate is her own," said Hursag solemnly. "I'm talking about yours. The labyrinth is deep, but I believe you were meant to go deeper than Uncle's maze."

"Are you implying that because this cave is deeper in the earth than the labyrinth, I belong here?"

"I am."

His frustration felt extreme. "You know as well as I do that no one wants me here."

"That will change if you become my child."

"In the uterine waters of our Cauldron of Rebirth," interjected Abruta, "your mind and body will return to a fetal state."

Colum's head jerked back as if he'd been slapped. "Is that even possible?" When Hursag first invited him to drink at her breast, he thought it was a bizarre prank.

"Of course it is," replied Abruta. "Haven't you already seen us shape-shift into all kinds of forms?"

"You mean I'll actually become an infant again?"

"Yes."

"What would happen to my memories?"

"They will be held in abeyance during your childhood, but once you reach maturity, they'll return."

Abruta placed her hand reassuringly on Colum's shoulder. "My sister offers you a chance to be reborn in our cave. This is a rare gift."

Colum thought of Dervor's heart constricting where she lay cramped in a narrow crevice of impenetrable darkness and silence. How could he leave the cave without her? He turned to Hursag. "Why do you want *me* for your child if men are such abominations?"

"The answer is simple. You are the only one capable of bringing in my milk. Even now, when I sniff you, a whiff of my milk rises into my nostrils." She paused. "Do you remember that day in London, when we followed you in the car . . ."

The memory flashed of walking home from work the day Uncle kidnapped him and being followed by a car. He had caught a glimpse of two older women in the front seat. "That was you in the car, wasn't it? You and Abruta."

Hursag nodded. "I have known for a long time now that I've wanted you for a son. The sight of you makes my breasts tingle. This birth is important to both of us, Colum. Say yes, and no part of you will be without my protection, strength, or love."

"If I'm so important to you, why didn't you kidnap me that day? Why did you let Uncle take me?"

"It was necessary for you to undergo the dragon's training, but I have always been with you. I came to you in your dreams, remember?"

"*The lion!*" he gasped. A strange calm came over him. How many times had the dream lion consoled and advised him at critical junctures? Her presence gave him courage when he needed it the most. "If I do this, will you ask the Queen to set Dervor free?" Colum looked earnestly at the old woman. "Will you give me that peace of mind?"

"There is no bargaining over this," replied Hursag. "Either you agree to be my son or not. If you agree, you will remain close to her. That is all I can offer."

Abruta's ten eyes swept outward to where Dervor lay in the cliff wall. "Kasi's own path has brought her to that rock, Colum."

"She came here hoping to be part of your sisterhood," he countered. "Instead she ended up being buried alive." He looked at the distant wall that held the woman he loved. "Can you see her, Abruta? Is she all right?"

"She lies in a quiet twilight between sleep and wakefulness. Her heart and lungs are barely moving. She sinks into the dark space around her, a space that will become her chrysalis. In it she'll have a chance to transform." Her ten eyes glittered in the firelight. "Meanwhile, my sister offers you a different fate than what you had as Uncle's faithful servant. She offers you the gift of sonship." The woman smiled. "Here you will no longer taste iron in the air."

"What will I taste in its place?"

"Ash, salt, and blood."

Colum breathed in the pungent, smoke-filled air, gripped by the gravity of his situation, and stared at Dervor's wall. A powerful desire overcame him to join her in her darkness, to wrap his arms around her and never be separated again. But Uncle's training prodded him out of such indulgence. If he stayed in the cave, he still had a slim chance to rescue her. He thought of Hursag's unmistakable regard for him and realized something in him trusted her. "I agree to be reborn if you are my guide," he said, taking a deep breath. "I do this for your sake and for Dervor's."

Hursag's face brightened. "Soon our hearts shall beat as one!"

CHAPTER EIGHT

The news spread throughout the cave, and everyone began to prepare for the upcoming birth. Soon the vaulted and cavernous space resounded with the women's joyful activity. Vegetables were gathered and animals butchered for the event. The smell of beer, along with wines fermented by wild yeasts in clay pots, wafted through the air. Savory and sweet pastries baked in beehive-shaped ovens made of mud and straw.

Colum sat by Hursag's fire thinking of how he was about to surrender his life to this woman. Uncle had only erased his memories of the labyrinth. As a newborn, he would lose not just personal history but the body he now inhabited. Far worse, he would lose his basic sense of himself.

Abruta sat nearby watching him. "What is on your mind, Colum?" she asked.

"I don't understand why all this fuss is going on over a mere man," he replied, a cynical tone in his voice.

"You may be a mere man, but Hursag is highly loved and respected by all of us. And she has never borne a child in our cave before, which makes your birth extremely special. Because you will gestate not in Hursag's womb but in the Cauldron of Rebirth, our *common womb*, the Queen has summoned all our sisters to be present, including those traveling in space."

Colum was genuinely surprised. "Women from the cave travel in space?" he asked.

Abruta nodded. "You should know that some of our sisters question whether you can survive a life as deep as ours, let alone flourish."

"And yet they're preparing to celebrate my rebirth."

"Yes, because they revere Hursag and would never deny her the child she so fervently desires."

"Is that supposed to reassure me?"

"What should reassure you is Hursag's love."

"I know she wants a child, but isn't she stirring up a hornet's nest by bringing a man into the cave? What does she see in *me* that would make her risk that?"

"Perhaps she sees the column that will connect our two worlds."

Colum shook his head at Abruta's nonsensical suggestion and changed the subject. "What happens in the cauldron?"

"Your body will dissolve, but not before its cells attune with Hursag's to become a fetus. Don't worry, it is a painless process." Abruta pulled her hood over her head and stood to leave. "I promise you this, Colum, I will not cease to look upon Kasi while she lies in the rock."

Tears filled his eyes at her words. "Thank you, Abruta."

Once she left, Colum stared in Dervor's direction. "I'm so sorry I can't do more, my darling," he whispered into the smoke-filled cave. *What an idiot I was to think we could just come here and be granted a solution to our dilemma. It was doomed from the start. Look at how you've already faded into oblivion for them after they were so fervent to have you as their sister. Now they bustle around as if you never existed. Shape-shifters at their core! How can I ever trust them when they're so mercurial?*

Colum watched the activity continue around him. Women were bringing in more plants, animals, fish, and firewood from the forest. They stuck posts in the floor and wound flowering vines around them. Steam from countless cauldrons moistened the air. The sounds of their shuffling feet, rustling robes, and excited voices never stopped. There was no day or night in the cave. They slept solely on the basis of how tired they were. Women everywhere festooned their hair and garments with a stunning variety of colorful, shining decorations. Colum breathed in the pungent cave air, realizing he was involved in an all-or-nothing gamble with Hursag. He was both totally dependent on her and way out of his depth with her.

Abruta arrived at Hursag's hearth. "It is time, Colum."

Everyone began to move en masse in the direction of another cavern. Colum took a final glance at the rock wall that held his lover's body. *I won't leave you, Dervor, no matter what happens. My love, I hope you feel me here. You're not alone. You'll never be alone. My arms will hold you even if I can't remember. My heart will always beat with yours.*

Although he had shed his editor persona long ago, a quote by the poet W. H. Auden popped into his mind: "We are lived by powers we pretend to understand."

By the time Colum and Abruta arrived at the hidden gallery, most of the women were gathered inside. The walls and floor of the chamber were smeared and daubed with red ochre. In the middle of the room, nine glistening stalagmites like gnarled tree trunks encircled a giant cauldron covered in strange markings. The cauldron balanced on an iron trivet, small fires gently warming the water from beneath.

Colum and Abruta moved slowly toward a narrow set of rough-hewn rock stairs. On either side, tightly pressed bodies parted to make way for them. The stairs led up to a limestone platform that abutted the cauldron's rim. Colum trembled as he climbed the stairs under the gaze of hundreds and hundreds of staring eyes. He glimpsed Sny below. She wore a loose robe instead of her usual leather pants, her hair entwined with flowers. There was not a trace of mockery on her face.

"Remember," whispered Abruta, "the dissolution of your adult form will not touch your essence. The resonance of your essence will be transferred through the cauldron's waters to you as a fetus."

Her words only made Colum tremble more. Aware that his entire existence was about to dissolve and reform, he tried to keep his focus on what was happening in the moment. Abruta put a firm hand on his arm to steady him as he stepped onto the platform.

"The water is so murky," he whispered.

"Each woman in the cave has contributed a few drops of her blood to mix with it," replied Abruta. "Some cut their flesh to provide the blood. Others gave menstrual blood."

Her explanation only made him queasier and more disoriented. Colum stared down at the crimson streaks of blood saturating the water like red dye. In a way, each woman there was taking part in the dissolution of his identity. The thought sent a chill up his spine.

"Our blood lends vitality to the water and will help revivify you once your current form dissolves," explained Abruta.

Seven women solemnly climbed the rock stairs to position themselves around him on the platform. "What's happening?" he whispered to Abruta.

"These women have made a solemn vow to be your advisers and protectors from this time forth. As have I." She turned to the woman on her left. "Allow me to introduce Ethliu. Ethliu has come from space to attend your rebirth."

The woman towered over him. Her burnished gold hair flashed in the torchlight, and a black sheepskin draped over her forest-green gown. She exuded an extraordinary sense of power and strength.

"You shall be a mighty son to my sister!" declared Ethliu, and her deep voice boomed against his chest.

Abruta turned to Colum's right, where a tall, willowy woman stood with sprigs of flowers in her dark reddish-brown hair. She wore a trailing cloak of willow leaves. "I am Huluppu," she announced.

"I remember you," said Colum. "I saw you change into a willow tree."

The Willow Woman gave him a tender smile. "Do not be afraid. We shall watch over the entirety of your rebirth to see that all goes well."

Huluppu and Ethliu carefully pulled off Colum's grey wool shirt. "You must go into the cauldron naked," explained Ethliu, nodding at his pants.

Colum tried not to be embarrassed as he stepped out of them in front of the large audience. The women placed their arms around each other's waists and began to sway from side to side, moaning as if in labor. Colum swayed too, and Ethliu gripped his arm to hold him steady.

The Queen arrived, adorned in a cape that shone with the silver-gold carapaces of thousands of beetles. Hursag walked naked at Lillake's side. The crone's sharp, bony clavicles rose above her drooping breasts. A spiral painted with blood covered her belly. Queen and crone ascended the stairs and stepped to the lip of the cauldron. Colum leaned closer, noticing for the first time that the cauldron's interior was lined with pink quartz. He knew the tremendous pressure it took to produce pink quartz and wondered if that kind of pressure was about to be exerted on him.

Bull-faced Amorpho, also one of his attendants, swung her arm out over the cauldron. "Colum," she exclaimed in a loud voice, "behold the font of your rebirth!" Amorpho then grabbed Colum and, to his great fright and embarrassment, lifted him high over her head and turned him in a slow circle for all to see.

When the circle was complete, the Queen intoned, "*Enter the waters of your rebirth!*"

The Bull Woman lowered her charge feet first into the cauldron. As soon as his flesh touched the bloody water, a cry escaped him. It felt as if he were free-climbing a high mountain, holding on to a firm crevice, and had to let go.

Amorpho released her hold on him, and he plunged deep underwater. Soon he floated up like a cork to bob on the surface. Hursag walked to the rim of the cauldron and jumped in, landing close to Colum. At once she wrapped her arms around him. All around the cauldron the women's swaying movements and moans became louder and more intense. The viscosity of their blood in the water rendered Colum sluggish, sticky, light-headed, and pliable. Held in Hursag's arms, he floated in eerie suspense. Thoughts tumbled in his mind as he fought to keep himself oriented to reality and maintain a sense of self. But the time for that self was running out, and he knew it. Language was collapsing.

I'm being reformed . . . re . . . born . . . in the waters of this . . . bloody . . . caul . . . dron. His mind loosened further under the pressure of the water. Colum searched frantically for words to finish his thought. *I do this . . . for . . . you . . . Der . . . !*

Warm amniotic fluid sloshed in rhythmic waves over his head, acting like a solvent to dissolve the snapshots of memories from his life. Words disappeared. He was porous, with no self-definition, which made him infinitely more susceptible to the power of the warm, blood-streaked water. He floated in a dreamlike, amorphous reverie, enfolded in the crone's loving embrace. Duration was now an uninterrupted rhythmic flow. He surrendered with a final sigh to the arms of the mother and, in the cauldron's timeless womb, let the bundles of habits, beliefs, and memories that held together who he was drift away.

The women watched as the pulsations of the bloody, viscous water turned into full-blown contractions, pressing Colum into an atom-splitting meltdown accompanied by a blaze of light so bright they jumped. Soon the head of an infant crowned above the surface of the water, and the breath of every woman present stopped.

"Behold! The son of Hursag slides forth from the outflow between his mother's thighs!" exclaimed Amorpho with a bellow of joy. Cries of delight sounded throughout the alcove.

Hursag held the newborn aloft as Amorpho reached down to receive him. The Bull Woman cradled his wet, naked body in her large arms, while Ethliu and Huluppu leaned over to help

Hursag out of the water. The new mother shook off her wetness like a cat and, taking the infant from Amorpho, held him up for all to see. A common burst of explosive joy shook the grotto walls.

"Hursag's child comes forth from the blood of us all!" shouted Ethliu.

"Our life blood surges through him!" exulted Yaga.

"How seamlessly he slips from one lifestream to another!" cried Huluppu.

"Hursag's heart and his beat as one!"

Another roar of approval sounded.

Ayylo, radiant with happiness, exclaimed, "Our brother shall never starve for our love!"

"This fledgling has come far to land in his mother's nest!" another rang out.

"In our place of origin he is reborn!"

"Our beloved Mammi has spawned a son for us!"

"Behold, our beloved brother has burst into form!"

A pinkish, cheeselike vernix covered the baby's skin. Ethliu leaned over and kissed the infant. "Sweet babe, firstborn son of our cave, you herald a new order of life for all of us," she whispered.

Panpipes and flutes began to play.

The Queen turned her dazzling emerald gaze on the new-born child. "Welcome to the Cave of the Dark Moon," she said, smiling.

The women began to leave the alcove and return to the main chamber. Their cries of jubilation resounded as they went. In the vaulted cave, they danced and sang and feasted to the music of drums, lyres, flutes, and bull-roarers. Laughter rang out. Bowls overflowed with honey cakes and berries. Roasted meat in skewers was offered everywhere, along with beer and wine.

A chair for Hursag and a fur-lined basket for the baby were placed next to the Queen to enable the women to view the child and praise the new mother.

Ethliu's golden hair framed her face like a halo. "Since Colum is now of your lineage, Hursag, he will share in your glory."

"He already shares it, sister, or he could never have brought in my milk." The crone beamed. "Will you leave after the celebration?"

"Yes, but if your son ever has need of me, I shall return." She stroked the infant's cheek. "Look how clear and bright his eyes are. How fine his color."

Hursag glowed. "He is a beautiful baby, sister."

Abruta looked at the newborn. "For most men, this cave is the last station on their way to death. But for Colum, it has become a fountain of life."

CHAPTER NINE

Colum slept on his mother's furs beside her. "He's a voracious eater," said Hursag to Abruta.

Abruta, sitting close to them, watched a trace of milk dribbling down the baby's chin. "He comes by his voraciousness naturally. After all, he is the son of a lion. His awareness now originates with you."

A hummingbird, wings flapping so fast they were invisible, hovered close enough to Hursag's face to share a brief glance with her.

"Zisitee," greeted the crone, smiling, "come whenever you like to see my son."

As if in acknowledgment, the hummingbird dipped her head and flew off.

Hursag looked down at her babe. "Look how his eyelids flutter, sister. Do you see what he's dreaming?"

"As a newborn, he is once again more star seed than human, and he dreams of the cosmos as all newborns do," said Abruta. She stroked the baby's small hand. "How different his life will be, sister, suckling at a lion's teat."

Colum sucked in vigorous gulps, immersed in the sensation of Hursag's warm, sweet milk flowing into him.

———

As he grew from infant to small boy, the dark chamber of the cave was the only landscape Colum knew. And he knew it well. He didn't have to go to the forest to hear birdsong or frogs croaking. The dizzying spontaneity of the women's constantly shifting forms provided him with all the nature he needed, and moving among them was as natural to him as breathing. Hawks, jaguars, and raccoons morphed seamlessly from animal to human and back again. The rhythm of the women tending their fires, preparing food, chatting, singing, dancing, and shape-shifting attuned him to their world of flux and flow.

Soon Hursag began to take Colum on forays away from her hearth. On one outing, he sat by the river building mud creations. His mother squatted close to him, scooping up her own handful of muddy clay and shaping it into the form of an animal. Colum stopped what he was doing to watch her scrape off the excess mud.

"What is it, Nana?"

"I don't know. Let's find out." With a sharp stick, she created the effect of fur on its body. Next the crone sketched a face, squished two dark pebbles in it for eyes, and added one for a nose.

"A groundhog!" he cried.

"Shall I sing to it?" asked the crone.

The idea excited him. "Yes, Nana, sing."

Hursag's voice lifted in a lilting melody. "Rise up, little brother," she sang, "rise up." She smiled at Colum. "Sing with me this time."

They sang together. "Rise up, little brother, rise up!"

The clay figure, still on its side, moved its small legs as if to stretch them and flipped itself upright. Hursag sang again, "Walk, little brother, walk."

"Walk, little brother, walk," sang Colum after her.

To Colum's utter delight, the groundhog slowly moved

forward. In a rush of excitement, the boy seized the ambling animal and threw it in the river.

"Swim, groundhog, swim!" he sang, but instead of swimming, the groundhog dissolved into muddy clay. The child reached into the river where it had been but to no avail. He shrugged his small shoulders in puzzlement.

"The water took him, my sweets," explained his mother.

He shook his head. "I don't even know that, Nana."

"Now you do. That's what water does to mud."

He gave her a forlorn look. "Oh."

Hursag leaned over to kiss the top of his ear. Her kiss made him giggle.

Another time, Hursag was washing their clothes at the river. Not far from her, Colum watched an iridescent green beetle make its way through the wet sand. He noticed it was having difficulty. Looking closer, he saw one of the beetle's serrated forelegs dangling uselessly at its side. Gingerly, the boy picked up the insect.

"It's hurt, Nana," he announced.

"Shall I fix it?"

He held it out to his mother, his eyes wide with anticipation. "Yes, please."

Hursag cupped her hands over the beetle and breathed into them, then carefully put the insect back on the ground. Colum squealed in delight as it scurried off on all six strong legs. To him, there was nothing his mother couldn't do. He trusted her implicitly. The space between them was always filled with love and delight.

"Where do you think the beetle is going?" she asked. "To drink at the river?"

The boy thought about it. "Maybe it will climb a ledge to look down on us." Then, with a grin, he said, "Or maybe it will steal crumbs from Yaga's hearth."

"What if she flies on top of Ayylo's head to shine like a pretty jewel?"

Colum clapped his hands happily. "Yes, a pretty jewel in Ayylo's hair!"

Back at their hearth, Hursag deposited her basket of wet clothes on the floor. At once the boy pulled out his freshly washed tunic and laid it on a flat rock by the fire to dry. It pleased him to do things he saw others doing.

Huluppu strolled over. Ivy fronds were threaded through her hair like ribbons and gave off a jadelike radiance in the firelight. Colum knew Huluppu was special. Unlike most of his animal sisters, she shape-shifted into a willow tree. What's more, his mother told him she was one of his seven protectors.

The Willow Woman held out a leather bag to Colum. "For you, little one, a gift from the forest."

Something in the bag was squirming. When he opened it, a baby rabbit jumped out. "Can I keep it?" he asked in awe.

"Yes, of course." Huluppu placed the rabbit in his lap and he gently stroked its grey fur. "I thought it was time you had a pet to play with." Next, she pulled a pouch full of clover from a pocket in her robe. "Feed her this, and I'll bring you more as you need it." Finally, the woman tied a strip of leather around the rabbit's neck with a rope attached, then tied the rope to a post. "We don't want her running away," Huluppu said, smiling.

Colum noticed a deer freshly tethered to a post at a neighboring hearth. The hearth belonged to a woman named Cardea. While his mother and Huluppu chatted, the boy wandered over to see the animal. The deer's gentle eyes stared into his above its moist, black nose. The next instant, Cardea brought a heavy hammer down on the animal's head, bludgeoning it to its knees. The deer teetered and dropped to one side. Colum started to cry.

Yellow-toothed Yaga padded over from her hearth so fast the skin folds on her cheeks bounced as she came. "Cardea, what were you thinking?" she chided. "You scared the little one!"

"Oh, sister, I never saw him there," said the woman, chagrined.

Hursag appeared, and Colum threw his arms around her with a sob.

"I never meant to frighten him, sister," Cardea said sincerely, then knelt down to meet Colum at eye level. "The blow was strong and swift, little one. The doe felt nothing."

Hursag took her son's hand. "Come, let us look at her." They moved closer to the fallen deer. "See how peacefully she sleeps? Her life will provide food for your sisters, and she will live inside them."

Colum stared at the deer and felt his mother's calm response to its demise. She squeezed his hand reassuringly, and the two of them returned to their hearth. Hursag lay down on a spread of musky fox and marten furs and pulled him down after her. Colum stared up at the dome ceiling and listened to his mother's soft breathing. With an acuity of vision born in the Cauldron of Rebirth, the boy watched a droplet of water make a long, swift descent from the dome. Suddenly, his hand flashed out to catch it. He used his index finger to push the shiny sphere of water on his palm into an elongated shape.

Hursag leaned over to blow on the droplet, turning its color from slate blue to pink.

"Orange, Nana! Make it orange!" cried Colum.

She blew again. Her small son watched, transfixed, as two streaks of yellow and one streak of red magically appeared, then slowly mingled to produce a bright orange.

"Green!"

"You make it green," she invited.

"I don't know how, Nana."

"Of course you do. Simply close your eyes and *see* the color green." He squeezed his eyes tight, and the crone smiled. "Nod when it happens."

He gave a vigorous nod.

"Open your eyes."

The boy stared at the droplet on the palm of his hand. "*It's green!*"

His mother laughed out loud. "Now you can play with colors whenever you like."

In Colum's excitement, his hand jumped and the bubble burst.

As a child of the cave, Colum learned to discern between the smells of each cooking pot. He was able to differentiate the odors of a woman's breath and know what she had just eaten.

He heard every rustle in the robes of the women who passed by. For him the robes themselves were like living fabrics with intriguing folds that entertained him with their shadow play. He could recognize individual voices in the cacophonous array of sounds surrounding him. Everything in the limestone chamber vibrated with life.

Hursag watched her son playing with his rabbit. "You've grown so fast I'm going to have to spin you a new tunic," she said.

Abruta had come over to comb flax at the crone's hearth. The boy knew she would comb until the clean fibers stood up "like the raised hackles of a dog." Abruta smiled. "You're such a meticulous weaver, sister."

"I'm doing this for Colum's new tunic. He plays hard, sister, as hard as he once labored in Nirah's labyrinth."

Abruta's ten eyes glistened in the firelight. "I wonder what will happen when he grows up and all those memories return."

The children who lived in the cave displayed spontaneity and throbbing aliveness. If they felt hungry or thirsty, they had only to stop at the closest hearth and their needs would be met. There were no rules. No one ever told them "no" unless they faced real danger. Mothers abided their children's explorations, allowing them to discover the mysteries of the cave at their own pace and on their own terms. As a result, the children had deep-seated self-confidence.

Colum's body grew and his mind developed in the cave's boundless presence. Soon he was running with other children in small packs. His closest friend, Iblis, was a dark-skinned girl with black hair and cerulean eyes. She was being raised by someone other than her birth mother. When Colum asked where her real mother was, the girl replied, "Flying in space."

The two of them loved to play a game with five short, spiky bones, the vertebrae of an animal. The object was to throw the bones in the air, then intercept them with the back of a hand as they fell and catch as many as possible, as fast as possible.

Iblis wore a moss-green tunic and a jangle of copper bells on one ankle. She tossed the bones high, catching four of them.

"You're so fast!" exclaimed Colum admiringly. Then it was his turn. He reached his hand out with blurring speed and caught all five.

"Not as fast as you!" cried Iblis. "Your hand flashes out like the tongue of a snake!"

The children played on, their breath and hearts rising and falling with each toss. After a few more rounds, they ran off giggling toward the river. Women and livestock leaped out of their way as girl and boy chased each other around a profusion of fires. When the children of the cave knocked things over or trampled through someone's furs, they were never made to feel guilty or embarrassed. The women just laughed, picking up and dusting off as needed. Theirs was a life of freedom and exuberance.

Colum and Iblis scooped the cool river water into their cupped hands and drank thirstily. Colum turned to Iblis then and asked, "What animal do you want to be when you shape-shift?" The question was a favorite topic among the children in the cave.

Her expression turned serious. "A raven like my mother, of course. What about you?"

"Oh, I want to be like my mother too."

"A lion?"

"A roaring lion!" He stared at the river. "Iblis, do you think everyone is happy with what they become?"

"I don't know anyone who isn't. Do you?"

"No."

"You ask the oddest questions sometimes, Colum."

"What if you don't change into a raven?"

"I wouldn't mind being an otter!" Her face lit up at the idea. "I love the water!"

"You'd be a great otter, Iblis."

"I'm hungry," she announced. "I'm going to find something to eat."

"Go ahead. I think I'll stay and swim awhile."

Colum threw off his tunic and dove naked into the river without waiting for a reply. The impact of the cool water on his chest shocked him, but his body soon adjusted. The boy swam to the other side of the river, an area without fires, women, or animals. He stepped onto the shore, shaking beads of water off himself like a duck and feeling invigorated. Colum leaned against a lichen-encrusted boulder, one of many scattered across the rough rock floor, and started to sing. It was a song he had made up and only sang when he went swimming. Then he startled, thinking he saw something move close to the cavern wall. It moved again. This time he barely made out a naked figure, thinly coated with rock dust, standing under the shadows of a crumbling ledge. At first, the boy wondered if the figure were a natural part of the cave wall, but then it stepped forward. The figure had small breasts and hips and, below its stomach, a pale triangular outline. She also boasted a head with round, recessed eyes, two holes for a nose, and no lips. Suddenly, she hissed at him, a slow inhale and exhale through a tubelike mouth. Colum's heart skipped a beat. Even in this cave, the creature felt alien.

"What were you sssinging?" asked the Rock Woman. The forcible passage of her breath through the hole in her lower jaw made her words sound like a low, sharp whistle.

"My water song," he answered.

"Ssso sssoothing."

The Rock Woman seemed as placid and ancient as the cave itself. Her reddish hair resembled wet sand and looked as if it would fall away if he splashed water on it. Her dusty odor resonated so deep in his chest it was hard to breathe, as if earth itself were infiltrating his lungs.

"Our cave never hosted a *boy* before," she whistled. A bat landed on the woman's head, then folded its dark wings as if resting on a rock ledge.

Colum stared wide-eyed at her, not knowing what to say.

The woman reached out a bony index finger to touch him between his brows. At her touch, stars, like bursting geysers, exploded in his head. She withdrew her hand. "I sssee it now."

The creature's next words blew through him like a wind. "You are not an intrusion but an upending."

The boy fainted.

He regained consciousness on Hursag's furs close to her fire. "How do you feel?" she asked.

"I had a bad dream, Nana," he groaned. "My head hurts."

His mother smeared duck grease on his burning skin. "I found you by the river with your forehead inflamed. It looks burned or badly scraped. What happened?"

Suddenly, he remembered. "You never saw anything like it, Nana! It had no eyes. I thought it was a talking rock, only instead of talking, it whistled through a hole." The boy shook his head. "It was *terrible*."

"You met the Rock Woman, my son. She's different, yes, but not terrible. She's the oldest woman in our cave, and no one can see her unless she wants them to. Many of our sisters have *never* seen her." Hursag was silent a moment. "You say she talked to you?"

"Yes, Nana."

"And you understood her?"

He nodded. "She touched my forehead with her finger. Is that why it hurts?"

"What happened when she touched you?"

"I saw *light*! All this light! Brighter than all the fires in our cave!" His voice shook at the memory. "Sparks of light were shining everywhere!" He clapped his forehead with both hands in histrionic despair. "It was crazy, Nana! I felt I'd die of all the light!"

"But you didn't, my son. The Rock Woman has honored you." Hursag looked gravely at him. "Didn't I warn you not to cross the river?"

He nodded sheepishly.

"Why do you think I did that?"

"So I wouldn't meet the Rock Woman?"

His mother took his face in her blue-veined hands to stare directly at him. "Yes, my son, and that's because you're too young to meet with her."

Hursag had submerged a pile of flax in water to rot away the unwanted parts of its stems from the tough fibers, and now she and Abruta sat combing the flax fibers next to the fire. Colum watched his mother work. He loved her sparkling amber eyes and how her cheeks were tinged bright pink in the firelight.

"Come sit while I comb your tangled hair," invited Hursag. The boy settled himself cross-legged in front of her. She began to draw her bronze comb through a section of his hair, disentangling the strands as she went. After a while, Colum's scalp started to tingle, and he began to fidget.

"Sit still," instructed his mother.

The boy lifted a hand to touch his hair. To his surprise, the smooth strands had been replaced by something that felt squishy and moist. What's more, there was a crawling sensation across his entire scalp. "Something's wrong, Nana," he said irritably.

"Sit still." The crone handed him a mirror made of black volcanic glass. "Look, my son, but no hysterics."

"Help!" he yelled. New cells in the connective tissues of his scalp were differentiating into carnivorous worms. All over his head, the boy's hair was changing into the flattened, segmented, soft bodies of leeches. The sight of the leeches sprouting out of his hair follicles horrified him. His entire scalp had become one flaming, maddening *itch* caused by the incessant tugging of the tiny bloodsuckers. As they wriggled out of subcutaneous regions on his skull, Colum reached up in a fury to rub them out.

"No," warned his mother firmly.

In a final surge, the insidious wormlike creatures replaced the last of his human hair. The boy leaped in a half twist to face his mother. "Get rid of them, Nana! I want them out of my head! I want my hair back!"

"They are your hair," she said patiently.

"No, they aren't!" he yelled.

Now firmly attached to Colum's scalp, the small, soft worms

squirmed under, over, and across each other, blindly stretching out their mouths to suck at empty air. With each movement the boy could feel them elongating, shortening, and elongating again. The leeches cast themselves into the air like hundreds of antennae, extending up and out in every direction, searching for nourishment. Steam from his mother's cooking pot rose to moisten their wormy flesh.

"You must get to know them, my son," urged Hursag.

Tentatively, plaintively, the boy reached up and brushed his fingers across their undulating suckers. Just as quickly, he dropped his hands. "I did it, Nana. I touched them. Now change it back," he pleaded.

"Touching them doesn't mean you know them," she replied.

Abruta cut a shallow slash across her palm with her knife and held it over his head. There was a delicate stir of excitement in the cluster of their . . . his . . . mouths. The next moment, the hungry leeches threw themselves at the oozing blood, piercing the woman's palm with their mouths and injecting a chemical to prevent her blood from thickening. Abruta's blood molecules coursed through the leeches, eliciting a satisfaction in them . . . and in Colum, as deep as the one he once knew drinking his mother's milk. The boy's body jerked in a convulsive hunger for more red blood, and in that moment, he knew what it meant to be a leech. Then Hursag touched his forehead, and the boy blacked out.

When he came to, he reached at once for his head. To his great relief, all he felt was human hair. "Was I dreaming, Nana?" he asked.

His mother looked at him with gentle amusement.

"No," said Abruta, "it was real."

He looked at her in fear and confusion. "Does this mean I'm going to shape-shift into a leech?"

"No," laughed the many-eyed woman, "it just means you're growing up and things are beginning to stir in you."

"But I craved your blood."

She ran her fingers through his hair. "Not anymore. There's not a leech left that I can see."

"Time for some stew and beer," said Hursag.

Colum ate two bowls of stew, stroked his pet rabbit for a while, and fell asleep exhausted from his bout with the leeches.

Abruta looked at him lying sweaty with a fur across his chest. "Colum has quite forgotten the man he was. Such a seismic shift for him to undergo."

The crone nodded. "Rebirth in our cauldron was never for the faint of heart."

Abruta took a sip of beer through her straw. "After the leeches, there's no doubt he carries the power of our blood. Puberty can't be far away now." The woman took another long sip. "I wonder what his animal will be."

Hursag smiled. "We'll find out, won't we, dear sister?"

Colum and Iblis rolled around the girl's hearth playing with a wolf cub she was keeping as a pet. Ash, food scraps, and other detritus caught in their hair as the threesome tussled.

Chortling at their rough-and-tumble antics, Iblis's foster mother, Twa, called out, "The perch is ready."

Iblis tied the wolf to a post, and she and Colum sat down to eat a fillet of salted fish and a pile of collards on a wooden platter. Fish bones soon lay strewn around the fire. Colum noticed tiny, soft feathers mixed in with Iblis's eyebrows.

Iblis finished her meal with a hearty belch. "I heard about your leeches, Colum. I don't think anyone has ever turned into a leech before."

"My mother says I won't shape-shift into one."

She let out a sigh of relief and moved closer to him. "I'm glad to hear that!"

Colum felt the warmth of her hip against his leg, along with an unfamiliar stirring in his chest and groin.

CHAPTER TEN

For several days, Hursag had been fattening beetle larvae on spicy meals of flour mixed with beer. At last she was ready to roast them. The crone blew on her fire, throwing off a cloud of sparks, and shoved the larvae underneath the hot coals on the edge of the fire. Before long, they were ready to eat. It was one of Colum's favorite meals. He loved the larvae's crispy exterior and cheesy, almond flavor.

The boy stood taller than his mother now, his hair a mass of brown curls. There was a scary wildness in his blue eyes. His tunic reached mid-thigh. A bronze-handled flint knife dangled on a strap around his waist. The youth was as good at throwing knives now as he was at catching small bones on the back of his hand or droplets in his palm from the cavern dome.

Finished with his snack, the boy headed off toward the river. Overhead, a bird pivoted ever higher on her wings. The fluidity and evanescence of the women never ceased to excite him. Skilled masters of their bodies, they created an impressive, ever-changing collage in the granite chamber that was his home. On the way to the river, he passed a woman morphing into a small songbird, then watched her fly off to land on the head of a friendly hippopotamus. The hippo stomped across the floor on heavy hooves, carrying the bird with it.

Colum arrived at the river in time to see a silver-scaled fish rise out of the water. While he was watching the fish, someone touched him on the shoulder.

"Iblis," he said, smiling.

"I was hoping I'd find you here," she said. "I feel so restless lately."

"What about?"

"I don't know. I have this terrible itch in my back." Iblis began to wriggle uncomfortably. "Scratch it for me, will you?"

Colum stepped behind her and saw something wet and ooz-ing under the girl's tunic. Suddenly, the skin over her scapula and the fabric of her tunic started to split apart, each dividing in two long lines on either side of her spine. Astonishment gripped her companion.

"You're changing, Iblis! It's happening!"

Wet, folded, blue-black feathers pushed up and out of the girl's shoulder blades. Iblis reached behind her to touch their edges, shrieking with delight. The feathers spread out like fans to dry quickly. She began flapping her wings, beside herself with joy.

"Your feet just lifted off!" exclaimed Colum. "You're flying, Iblis!"

She rose several feet in the air on awkwardly fluttering wings, then came crashing down and rolled on the ground. Other women came running over to witness her transformation. Unfazed by the fall, Iblis pumped her wings harder and she rose once more, even higher. The girl fell again. This time she landed on her feet and stumbled forward several steps. Colum reached out to grab her arm and steady her. The growing crowd of women shouted their encouragement.

"Iblis, you're a raven!" cried one woman.

"Look how strong and iridescent your wings are!" exclaimed another.

"How proud her mother will be!" exalted a third.

"Iblis the Raven Woman!"

The girl threw her arms around Colum, out of breath and shaking with pride. Summoned by others, Twa, her foster mother, now came running. When she arrived, Iblis lifted off and flew in a wide circle to impress her. By now, she had enough control to land without so much as a skid.

Twa hugged the girl warmly. "Your mother must be summoned at once! We shall have a great feast to celebrate your wings! You will return to outer space with her as a fellow raven!"

Iblis turned to Colum, her face radiant. "You're next, brother. And if I'm in space when you shape-shift, I promise to return for *your* celebration!"

Colum was happy for her but sad to know his friend would soon be leaving. Iblis deserved her moment of glory without him spoiling it, so he decided to wander off by himself. Recently, he had been going to a more desolate area of the cave. Why, he couldn't say, but whenever he went there, his heartbeat quickened, especially near one section of rock wall.

He touched the wall, and suddenly, hot tears rolled down his face. The only other time he had cried this hard was when his pet rabbit died. He loved that rabbit. It would thump its back legs in rhythm whenever a drum was played, for as long as it played. And it growled if anyone but he came too close while it ate. When the rabbit died, he'd wrapped the limp, soft-furred body in moss and a small woven cloth and placed it in a shallow hole between two boulders by the river.

When he asked, his mother told him his tears came from "a place of grief." He loved his pet for itself alone, the way his mother loved him for himself alone. He understood his feelings for the rabbit, but why did the rock arouse such grief in him?

Colum returned to his hearth to find his mother snoring on their pile of fox and marten furs. He curled up next to her and fell asleep, and while he slept, he had a dream. He dreamed of a woman lying on her back in a cramped space that had been hollowed out of rock. The woman's fingers fluttered across her stomach like spread-out fans. Her breathing was shallow. Hardly any breath at all. And the darkness that surrounded her poured out of an even greater darkness. The woman, as if aware he was watching, called out, "*Is anyone there?*" Her voice sent a thud of dull horror into his heart, and he woke up gasping.

Hursag's eyes flashed open at the sound, one of her bony legs draped over his. "What is it, my sweets?" she asked, seeing at once the unfocused dread on his face.

"She hurts, Nana."

"Who hurts?"

"The woman in the rock."

"You were dreaming, my son."

"No, Nana, it was *real*," he said emphatically. "She *knew* I saw her."

"Are you sure?"

A shiver rippled through him. "She asked if someone was there."

"What did she look like?"

"I don't know. She was covered in dust, and I only saw her eyes when she opened them. They were like an owl's eyes . . . large and staring."

"Very well," said Hursag, throwing off their furs and standing up decisively. "We must consult with the Queen about your dream."

Mother and son headed for Lillake's throne, striding past the burning fires that kept the cave's inky blackness at bay. They arrived to find the Queen sitting regally on her iron chair as if she expected them. Her blue-black hair fell in glittering waves over her shoulders, and she wore a gown of silver cobwebs. There were no attendants in sight.

"Something has upset you, sister," said the Queen.

"Yes, Mistress. My son has seen an old friend in a dream."

"And who might that be?"

"Kasi, Mistress."

Lillake raised an eyebrow. "Such a precocious child he is." Her gaze made Colum feel lightheaded. "It seems he and Kasi are more deeply connected than we realized. What do you propose, sister? Shall we erase the dream from his memory?"

"I fear it will only recur."

"As do I. What then?"

"Perhaps the time has come for him to remember."

"Follow me, then."

The Queen rose from her throne to lead Colum and his mother to the wall with Dervor's vault. Lillake raised her arm and a mist surrounded the area to hide them from prying eyes. At the Queen's command, the rectangular vault slid out of the rock, hovered a moment in the air, then drifted gently to the cave floor. Dervor lay inside, her hair long and matted, her skin as dry as paper. Her large, grey eyes stared blankly into space.

"Sit up, Kasi." The Queen's rich, dark tones resonated with a power not even the dead could resist.

Dervor quivered in her attempts to obey, crumpling twice. It was obvious the gaunt woman had no strength to comply. Lillake leaned over and lifted Dervor out of the vault as if she were a sheet of weightless paper, then placed her in a sitting position on the floor with her back against the cave wall.

Colum knelt in front of her, hardly believing his eyes. Hesitantly, he took one of her paper-thin hands in both of his, where it rested passively.

"Is she the one in your dream?" asked the Queen.

"Yes, Mistress." His chest tightened at the sight of Dervor's glassy, absent eyes. "Something's wrong with her."

The Queen gave a sympathetic nod. "Don't worry, child. I will send her back to the place she's from, and she will receive the care she needs there."

The youth gave Lillake a puzzled look. "Does she have a mother waiting for her?"

"No, I'm afraid she has no mother."

The thought of someone not having a mother turned Colum's puzzled look into one of distress. He turned to Hursag. "Can we take care of her, Nana?"

"No, my son. Our cave isn't her home."

"Then why is she here? I don't understand."

"She was visiting us," explained the Queen.

"I feel I know her, but how?"

"You know her from another time and place," said Lillake.

"Not the forest." He frowned. "I've never been in the forest. I've never been anywhere except the cave."

The Queen spoke gently to him. "I can help you remember, if that is your desire."

The youth shrugged, unsure what he wanted. He felt eerily close to this dust-ridden, emaciated woman with the huge, hollow eyes. She seemed an eternity away, so utterly foreign, and yet so strangely *familiar*.

Lillake turned to Hursag. "I leave the decision to you, sister. Shall I return his memories?"

"It seems that the time is upon us, Mistress," replied the crone. "His memories are beginning to return on their own."

"I agree." The Queen leaned over and whispered into Colum's ear, "*REMEMBER*."

Partial, fleeting images floated through his mind. Lifting blocks of iron, one on top of another, to form a wall . . . jumping out of an icy shower . . . a woman with large, grey eyes sword-fighting with him. Colum's heart beat faster at the sight. Who was this strong female fighter who wielded such a ridiculously long knife? It didn't occur to him to associate her with the half-dead woman leaning against the cave wall. As if reading his mind, the Queen waved her arm over him and the two female figures meshed. Colum suddenly realized they were the same person, and somehow he knew her. The knowledge flooded him with an almost painful tenderness and love.

"*I know her*," he said, as if to himself.

The crone nodded. "Yes, my son. You were good friends."

"But how do I know her, Nana?"

"You shared another world together before you became my child."

"*Before* I was your child?" He felt dizzy. "What world?"

"You saw glimpses of it just now, my son. We are going to send your friend back to that world so she can be healed."

"It's cold there. There are no warm fires in that world," he said. The very thought made him shiver. "Why can't she stay with us? You can heal her, Nana. You can heal anything."

"I fear not all your sisters would welcome her."

It bruised Colum's heart to think of sending the woman back to that world of desolate tunnels. "Our sisters don't know her yet. When they get to know her better, they'll want her to stay. I'm sure of it, Nana."

Lillake addressed him. "I'm afraid she cannot stay."

"But . . ."

"Let go of her hand, Son of Hursag. It is time for her to return from whence she came."

Knowing he could not go against his Queen, the youth hesitantly let go of Dervor's hand, then watched it float to her side as if it were immune to gravity.

"Step aside," said Lillake.

With a pounding heart, Colum leaned over to kiss Dervor's pale forehead, then moved to one side. "Will I ever see her again?" he asked.

"All things are possible," answered the Queen.

Hursag helped a swaying Dervor to her feet. Abruta arrived, emerging from the mist as though summoned. She carried a black robe draped over her arm. The many-eyed woman carefully dropped the robe over Dervor's head and pulled its hood forward to obscure her face. The mist was beginning to dissipate.

Abruta placed her arm around Dervor's slender waist, then walked with her in the direction of the tunnels that led outside. No one seemed to notice the figure in the black robe who stumbled along at Abruta's side.

Colum strolled through the cave with Iblis during one of the rare times she wasn't flying around in her new raven form. There was less exuberant, silly play between them now. They were both discovering a newfound poise and sense of themselves.

An owl flying overhead dipped close enough to muss Colum's hair before soaring up again. "Imbolc is having fun with you," laughed Iblis. "She likes you, Colum. And she's not the only one." The girl stopped strolling long enough to kiss him on the lips. "*I* like you." As if embarrassed, Iblis transmogrified and flew into the air. Soon he heard her piercing caw from the other side of the cave.

Colum sauntered slowly to the river. When he got there, he sat on a rock, pulled a three-hole flute out of his waistband, and began to play. The tune's sweetness made him think of Iblis. Soon her mother would return, and the two of them would fly away into outer space together. He felt disgruntled. So many of their friends were shape-shifting, yet the only change he could muster was a head full of leeches. The youth played a few more notes and ruminated with a pang about how life in the cave was changing for him. Who was the strange dusty woman in the rock? Why did he have such strong feelings for her? And what were the strange visions she stirred up in him all about? The Queen had called them his "memories," but memories from where? Was he the only one in the cave with memories of another life?

Colum replaced his flute in his waistband and swam across the river. On the other side, he looked for the protruding ledge that held Ayylo's hearth. He saw smoke coming off the ledge and started to climb. He could feel the constant adjustments his muscles made as he went. When he was halfway up, Ayylo leaned over the ledge, her hair spilling into space.

"Colum!" she called and reached out her hand to help pull him up. "Welcome, brother. What brings you so high?"

He stared out at a stunning panorama of the cave with its crimson, creamy-yellow, and grey stalactites and stalagmites dispersed everywhere. The ones with crystals embedded in them sparkled in the firelight below. "I love the way the cave looks from up here."

Ayylo stretched out like a tawny lion on a pile of pelts and patted them for him to sit next to her. "I'm glad for your company, brother." A small fire burned in a rock alcove. The flickering light made Ayylo's vibrant green tunic shimmer on her body like a leaf in the forest.

"This is the best place in the whole cave!" the youth exclaimed.

"I think so."

He watched a slender cobalt-blue serpent slither up Ayylo's left hip and over her left breast. It wrapped itself twice around her upper arm where it shone like a colored jewel. The Queen's daughter stroked the snake's flat, smooth-scaled head with her index finger.

"So many of my sisters are shape-shifting," said Colum, looking at the snake.

"Didn't your hair turn to leeches?"

"Yes, but I don't want to be a leech!"

"It just means your body is getting ready to change. The timing is different for everyone." Ayylo held out a bowl of red fruit. "Have some cherries, brother. I picked them from a grove of trees in our forest."

"I don't think I've ever had a cherry." He popped the red berry in his mouth, then bit down tentatively until his teeth reached the pit. The flavor exploded in his mouth. Bursting darts of tangy sweetness struck his tongue, the sides of his cheeks, and the back of his throat. He could feel his taste buds swelling.

Ayylo smiled. "Good, aren't they?"

He snatched two more. "Once I can go into the forest, will you show me where the cherry trees are?" he asked eagerly.

Ayylo's green eyes sparkled. "I promise, brother. You'll fall in love with our forest. Life of all kinds flourishes there."

Colum loved the way this beautiful woman confided in him. "I've seen things lately, Ayylo."

"What kind of things?"

"I've been getting visions of tunnels filled with a blue light. A blue I've never seen before. My mother says they're old memories."

"Visions from your dreams, or when you are awake?"

"Awake. I can be walking around the cave and suddenly I see them."

"How do you see them?"

"In my head. The way I see you when I'm not with you."

She gave him a curious look. "When did this start?"

"After the Queen took a woman out of a rock wall." He pointed in the general direction of Dervor's rock vault.

Ayylo thoughtfully stroked the slender serpent coiled on her arm. "You were with my mother when this happened?"

Colum nodded. "The strange thing is, when I see the tunnels with the blue light, I feel as if I've been there."

"And the woman in the cave wall? Do you feel you know her?"

"Yes and no." Colum felt distressed at her question. "My mother says the woman comes from the tunnels with the blue light. I had a vision of the two of us in them play-fighting with long knives. But how is that possible?"

The blue scales of the serpent on Ayylo's arm shimmered in the firelight like prisms of water. The Queen's daughter picked up her flute and began to play. The flute was made of green rushes held together with beeswax and split willow twigs. Ayylo had told him once that she'd made it herself. Colum stared across the expanse of the cave, listening to her joyful melody. The music lifted his mood and made him forget all about his new memories. At last Ayylo's lips slipped off the reeds of her pipe. "I have a feeling your mother is calling you," she said, and they parted.

Colum returned to his hearth to find Hursag preparing some spiky vegetables for a stew. She cut off their black poisonous leaves and began chopping the vegetables into small pieces. The youth watched her dump the pieces into a simmering pot, then add some flour and spices. How often had his mother joked that this special vegetable, with its sweet, earthy flavor, must be cooked until it was "as soft as your earlobes"?

After finishing a bowl of stew, the youth lay on his back on their strong-smelling furs. He bunched a fist behind his head and stared up at the smoke billowing from countless fires toward the cave dome. The thick, pungent scents of cooking pots wafted over him from all directions, causing his nostrils to flare. Hursag settled herself next to him.

"Nana, who is the woman in the rock?" he asked.

"Someone you knew long ago."

"But not in the cave?"

"No, my son, not here."

"Do all our sisters have lives somewhere else?"

"Not everyone."

Colum gazed at the granite dome above him. For him, it might as well have been the dome of heaven. "I don't understand, Nana. How did I get from those blue-lit tunnels to here?"

"You left them to visit our cave, and in the cave, you were reborn as my son."

"But I've always been your son, Nana."

She looked tenderly at him. "Do the new memories make you afraid?"

"Sometimes." Colum pressed his face into her smoky hair. "But not when I'm with you."

"Let the memories come naturally, my son. Don't try to resist them or understand them." She kissed the top of his head. "You may ask me about these memories at any time."

"Will I go back there like the woman did?"

"No, my son, your life is with us now. Hers was not."

The deepest love for his mother filled the youth. He leaned over and kissed her creviced cheek.

CHAPTER ELEVEN

On the spur of the moment, Colum decided to visit Ayylo. He strapped firewood to his back as a gift to her and took a different route to the river, one he thought might be faster. He moved through the high-vaulted limestone cave, taking in the undulating faces and forms all around him. Lizards, hedge-hogs, bears, aurochs, swans, hyenas, and many more, crawling, tumbling, hurtling, and hovering in every direction. The youth stopped to have a short, friendly conversation with a female rhino who stood at her fire burning animal bones. He walked on through the bizarre subterranean bestiary and found himself comparing it with the sterile hallways of his new memories.

At last Colum squirmed between two large stalagmites to arrive at the base of Ayylo's ledge high above the river. White calcite glistened in the limestone wall below the ledge. Soon he was climbing up the cliff with the firewood on his back.

"You brought me wood!" Ayylo beamed. "And just when I was running out."

Colum unloaded his treasure in a bin next to her fire. "I'm always coming up here to eat your food and drink your wine, Ayylo. It's time I gave you something."

The Queen's daughter looked at his forward-creeping shiny brown curls, like a newly leafed tree, and his well-proportioned boyish face. "Just to see you, brother, is enough of a gift."

After adding wood to her fire, the Queen's daughter sat at the edge of the high wall with her legs dangling down. Colum joined her, and together they gazed out at the panorama below.

"I love being up here with you," he sighed.

Ayylo's luxuriant mane of golden-red hair flowed down over her perfectly rounded shoulders. She leaned forward and pointed excitedly at a hearth on the cavern floor. "Oh, look! It's Zamar with her new man."

Colum made out a tall, muscular fellow with black hair. It was rare for him to see a man in the cave, but even he knew about Zamar's insatiable sexual appetite. You couldn't live with these women and not be aware of what went on.

"A *new* man?" he asked, confused.

"Yes. She wore the last one out, then missed him so much that patches of her hair fell out in grief."

"Did she love him?"

"Not the man. She loved the sex she had with him. It's hard for Zamar to find someone with enough endurance to satisfy her cravings. The last man was far better than most." She looked again. "I heard this one is an engineer."

"What's an engineer?"

She looked at him in surprise, as if she'd forgotten the young Colum had no way of knowing. "An engineer uses special tools to build things."

A cry of pleasure reached their ledge. When Colum looked down, he saw Zamar straddling the large man. "Stiffen your organ, honey man. I want it up in my throat this time!"

Zamar gripped the engineer's shoulders, riding him in a frenzy of furious motion that shook him like a rag doll. Her dark hair fell in long waves, covering her sweaty back and fleshy buttocks. Colum had the feeling that sex with her was a lethal threat.

"They'll be at it for a while," said Ayylo. "The only thing that matters to Zamar is a man's sheer staying power."

Colum looked away feeling oddly disturbed to see the poor man treated this way, but why? Didn't he make himself fair game by trespassing on their bridge? At the same time, the blurry image of a woman's face came to him. It was the face of the woman buried in the rock. It was the face of his *special friend*. But why was she so special? He looked again at the engineer thrusting into Zamar, and suddenly Colum's own organ began to harden. On hearing Zamar moan in pleasure, he imagined himself in the engineer's place and his special friend in Zamar's place, and he broke out in a sweat. The youth shook his head vigorously and the scene vanished.

"Don't let this upset you," said Ayylo, seeing the distress on Colum's face. "A whole different experience awaits you, brother, one you'll find utterly delightful. I'll see to that. I am very generous with those I love."

The youth had no desire to discuss what had just happened to him. "Will Zamar return the engineer to the forest when she tires of him?" he asked.

"If he pleasures her well enough and long enough, she might. She'll erase his memory of us first, of course."

Colum left Ayylo's perch to sit by the river and ponder what just happened. Why did making love to the woman in his mind feel so real? And real to whom? The hardest thing about his returning memories was the sense they didn't belong to him. There was no way he'd ever made love to the woman in the rock. But then, why did it *feel* as if he had? Why did he feel himself swooning in the pools of her grey eyes? Who was the man he'd seen sword-fighting with her in the labyrinth? It still astonished him to conceive of the man *in any way* as himself.

A small circle of river shimmered silver in front of him, and out of it the Fish Woman, Ketu, rose up. Smooth brown skin covered her upper body, and beautiful silver-green fish scales shone across her lower half. Greenish-yellow seaweed, like fronds of hair, streamed over her shoulders.

Ketu's large, watery blue eyes stared at Colum. "Shall we race, brother?"

"Yes!"

Ketu took off, and the youth dove into the river to swim after her. He could barely keep up with the Fish Woman's ecstatic pace. A little later, tired but exhilarated, Colum climbed out of the river to make his way back to Hursag's hearth.

"Did you have a good time with Ayylo?" asked the crone.

"Can you see that far away, Nana?"

Firelight flickered on her face. "I don't need eyes to track you."

"We were watching Zamar and her man."

"Oh?"

A pig snuffled close to their hearth, and Hursag shooed it away. Colum drank some water and nestled close to Hursag on their furs. "Tell me a story, Nana. One about you."

"Very well. I shall tell you how I came to be here."

His eyes widened. "Weren't you always here?"

"Oh, no. I come from a faraway place."

"Why did you come so far, Nana?"

She mussed his curly hair, smiling. "To find you, of course."

Colum always felt an unfiltered acceptance with his mother. To be with her filled him with a sense of peace. "Did you fly here with the Raven Women through deep space?" he asked.

"I flew through deep space, but not with the Raven Women. Lions don't have wings."

"How did you fly then?"

The crone's eyes grew distant. "In a ship that sailed through the heavens. A girl chasing her brother."

"You have a brother?"

"Yes," she said, nodding. "He came here before me. I sailed and sailed, restless and excited, until at last I descended under the canopy of Earth's blue sky."

"Earth?" He knew about blue skies from descriptions of the forest.

"Earth is a huge, spinning rock in deep space. It circles around a fiery star. There are many, many forests and rivers on Earth."

"And tunnels with blue lights?"

"Some." Hursag smiled again. "My ship landed close to a spread of marshes—wet, squishy places. I found this Earth to be vibrant, unspoiled, and breathtakingly beautiful. Many of its life-forms were similar to those on my planet, another spinning rock in space. But I did discover some fascinating differences." Colum listened, enthralled, watching the flames of their fire create shadows on his mother's craggy face. "At the time that I landed, the earth had recently undergone a great cleansing. Humans were few. Occasionally, I assumed the form of a fish and swam among the marshes with other fish for company."

"You shape-shifted into a fish when you came?"

"In those days, I could take on any form I desired. As a fish, I pulled cool water into my gills and sheltered in the wet shade on blistering-hot days, listening to the wind that rustled the reeds."

Hursag's melodious voice entrained Colum's mind with her vision, and he began to "see" what she was describing as if he were underwater himself. He scarcely breathed as she continued her story.

"Once, I became a beetle. I walked along the ground sweeping my toothed legs to remove obstacles until I reached some tasty carrion. I lived secretly, rolling my eggs in spheres of dung and placing the spheres in hollowed-out burrows in the ground. When the rains came, they soaked through the earth, dissolved the hardened dung, and released my offspring into the air. As a beetle, I learned the importance—no, the *necessity*—of gestating in darkness to prepare for one's moment of bursting forth into light." Her amber eyes flared. "You know this secret, too, my son."

"I do?" As soon as he asked the question, a memory returned of a sea of lava ablaze with flames. "Oh, Nana, I see myself swimming in fire and not being burned!"

"Darling child, that's because the man-you-were did swim once in Earth's red-hot core. You swam deeper than I ever have." Her ash-stained hand stroked his face with infinite tenderness. "In such depths, our essence is touched."

Colum didn't understand everything his mother said, but he could feel her love for him pulsing warmly in his veins. "I'm glad you sailed to the earth, Nana, and I'm especially glad you found me."

The crone picked up a clay pipe with a long stem, filled it with tobacco, and tamped it down. She lit the pipe with a stick from the fire. "Ahh, the pleasures of life," she said, drawing in the smoke. After a few puffs, Hursag held the pipe out for them both to admire. "Many sea creatures had to fall, my son, and become compacted enough to form its clay." Her eyes sparkled. "What I hold is mostly solid sea foam!"

"Sea creatures like Ketu?"

"Well, Ketu is most definitely a creature of the water, and all rivers do run to the sea. So, yes, like Ketu." Hursag took another long draw on her pipe. "Now, since I told you what it's like to be a beetle, I'd like to hear what it's like to be a leech."

The youth shuddered at the memory. "Oh, Nana! Your whole body is constantly searching for blood. It *hurts* to be that thirsty for blood."

"An all-consuming hunger," she said with a nod.

"It was their craving for blood that roused them up and out of my scalp."

Hursag puffed on her clay pipe. "Some truths can only be lived."

Suddenly, they heard a scream and turned their heads in the direction of Bruha's hearth. Bruha was a sister who shape-shifted into a hippopotamus, and at the moment, she was prodding a red-haired man toward her tethering post. Colum stiffened at the sight. The man's hands were tied and his clothes were torn. There were abrasions and bruises on his chest and arms. Terror filled the man's eyes. Other than Zamar's lovers, it had been a long time since a man had been captured and brought into the cave. Bruha certainly wasn't about to make love to the man. She'd crush him if she tried. What did she want with the captive? Colum left his mother to wander over for a closer look.

The bulky contours of Bruha's torso and thighs were enormous. She had short, bristly hair and, instead of feet, retained the dead, grey, horny cuticles of her stumpy hippo pads. The entire effect was intimidating, and the redhead seemed barely able to contain his panic. Colum stepped into the circle of her hearth.

"Greetings, little one," said the Hippo Woman. She tugged at the ropes around the man's wrists to make sure they were secure before tying the rope to a post in the ground. "How can I help you?"

"My mother has some excellent tobacco. Would you like to have a smoke with her?"

Bruha smiled. "I just might at that."

"I can watch the man while you're gone."

"Only if you promise not to go near him. These outsiders are tricky and can be quite dangerous. And you're too young to know what to do if something goes wrong."

"I'll keep my distance, Bruha, I promise."

The woman clumped off.

Once she was out of hearing range, the redhead croaked, "My God, that thing isn't human! Did you see those feet!" His eyes darted around to stare at the strange creatures around him. "Where the hell is this place?" He looked at Colum. "Why aren't you tied up? Never mind. You have a knife. Quick, cut this goddamned rope!"

"It won't do any good. They'll stop you before you get to the next hearth."

The stranger's face twitched with fear. "I must be dreaming. This can't be real."

"It's real to me," said the youth. "And let me guess. The woman who just left?"

"You call that creature a *woman*?"

"I do." Colum met the man's gaze. "She probably caught you trespassing in her forest just now."

The captive's eyes rolled in distress. "Please, cut this damned rope before *whatever it is* gets back."

"I can't." Colum dipped a gourd into Bruha's pot of drinking water, placed it on the ground within the man's reach, and stepped back.

The fellow winced in pain as he gulped the tepid water. "I think my shoulder's dislocated."

Colum noticed how the man's arm dangled at his side. "What's your name?"

"Jack."

"I'm Colum. What happened in the forest, Jack?"

Thin fumes of smoke drifted upward from Bruha's fire. "I was fishing when that *woman* came clomping up from behind and knocked me out. When I came to, my arms were tied." His voice shook. "Why do you think she brought me here?"

"I don't know."

"How did you get here?"

A piercing screech from an adjacent hearth made Jack jump. He turned toward the sound in time to see a woman turn into a falcon, then fly away. "What the fuck was that!" The sight made him blanch, and in a panic, he struggled to pull loose from Bruha's rope.

Colum was confused. "You act as if you've never seen a person change form before."

"You're fucking kidding me. Humans don't turn into birds!" Sweat beaded on Jack's forehead. "Christ, man, cut this rope before that thing gets back!"

"I can't, and like I said, even if I did, you'd never make it to the tunnels." Colum gave the man a puzzled look. "How did you find the forest?"

"I walked over a bridge into the woods the way I always do. To go to this lake I like to fish in." The redhead shook his head. "Only this time, the lake was different. All these big fish were leaping out of the water. Fish I've never seen before. And the sun was shining so bright on their scales I was nearly blinded."

"You've been to the lake before?" asked Colum.

The man nodded. "Every summer, I take a week off from work and go there to fish. I've done it since I was a kid." The stranger's voice dropped, and he strained against his rope. "Oh, bloody hell, she's coming back. You've got to help me!"

Bruha thumped toward them through the smoky light of scattered fires.

"Bruha," said Colum when she arrived, "can I take this man to my hearth?"

"Whatever for?"

"I've never had a man for a pet."

The Hippo Woman stared at him, rubbing her chin. "Men can be more dangerous than wolves, little one. I'm not sure that's a good idea."

"I played with a bear once. Remember?"

With a bellowing laugh, Bruha slapped her hand on her huge flank. "So you did!" She untied Jack's rope from the post. "Let's go ask your mother if she approves of this strange request of yours."

After speaking with Bruha, Hursag pulled her son aside. "I fear this will not end well."

"Please, Nana. I've never been around a man before."

"If I agree, you must keep him tied up and not allow yourself to get too attached. A man loose in our cave would cause great havoc, I'm afraid."

Once Bruha left, Colum secured Jack's rope to their tethering post. Hursag reset the captive's shoulder, then brought him water and a dish of stew. Jack's hands were trembling so violently that he spilled the water.

Later, when Hursag had left, the man asked Colum, "You're a man too. Why are you free to walk around?"

"This is my home. I was born here. The woman who fixed your arm is my mother."

Jack's mouth dropped open. "That hag?"

Colum's cheeks reddened at the insult. "Let me give you some advice. If you ever hope to leave this cave, you better start showing these women some respect."

Several feet away, a woman flipped her legs in the air like an overturned insect and buzzed away. Jack slumped to the ground in shock.

Colum needed to think and left the man to do his own pondering.

As he walked away, the words *River Styx* flashed in his mind, triggering another memory from his life in the blue-lit tunnels. A man was telling him about the Greeks and their sacred river Styx. He explained how the river separated the "land of the dead" from the "land of the living" and how even the gods were afraid to dip their toes in its . . . how did the man put it?

"Terrible and wild" waters. Colum glanced back at Jack, whose head was buried in his arms.

Is that how the cave feels to him? Like crossing from the land of the living into the land of the dead? Did I make a mistake bringing him to my mother's hearth?

When he returned, Hursag was sitting by their fire.

"Thank you for letting me keep Jack," he said sheepishly.

The crone sprinkled powder into a cup of water and stirred. "Take this to him. It will help him sleep."

Colum brought the man some furs along with the sleeping potion. Exhaustion and the contents of the liquid drew Jack into a deep sleep.

"What kind of game are you playing with that man?" asked Hursag as she pulled her hair up in a messy bun.

"It's not a game, Nana. He's terrified."

"He crossed the bridge to our forest of his own accord. No one forced him to."

"Maybe not, but Jack told me that he crossed it every summer to fish in a lake he always fished in. Only this time, the lake happened to be our lake in our forest." Colum stirred the embers of the fire with a stick. "I don't think he had any idea he was in our forest."

"It's true the way into our forest opens and closes at will. Still, it is always a choice for the one who enters."

"But why would the forest open to Jack?"

"Perhaps something in him wanted to come."

Colum gave her an eager look. "Maybe he wanted to learn how to shape-shift, Nana."

"I doubt that."

"Why?"

The crone sighed. "His human form is too hardened to change into another one. He's been too set in his ways for far too long."

"You said the woman in the rock, the one from the blue-lit tunnels, could shape-shift."

"She was different."

Colum was silent a moment, then asked, "Why was she in the rock, Nana?"

"She tried to kill one of our sisters."

His eyes filled with shock. "No!"

"I'll tell you the whole story one day, but right now, you're not ready."

Colum, who trusted his mother implicitly, dropped the subject to look again at the man sleeping at their hearth. "If Jack is as hardened as you say, Nana, then he doesn't belong here. Perhaps the forest made a mistake when it let him cross. Can't we just put him back on the bridge and let him return to his world?"

"The choice has been made. It cannot be undone."

"But he didn't know he was entering our forest."

Hursag's wrinkled hands smoothed her robe. "Something deeper than Jack's mind brought him here, my son."

Colum was sitting with Jack at the tethering post when Sny and Kle-Ptuza strolled over.

Sny leaned toward Jack and started sniffing him. "Your pet's sweat reeks of fear," she announced derisively.

Kle-Ptuza's metallic eyes glared at the captive. "I'd say this one is a *mule*, don't you think, sister?"

"Oh, yes," replied Sny. "He could definitely use a nose rope, and I'm the one to lead him by it. Perhaps I can persuade Bruha to make a trade with me." She cast Colum a cold look. "Once you tire of your pet, that is." The two women strode off, laughing.

Jack let out a nauseating groan. "They want me dead."

"They're hunters, Jack," cautioned Colum. "The tall one, Kle-Ptuza, is a raptor, and Sny is a panther. I'll do my best to keep you away from them."

The redhead was trembling violently and leaned against the rock to steady himself. "They just came to your hearth. How do you intend to keep them away from me?"

"Don't worry. You belong to Bruha, and they'd never risk offending her. And I'll ask her not to trade you to either of them." Colum put a reassuring hand on Jack's shoulder. "Just try to be friendly to the others. Once they get used to you, these women will start to see you as a harmless pet, and at least you'll have a place among them that doesn't threaten anyone."

"So that's the plan," said the captive nervously. "Win them over so they relax their guard, and I can look for my chance to escape."

Colum didn't reply.

CHAPTER TWELVE

Since Bruha seemed in no hurry to reclaim her prize, Colum began to take Jack on short walks. As Hursag's son, Colum was greeted with open affection wherever he went, and because of him, his new "pet" became increasingly tolerated.

The two men sat by the fire together. "Didn't you ever want to be something else?" asked Colum.

"As a kid, I thought it would be exciting to be a pilot and fly airplanes." Jack pressed his lips tight together. "But you mean shape-shifting, don't you?" He sighed. "Well, maybe a horse. They're such beautiful animals, and whenever I saw a horse in the movies, I wanted to be on its back galloping like the wind."

"What's a movie?"

Jack shrugged. "Pictures. Pictures of people and things that move on a screen."

"Screen?"

"It's like a big piece of white cloth." Jack looked closely at him. "You've never been out of this cave, have you?"

Before Colum could answer, Hursag came over with a platter of fried perch. As the two men began to eat, an eagle swooped down, caught Colum's fish in its talons, and flew off with it.

"You're welcome, Lael!" he called out. His mother slid another fish onto his platter.

"To tell you the truth, Colum, there's no animal I want to be. I was born a human and I want to stay one."

"What was your life like before Bruha found you?" asked Colum with genuine curiosity.

Jack's hair was stiff with dust and flying ash as he bit into the perch's white flesh. "I worked in an office all day. Then I went home to my wife and kids. My wife is a nurse."

"What's a nurse?"

"Someone trained to take care of sick people."

"A healing woman. We have those."

"I guess so," said Jack, picking at the dirt under his cracked fingernails.

"And you mentioned children?"

"Two." Jack's eyes brightened. "Billy's five and Camilla is eight. They're smart. Funny, too. You should see Camilla . . ." Jack trailed off as a tall woman with smooth jets of black hair streaming down her head approached the hearth. She held out a string of ripe, bulging onions to Hursag.

"A gift for you, sister."

Hursag took the onions. "So yellow and fresh. They will make our next stew quite tasty."

Colum stood up. "Welcome, Zamar."

The woman smiled warmly at him. "It is a pleasure to see how fast you're growing and how strong you've become, little brother." Zamar then took a long look at Jack still sitting by the fire. "Stand up," she ordered. As soon as the man did, she reached out to run her fingers through his hair. "So red . . . *like fire.*" In a flash, she unzipped his pants and thrust her hand inside. "Oh, yes, this one has potential!"

Jack blushed violently at Zamar's brazen act and instinctively backed away from the desire that burned in her eyes.

The tall woman turned to Colum. "I asked Bruha if I could borrow your pet for a little while, brother." Zamar gave him a friendly wink. "I promise to have him back before he's even missed."

Jack shot Colum a frantic glance.

"Of course, sister," said Colum, and he tried to give Jack a look of encouragement. "I hope he pleases you."

Shortly after Jack departed with Zamar, Ayylo arrived at the hearth.

"Where's your mother?" asked the Queen's daughter.

"Foraging in the forest."

Ayylo wore her green tunic and sat gracefully on a flat rock by the fire. "I saw Jack with Zamar just now. I doubt he can match her engineer's stamina, but perhaps he can appease a small part of her lust."

"I hope she doesn't hurt him with her rough sex."

Ayylo's green eyes stared in the direction of the tall woman's hearth. "Zamar is aware that Jack belongs to Bruha. She wouldn't risk bringing him back in less than one piece. Who knows? Jack may even enjoy his time with her."

"I doubt it."

The fire's flames highlighted the golds and reds in Ayylo's hair. Colum sat on a nearby rock breathing in the slight musky fragrance that rolled off her. The nearness of the Queen's daughter filled him with strange, wild, unpredictable sensations. All at once her nose twitched, catlike, and triggered in him the memory of another tawny cat. One that had been his staunch companion. But from where, and when? There were no cats in the blue-lit tunnels where Dervor lived. A memory flashed in his mind of high cliffs facing a huge body of water, the cat at his side.

"Ayylo," he said quietly, "I have this memory of a cat. A cat, not a lion. And somehow it makes me think of you."

Her emerald eyes glittered in the firelight. "Did the cat bring you many nice gifts?"

"If you call mice and rocks and insects gifts."

"Oh, I do."

"Are *you* the cat I'm seeing? Do we know each other from somewhere else? Is this my memory?"

The Queen's daughter leaned forward to look into his eyes. Her intoxicating scent wafted over him, creating a desire so intense it threatened to unravel his senses. "I believe so, brother." She stood up, purring. "I must leave now, but I promise, once you shape-shift, I'll show you how a Cat Woman makes love."

"I hope I change soon," he said, feeling vertiginous.

As Ayylo walked away, a vivid image of Dervor's face appeared in his mind's eye, along with an aching sadness at the unbridgeable distance that separated them. Not even the Queen's daughter had the power to erase the woman with those large, grey eyes from his heart and mind.

Hursag returned from the forest. "It's pouring rain out there!" she exclaimed, unstrapping a harness that held a basket of foraged goods from her shoulders. The crone shook herself like a dog, then changed out of her wet robe.

"Sit by the fire and let me dry your hair, Nana," invited her son.

Hursag's amber eyes sparkled in the firelight as she sat. To Colum, her presence made the whole cave feel more spacious and welcoming. As he vigorously dried her hair with a cloth, two figures came toward them.

"Zamar must be finished with your pet," said Hursag and stood.

Zamar pushed Jack forward with a look of disdain. "Too vapid for my taste," she sneered. "Nothing but a bleating lamb." She turned without further ado and left.

Jack stumbled to the safety of the large rock near the tethering post and sat with his knees to his chest. When Colum brought him water, the redhead drank thirstily. There were bruises on the man's face and his lower lip was bleeding.

"I'm sorry I couldn't stop her from taking you, Jack," said the youth. "There are limits to what I can do for you."

A dry sob shook the man. "Fucking her is like . . ." Without finishing the sentence, he turned his face to the rock and soon fell into an exhausted sleep.

Colum watched the fire next to Jack when robed figures began moving en masse toward one end of the cave. Colum shook his sleeping pet awake. "Jack, the Queen has summoned us. I have to go."

"I'm not staying here alone."

Colum grabbed his arm to help him up. "All right, let's go."

After hustling through the crowd of women, the two men climbed a boulder for a better view. A giant black arachnid stood in front of Lillake's empty throne.

Jack's mouth fell open. "What is *that*?"

"Our Queen," replied Colum. "She has shape-shifted." He felt the spider's powerful magnetic force pulling him to her and knew she was pulling the other women with equal force.

The huge, black spider started to move through the cave in a slow, steady, zigzag pattern. Women on every side of her parted to make way. Gossamer threads spewed out of the arachnid's abdomen as she crept along, creating a web of her own froth and protein. Lillake moved on large, hairy, bent legs, back and forth and sideways, spinning translucent spider silk out of herself and forming crossties and nodes at critical junctures to reinforce her netting. The Queen's web rose in glistening spires as it extended into every nook and cranny of the cave until at last the web was complete and the giant spider stood still. With a ceremonious nod, the giant spider beckoned her women to climb on.

The web's incandescent filaments coursed currents of energy into everyone who made contact with them. Most women, though not all, began to shape-shift. With increasing abandon, their various forms started to leap, spin, and somersault in a joyful, riotous dance on the Queen's membrane. Her delicate, sensuous, yet powerful silver threads rippled with the surging bodies.

Abruta, seeing Colum and Jack on the boulder, came over, her ten eyes filled with wild joy. "Dance, Colum! Dance with us, brother!" she cried. The next instant she was gone.

Colum shot Jack a quick glance. "I have to dance!"

"You can't leave me here. I'm your pet, goddamn it. You're responsible for me."

"You'll be safe on this rock."

"*Don't go!*" Jack began to hyperventilate.

"I have to. Look, the web isn't touching this rock. If anyone comes too close, just slip into a crevice until they're gone." The youth leaped off the rock and raced to the web to join his sisters in their wild, pulsing dance.

"Brother!" called Iblis, darting Colum a quick, radiant smile before turning into a raven. Her black wings flailed in the air, balancing her as she zoomed up and down on the web.

Women flowed in undulating waves across the Queen's web, drawing on the power of her silver threads for their renewal. Only the dance existed, and the air filled with an awakening joy.

Colum caught sight of Bruha's fluid movements, marveling at how there was nothing ponderous about a hippopotamus dancing on Lillake's web. He somersaulted across several glistening strands of web to reach her, and they jumped rapturously together. A large praying mantis soared high in the air on one side of them, her slim, pale green body landing with a single bounce on the silk ribbons. The mantis playfully ran her feelers through Colum's hair before careening off in a new direction. The momentum of the youth's next leap took him far from Bruha. This time he rose halfway to the dome, his curls spraying out like a corona. He landed on another strand next to a woman with feathery wings. She turned her owl's head around to stare at him with glowing, bronze-colored eyes. As if in greeting, the owl's throat swelled, and she let out a "*WHOO—HOO—HOO—OO.*" The sound resonated with so much love he nearly fainted.

Women laughed and cried as they crossed paths, airlifted on the shimmering streamers of Lillake's web. Boundaries blurred. Essences mingled. The Queen's silken wheel glittered like a great shining star, illuminating the beauty of every form that danced on it. At times, the Great Spider plucked the web's filaments like strings on a violin to send her vibrations flowing through the cells of everyone present.

"The net of our Spider Queen holds us all!" cried one.

"Ee-ahh! Blessed Web of our Mistress!"

At some point, Colum found himself on the same pulsating

strand as Sny. Together they spun like quicksilver into the air, eyes blazing with utter delight.

All over the cave, the lofting crescendo of the dancing women began to peak, then peaked again, threatening to set Colum's heart ablaze. At last the web began to lose resiliency, lowering itself like a gentle blanket, then vanishing wherever it touched the cave floor. Some women swooned. Some lay down serenely where they were. Others staggered around, still in a trance. All the women shimmered with a kind of glory, as if the Queen's web had transcended the cave's limitations to merge with the starlit universe.

For Colum, everything had become fresh, luminous, and beautiful. He sat on the floor shaking with the wonder of it all. Yaga plopped herself beside him and flung her arms around his shoulders. The old woman's tear-streaked face glowed with unabashed happiness.

Jack, who had watched the dance in a state of terrified attention, scrambled off the rock and hurried to Hursag's hearth. When Colum arrived, the redhead looked at him with suspicion.

"*They're she-demons!*" exclaimed Jack in a low, harsh voice.

Colum was still floating in an aftermath of bliss. "What are you talking about? Who's a demon?"

"All of them!" A bunched muscle showed in Jack's lean jaw. "Zamar didn't borrow *you*. If she had, you'd know, like I do, that one day these women will turn on you. Don't think they won't."

Hursag arrived at her hearth in time to hear him. She walked up to Jack. "For whatever reason, you've been drawn into the circle of our cave." The crone's golden-brown eyes stared into him. "I'd advise you to adapt while you can. *Men are nonessential goods to us.*"

The man retreated white-faced to his rock.

Colum strolled over to Bruha's hearth. The Hippo Woman stood, stirring her pot.

"Greetings, sister," said Colum, holding out a bag. "I've brought some Nara roots. They're from my mother to thank you for loaning me Jack." He glanced at the mash of greens in her pot.

Bruha opened the bag. On seeing the roots, she slapped her thigh in glee. "My favorite! You don't know it, brother, but these are especially hard to find." She shook her head, puzzled. "I don't understand how your mother, as a meat-eating lion, always knows where the best ones are."

Bruha sprinkled millet in a pan over her fire. When the millet began to crackle and pop, she pulled four Nara roots out of Hursag's bag. The Hippo Woman sliced the roots lengthways and laid them in the pan to fry. Colum watched silently as a few millet seeds popped out of the pan to burn in the fire. Soon a pleasant aroma rose from the frying Nara roots. Bruha put them on a platter, adding some of her mashed greens to share with her guest. They sat down across from one another.

"Tell me, little one, how does it go with your pet?"

"Well, sister, I'm learning what a man is like."

She snorted. "Not much to learn, if you ask me." Colum scratched his forearm, then scratched it harder. "Did something bite you?" asked Bruha.

He shrugged, trying to ignore it, but the irritating itch became more intense.

"Let me take a look," offered the Hippo Woman.

Colum stretched his arm out for her to examine. She turned his arm first one way, then the other. As she did, a damp red patch the size of a large bottle cap broke out on his forearm and clear, thin moisture started to seep out. Colum stared transfixed as a bulge of new tissue rose up out of the patch in his arm.

Bruha seemed equally enthralled. "What are you feeling?"

Sweat broke out on his forehead. "Pressure. Like a tight squeezing, and it's getting stronger." His arm started to jerk involuntarily. "It feels like something is wriggling and twisting inside my arm."

The bulge stretched longer and tauter under his flesh. Then the skin split apart like fabric ripping. The initial bulge was now a pulsing, wet, cordlike object.

"It's not a leech," said Bruha.

Colum let out a guttural grunt, then shook his arm as if to force the object out.

"Stay still," cautioned the Hippo Woman.

Now they both heard a loud, squishing sound, similar to a boot being sucked out of mud, and the object's head burst through his skin. It was flat with two slits for eyes.

"A snake!" Bruha cried.

Colum blinked in shock. The scales of the serpent were black except for a bright scarlet band around its neck. Still damp from the fluid in Colum's tissues, the serpent raised its head and let out a sharp, sibilant sound like steam escaping a locomotive. Colum grabbed the reptile's neck in a quick, reflexive action. His instinct was to fling it aside.

"Don't hurt it, little brother," warned Bruha. "The snake issues from you and is part of you."

Colum gripped the creature's neck tighter. "Let's take it to my mother. She'll know what to do!"

Bruha rubbed her double chin, mystified. "Yes, let's."

Colum raced to his mother's hearth with Bruha clomping close behind.

Hursag stared at them. "What's wrong?"

The Hippo Woman placed her hands on her broad hips. "A serpent has emerged from Colum's arm," she said with an indecisive shake of her head. "If you're shape-shifting, brother, this is a strange way to do it. I've never seen this kind of transformation before. He *is* the first male child to be raised in our cave, and we have no precedence for how a male will make his changes." The whole thing seemed suddenly too much for her to ponder. "I leave it to you to sort out, sister." Bruha turned and clumped away, calling over her shoulder, "Many thanks for the Nara roots!"

Colum was holding the serpent's neck in a death grip.

"You hold it too tightly, my son. Snakes only have one lung with which to breathe."

The youth eased his grip slightly. Immediately, a second

unnerving hiss sounded. The serpent's forked tongue lashed into the air.

"I suggest you let it go and see what happens."

Colum trusted his mother enough to slowly release his fingers from the reptile's neck. It reared up to face him but made no attempt to strike.

"Neither of you can live without the other," said Hursag. "The two of you are as one."

"No, we're not! If we were, *all* of me would turn into a snake!" The serpent's golden eyes stared at him. "Why is this happening to me?"

"I think that by dancing on the web, you may have accelerated things." Hursag reached out to stroke the serpent. "Feel its skin, my son. Feel the silky smoothness of its scales. Look how striking this bright band of red is against all the glistening black."

His lips formed into a tight, grim line as he cautiously touched the creature. Still resting on Colum's arm, the serpent arched its neck to rear backward away from the hand that so recently had tried to strangle it.

"Go ahead, stroke it," encouraged Hursag.

Colum touched the snake lightly to and fro, afraid to rest his hand too heavily on the creature. To his surprise, the snake's slanted eyes half shut, and it lay down. Slowly, the slithery form began to sink back into Colum's arm, and the viscous ribbons of his separated flesh knit back together. A thick, ropelike cord wriggled briefly under Colum's skin before thinning into smooth muscle. Within seconds, all residual redness and swelling had vanished, leaving only a mild itching sensation.

"Will it come back?" he asked.

Hursag's bright eyes regarded him with amusement. "Let's hope so, my son."

"Where has it gone?"

"It hasn't gone anywhere. It is part of you."

He frowned. "Why can't I be like Iblis? Why didn't all of me change into a serpent?"

She thought for a moment. "It may be that your returned

memories are interfering and the man in you resists—no, *fears*—a full union with your serpent nature."

"Nana, if . . ." He shook his head. "When I turn into a snake, will I still have my own mind?"

"Not at first. It takes practice to retain your human point of view, though it's not impossible," she replied. "Not all of our sisters desire human consciousness in their animal form. They enjoy giving themselves over fully to their alternative form. Others prefer combining the two."

"Like Bruha with her cuticle feet?"

"She does it with her physical form. You're talking about consciousness."

"What about you, Nana?"

Hursag beamed. "I never lose my human consciousness."

He gave her a kiss. "I'm going to the river. I need to be alone."

Colum sat by the gently flowing water and tried to sort through what had happened. He wondered what it was like to be a limbless animal with a gaping mouth, split tongue, and no ears.

Is my animal soul really a reptile? The poor snake must have been as confused and frightened as I was. Next time, I'll welcome it. After all, as my mother says, it's part of me.

CHAPTER THIRTEEN

Despite Jack's inability to satisfy Zamar fully, she came back several times to fetch him. Sometimes she simply sent word. Most of the women took his presence for granted now, so occasionally he even walked without an escort. His face boasted a frizzy red beard, and there were dark circles under his eyes. He wore a grease-stained tunic frayed at the sleeves.

Jack returned from one such visit and, upon reaching Hursag's hearth, slumped on a rock. Colum handed him a bowl of warm stew, which the man ate ravenously. A new black-and-blue bruise could be seen on his shoulder. He often came back bruised, the result of Zamar's enthusiastic "lovemaking." Colum found some of his mother's salve and spread it on Jack's shoulder.

"I think she's actually grown fond of you," ventured Colum.

Jack wrinkled his nose in disdain. "She's like a sow with all these bristly hairs around her belly button."

White ashes flew in the air as Colum added a few sticks of wood to the fire. He knew the tension of Jack's situation never really eased, but at least it seemed the redhead's trysts with Zamar no longer terrified him.

"Where's Hursag?" asked Jack.

"Visiting somewhere."

"You love that old woman, don't you?"

"She's my mother. Of course I do."

"What a piece of luck for me that you're *her* son." Jack stared at the fire. "Strange, I never used to question my life. I drifted through the days going along with whatever happened. Just passing time, as if there's no end to time." A vein swelled on his forehead. "And what happens? I find myself in a place too weird, too frightening, for me to drift. A place where any moment I could make a deadly mistake." He began to tremble. "I've lost everyone I love, and now I'm having all these feelings about them. I have so many regrets."

"What kind of regrets?"

Jack wrapped his arms around himself defensively. "I keep thinking if I were home I'd never take my wife for granted again. I'd show her how much I love her every single day." He stared at the fire again. "I miss her so goddamn much."

Hursag had left Jack a pile of sinewy animal fibers to twist into a long, thick rope. Colum helped him with the rope for a while, but, after his time with Zamar, Jack soon fell into an exhausted sleep. Colum covered the man with a fur, then headed for the river.

Soon he was on top of Ayylo's ledge, where the two of them dangled their legs over the rock precipice, staring down at the river below. Its water had slowly created the cave they inhabited, dissolving weaknesses in its granite, widening its cracks, eating into the softer parts, and breaking through fissures to enlarge the space.

Ayylo broke their reverie first. "There's fire in your eyes, brother. I saw it when you leaped onto my mother's web." Her honeyed tones evoked in him the thrill of dancing on the web.

He nodded. "I saw fire in everyone's eyes."

"Yaga said your arm turned into a snake after we danced."

"How would Yaga know? She wasn't there." He laughed. "Of course, the whole cave must know by now! What happened is that a snake came out of my arm."

The Queen's daughter pressed playfully against him. "That's a good sign, brother."

"A good sign? Why do you say that?"

"Because now we know what animal you'll become. And a serpent is very special." The sensuality of her gaze made him quiver. "There are only two other serpents in the whole cave, and my mother is one of them."

As he returned from the river, Colum saw Yaga hobble over from one sister's fire to another's. He knew the hobbling was a joke. The crone could move as swiftly as a gazelle, which happened to be her animal.

Back at his mother's hearth, Colum watched as Hursag pulled a squealing goat toward her fire and dispatched it with a sharpened dagger. Jack was there to grab a bowl and hold it out to catch the blood. Colum joined them in stripping off the goat's hide and cutting out its entrails. Hursag lubricated the sinewy fibers with fat before beating the tendons with a wooden mallet. She was careful to use just enough force to separate the tough cords without breaking them. Finally, the three of them ripped the tendons into separate strands. At last, Hursag was ready to make a fresh goat stew. The crone left the fire to walk while it simmered.

Jack stared in dismay at the basket of sinews she'd left for him. "She wants me to make the rope I've been working on longer," sighed the redhead. A layer of ashen dust framed his eyes.

"I'll help," said Colum. To form a durable rope, the men began twisting the short fibers of the sinews tighter than the long ones.

"I've gotten pretty good at this," commented Jack after weaving awhile. "I'm almost as fast as you are."

"You're stronger than when you first came, too."

"That only means I'll last longer." Jack made no attempt to keep the cynicism out of his voice.

Both men looked up as Amorpho, accompanied by Iblis, arrived at the hearth. The girl's skin and hair were as black as a cave tunnel without torchlight. Colum smiled at her, and the face of a man with the same black skin shimmered in his mind, accompanied by a feeling that the man was a close friend. *He must be a friend of the Colum who lived in the labyrinth.* Colum gazed at Iblis. *What a beauty she has become!*

"Is your mother's goat stew ready?" bellowed Amorpho. "I've been smelling it for some time now. Your mother keeps some of the herbs she uses a secret, and whatever they are, they always make her stew better than everyone else's."

"I'm sure it must be, sister. Let me fill a bowl for you." The youth jumped to his feet and filled her bowl to the brim. "What about you, Iblis?"

"No, Colum, my food is waiting for me at my own fire," said the girl cheerfully. She kissed his cheek and scampered off.

Amorpho plopped her large frame on a flat rock to eat. The Bull Woman's wide eyes, strong jaw, and muscular body intimidated Jack, who retreated with rope and fibers to the tethering rock. After finishing two bowls of stew, Amorpho pulled a pipe out of her voluminous robe and stuffed it with tobacco. Colum grabbed a burning stick from the fire to light the pipe. In the glow of the fire's low flames, his guest placed it firmly in her mouth and inhaled.

After a few puffs, Amorpho grinned. "Watch this," she said, and the exhaled smoke began to divide. Some smoke curled up toward the dome and some down to the floor. Colum wondered if she split the air current in her lungs in order to blow it both ways. The whole time she smoked, the woman never blinked as if she were in a mild trance.

Several puffs later, she spoke again. "You forged iron in another life. Isn't that right, little brother?"

"I'm not sure," replied Colum with a shrug. "I've been having these strange visions lately. My mother says they're memories. They seem to belong to a man who lived in a labyrinth and forged iron." A lost look came over the youth. "I guess the man was . . . is . . . me."

"Our cave has a few small crucibles for forging. We must forge something together one of these days. Perhaps, if we do, you'll remember more." Amorpho's large brown eyes narrowed. "Why, just looking at you I can tell you're aligned with the iron."

A rush of excitement filled Colum at the idea of forging. Was that the man's excitement he felt? "I'd like that, Amorpho!"

The Bull Woman filled and emptied her pipe several times, while Colum lay sideways on the furs and watched the fire spit flames. There was something deeply satisfying about enjoying each other's company in silence. At last the Bull Woman hefted herself to her feet.

"Your time as a pup is coming to an end," she announced. "Once you shape-shift, you'll be seen as a man in our cave." She placed her large hand on Colum's shoulder. "Remember, I am one of your protectors. Which means you can consider me your ally in all things."

"Thank you, Amorpho," said Colum, touched by her support. "I'm truly fortunate to have someone like you as an ally."

As soon as she left, Jack returned to the fire. He sat on the rock still warmed by the Bull Woman's enormous buttocks and rubbed his forehead.

"Headache?" asked Colum.

Jack nodded. "I'm not sleeping well. I keep wishing this is all a dream, and that I'll wake up in my own bed in the morning with my wife beside me and my kids pouring themselves cereal in the kitchen and spilling the milk." Then, with a nervous twitch, Jack whispered, "My god, Sny's coming this way."

The Panther Woman stepped onto their hearth, pinning Jack with her gaze before he could retreat to his rock. "Still alive, I see." Her voice dripped acid.

Colum tried to stay calm. "What can I do for you, sister?"

"Just thought I'd check on your *pet*," answered the huntress, her hot breath spraying Jack's face. Sny's strong fingers grabbed his chin and jerked it up for a closer look. "Did you enjoy your little fishing expedition in *our* forest?" She let him go, then turned to Colum, asking with malice in her voice, "You realize his presence insults us all, don't you?"

"Not all our sisters feel the way you do, Sny. Zamar seems to enjoy having him around."

"I'll grant you men have their uses, but once in our cave, their lives have a penchant to be cut short." She drew her knife, pricking the skin under Jack's chin with its point. "I wouldn't mind tossing *his* cock and balls in a pot to season my broth." The huntress turned toward Colum, pushing her face close enough for their noses to brush. "This one came to meet his fate, brother, not play the role of your precious pet." With a rasping laugh, the Cat Woman whirled on her heels and strode off.

"Oh, shit," said Jack with a stricken look. "Here comes the other one!"

A profound wariness came over Colum. "Remember, Jack, you belong to Bruha. Neither of them dare touch you."

Kle-Ptuza crossed into Hursag's hearth uninvited and strode over to the captive. She gripped the tunic under his chin and, with a tight twist, used it to lift him onto his toes until his eyes were level with hers. Her unnerving stare caused a wet spot to appear below the navel on Jack's tunic. "Oh, poor scared thing, did you pee on yourself?" The Raptor Woman dropped him, laughing, then looked at Colum. "Shall I demonstrate, brother, how to eviscerate one's prey?"

"I know how to prepare prey, sister," replied the youth as calmly as he could.

To Colum's great relief, he saw his mother walking toward them. Kle-Ptuza gave Jack a shove backward and her sharp eyes glared at Colum. "All men are a blight, a disease to be purged. No man shelters here for long." The copper-haired woman left before Hursag arrived.

Jack retired to the rock, and Colum sat by the fire with his mother.

"What did Kle-Ptuza want?" she asked.

Colum composed himself with difficulty. "She's a raptor, Nana, and to her, Jack is prey." He sighed. "She was just having her *fun* with him."

"Ah, I see."

The youth stared at the flickering flames of their fire, listening to sounds of music all over the cave. He knew each instrument: panpipes, vulture-bone flutes, water flutes, bells, and drums. Somewhere a woman blew into the holes on her raven-bone whistle. In the distance another woman played a melody on a lyre, one that Colum found both haunting and musically interesting.

Musically interesting? Where did that thought come from? Is that the way the man in me perceives it?

The crone broke into his reverie. "You look disturbed, my son."

"I wonder what it's like to live in Jack's world, a world where you can't change your form."

"Aren't your new memories showing you that world?"

"I get pictures, but I don't know what it *feels* like to be the man in the labyrinth." He frowned. "Or to live in a world without our Queen's web to dance on."

"Ah, the ecstasy of Lillake's web." Hursag nodded. "No matter how old any of us become, her web fills us with endless vitality." As if she were drawing on it, the lines and sags vanished from Hursag's face, leaving her skin young and radiant.

Colum felt a rush of joy. "Oh, Nana, you're so *beautiful!*" He leaned against her chest and felt her heartbeat once more steadying him.

Hursag ran her fingers through the soft curls of his hair. "You were born to explore life's *deeper* structures, my son." She held him closer. "I am so happy I found you in the world. The chances were slim, but I never gave up hope."

She started to laugh, and soon he was laughing with her. They laughed until they rolled off their sitting rocks. They laughed so hard they had to press their hands against their aching sides to ease the pain. Jack stared at them across the furs as if they were crazy. At last mother and son wiped the tears from their eyes, panting for breath. Hursag flung an arm around Colum, and he felt her fierce love burn through him.

Later, Colum strolled to the river in time to see the shine of Bruha's huge, sweaty hippo flanks disappear into the water upstream. Soon her head broke through the surface, and, spotting Colum, she paddled toward him with her short legs with graceful glides as if she were a river horse. She submerged again, only to pop high into the air and come splashing down like a waterfall close to where he stood. Bruha rose out of the water and, snorting and wheezing, shape-shifted back into human form.

"Walk with me back to my hearth, little one."

When they arrived, she had Colum take a brush of light bristles and scrub the tough skin on her sides, working the contours.

"Ah!" she sighed. "What a good cub you are. Up . . . up toward the shoulder blade." Colum finally put the brush down and began to massage her back, rolling his forearms like waves in an ocean. He went up one side of her spine, then the other. "Oooh! Ahhh! Ummm!" It took considerable effort to cover such a large body with enough pressure for the Hippo Woman to feel. But it made the youth truly happy to see Bruha's eyes close in rapture and hear her moan with satisfaction. When he finished, the Hippo Woman beamed at him.

"I was nearby when Amorpho pulled you all wet and shiny out of our Cauldron of Rebirth. Now look at the strapping young lad you've become! And soon you'll be strutting through our cave as a man!" Bruha got on her feet like a small mountain pushing up out of the earth. She grinned. "Just listen to my stomach rumble. It must be time to eat." The woman laid out a platter of aromatic raisin cake and passed him a straw to sip beer from her common pot. Colum enjoyed Bruha's company. She told funny stories about their sisters, accompanied by full-throttled, head-thrown-back cackles over their misadventures.

When at last Colum got up to go, Bruha, in a genial mood, said, "Keep your pet for as long as he pleases you, brother."

"Thank you, Bruha."

Colum left the Hippo Woman's hearth and headed for Ayylo's cliff. He climbed up, listening to the lilting notes of her flute. He thought about how each hole in the flute's hollow bones facilitated a different pitch. *There is that man in me again wanting to know how things work.*

The Queen's daughter laughed as she helped pull him up over her ledge. "Ah, Colum, a visitor at last!" She looked frighteningly beautiful in her light green tunic with its diaphanous weave. "I saw Sny and Kle-Ptuza visiting at your hearth awhile ago."

"They came to torment Jack," he said darkly.

Ayylo picked up her flute and, with lips stained red from eating berries, started to play again. The music sent gentle, soothing waves through Colum, and he lay back to stare up at the stalactites hanging from the rock dome like sparkling icicles.

Ayylo put the flute down and said playfully, "Open your mouth." She dropped two red berries into it.

The burst of sweet acidity went straight to the youth's brain, and he sat up. "What's a wife, Ayylo?"

"Why do you ask?"

"Jack has a wife."

"Yes, well, in Jack's world, a man and a woman may choose to live with one another. Some have children and grow old together. A woman who does this is called a wife."

Colum grew thoughtful. "Have you ever been a wife, Ayylo?"

She shook her head, smiling. "Not me, brother. It's not in my nature."

"You had a father, Ayylo. Did you know him?"

"I did. When I was young, my mother built a hut in the forest so I could spend time with him." Her luxurious golden-red hair fell in soft eddies over her shoulders.

"Did he ever come to the cave to see you?"

"No, it was safer for him not to."

"What was your father like?"

Her green eyes held a faraway look. "His hair was red like Jack's. And he had the most wonderful laugh. I can still hear it if I try." Her gaze returned to him. "He lived so long ago, Colum, I can't see his face anymore. As soon as I shape-shifted, my mother sent him back to his world." She was silent for a moment. "What makes you ask?"

"I was thinking about how all of us have a father. And yet there are only mothers in our cave."

"Does it matter?"

"It makes me wonder if I belong."

She flashed him a radiant smile. "Of course you do! You're as much a part of this cave as I am!" The Queen's daughter walked to the cliff's edge and balanced on her tiptoes with outspread arms. Cavern breezes blew the bottom of her thin tunic up to mid-thigh. "Come, Colum! Stand next to me!" The youth joined her on the cliff's edge, and she turned to look at him. "If only you could see how *wild* your visage is!"

The two of them went back to Ayylo's fire and drank red wine together. The youth reached out to stroke her shiny hair. "My mother spins a luminous web for us to dance on, brother," she said, smiling. "She spins it not only in our cave but in the starry reaches of space."

"For our raven sisters to dance on?"

"Yes." The Queen's daughter put down her cup and started to caress Colum's chest. A musky, intoxicating, erotic scent rose off her like waves of catnip. "I desire you," she murmured, "the way my mother desired my father."

"What do you mean?"

"My father was the only man she deemed worthy to sire her child." Ayylo shook her golden hair like a lion's mane and kissed him on the lips. "One day I hope to have a child with you, brother."

Colum knew the flush in his cheeks and flutters of excitement in his stomach came from more than the fire and wine.

Ayylo purred. "But before I can offer you the friendship of my thighs, you must shape-shift in your *entirety*. You're on the cusp of being a man, brother. I know you feel the changes within you, and your memories of having been a man will only accelerate those changes."

CHAPTER FOURTEEN

Colum was sitting by the fire when he saw Jack approaching. The man kept his head down as he wound his way toward the hearth, shying away from the more aggressive women. A leather band held his red hair off his forehead and kept it from tumbling over his shoulders. Most of the women saw the captive as Colum's "pet" and largely ignored him. Despite the dark circles under his eyes, there was a new hardness to his body. At last the man reached the relative safety of Hursag's hearth. "I didn't see Zamar take you this time," Colum said.

Jack sliced a piece of roasted deer flank onto a platter and sat next to him. "You were off somewhere when she came." He began to eat with relish.

"How is Zamar?" asked the youth.

"She's like a goat in perpetual heat. She never changes." He sighed. "Sometimes I think she'll swallow me whole." Jack looked up from his platter, oblivious to the grease smeared on his chin. "Thank God that engineer takes the brunt of her cravings."

"You look tired. Why don't you get some sleep?"

Jack went to the tethering rock, curled up on a pile of furs, and fell asleep. After he was asleep, a young girl, around seven or eight, approached Colum. Her doe-like eyes sparkled in the firelight, and sprigs of white berries decorated her light brown hair.

"Welcome, Ast," greeted Colum, smiling.

She smiled back shyly. The girl had always been like a skittish cat around him, and her visit seemed an act of trust. "My mother and I picked oranges from our grove, brother. Would you like to try one? They are so juicy." The fire cast a glow on Ast's smooth, young face.

"I'd love to."

"Come with me to our hearth and I'll give you some to bring back."

She took off, and Colum followed her through a maze of cauldrons. They passed Strix's hearth. The crone was boiling pigments in a vat to make dye, and her white hair, wet with steam, stuck damply to the sides of her face.

"Where are you two off to?" she called out.

Pulled on by his youthful guide, Colum shouted over his shoulder, "Ast picked oranges from the grove and wants to share them!"

"Oranges?" returned Strix. "The orange trees in the forest are barren now."

Colum's heart nearly stopped at her words. He whipped his head around in the direction of his mother's hearth. Through the swirling smoke of multiple fires, Colum saw Sny striding toward his hearth.

He shook Ast's hand off his arm and took off at a sprint. But he hadn't made it far when he heard screams of anguish. The fear gripping Colum's chest turned to dread.

Dashing full speed through the firelit cave, he arrived to find Jack slumped over on his knees. The redhead's arms hung limply at his sides as if broken, a look of fixed terror on his face. Blood sluiced down his forehead from a gash in his scalp. Sny's metal dagger was wet with his blood. She looked up at Colum fiercely, clearly exhilarated.

"*No!*" Colum cried, fighting an impulse to fling himself through the air and grab the dagger from her hand.

The Panther Woman turned sharply on Colum. "Come to save your 'pet,' have you?"

The contemptuous sound of her voice awakened in him a memory from the labyrinth. Colum, the man, was holding his head in agony. Only this time, instead of just a mental picture, Colum, the youth, could feel the searing pain of Sny wreaking havoc in his . . . *their* . . . brain.

A profound caution seized him. "Jack belongs to Bruha, not me."

Sny gripped her knife harder, her voice dripping with malice. "She's not here, is she?" With a sneering laugh, she pointed to the redhead. "Oh, look, he's shitting himself like a baby."

Colum knew that taunting him gave her a visceral thrill. Sny knelt down on one knee close to Jack, an insolent glee in her eyes. Then she grabbed Jack's head, pulled it backward, and drove her long dagger up through his nose. The blade burst through the redhead's cribriform plate deep into his brain. He gave a violent, convulsive jerk and sagged. A line of froth formed on Jack's mouth as Sny withdrew her knife. The Cat Woman leaped to her feet and kicked the body aside.

Colum watched with breathless horror as vacancy filled Jack's eyes. The next instant, the horror was usurped by an anger that came with the force of a trembling earthquake. Before she could see it coming, he rammed his fist into Sny's chest. The powerful blow sent the huntress flying backward. She landed on her back, dazed and gasping for air. In a sudden rebound, Sny jumped into the air, transforming into a black panther with claws extended.

A large crowd of women were gathering. They formed a wide circle around the two opponents, watching as the panther dropped on Colum, digging her front paws into his chest. Agony raked him. The blue-black feline let out the terrifying, guttural cry of a predator mauling its prey. The gash over Colum's ribcage sprayed blood in the air, and he crashed to the floor under her weight.

Something stirred deep within Colum's sensory nervous system, setting in motion a profound inner mobilization and organization of forces. The youth's body entered a flux of instability, softening and molting. His human outlines began to blur. Capillaries in his skin allowed his body to stretch lengthwise. Soon his form was twice the length it had been. Colum's extremities shriveled and disappeared, along with his protruding ears and nose. His head elongated. A gaping mouth cut across the breadth of his face, revealing fangs, mandibles, and a forked tongue that flicked in and out. Layers of muscle, lymph, and bone reconstructed to produce the radically new shape of a serpent. His new black-scaled body was all sinew and muscular hardness, boasting a band of red scales around the neck. For a moment, Colum's thoughts swirled uselessly. Powerless to resist, the youth felt as if death were ripping through him. Then, as his human side became more and more remote, his thoughts vanished completely.

His breathing turned shallow and fast. A sense of awareness spread in a diffuse way over the entirety of his reptilian body. He saw, if only dimly, *through his skin*. Temperature-sensitive pits on either side of his head picked up Sny's heat. With no ears to hear, all sensations had turned to heat, light, and vibration, but the new sensory data was sharp, clear, and immediate.

Some women jumped back, while others stared mesmerized at the oversized dark viper with red neckband, flaring pits, and golden eyes.

"Colum the Serpent!" exclaimed several voices in chorus.

Amorpho bellowed, "Behold, the Ironsmith, forged in volcanic pyrite!"

"Creator and Destroyer is he!" cried another.

"Behold the true shape of our brother!"

Oblivious to their words, the viper riveted its attention on the creature in front of him.

He was *all* snake now. There was no train of rational thought left, only the cold reptilian depths of somatic awareness and a drive to survive. He existed as one long throat filled with nerves.

Lush, textured skin with smooth scales pulsed over his viper muscles as he studied the panther through lidless eyes.

Even the panther seemed momentarily stunned by the transformation. Soon, though, her rumbling growl, deep and menacing, filled the air, and she sprang into action. The black cat hacked viciously at the snake with her front claws, ripping the skin down one side of its neck. Blood gushed, spattering the rough rock of the cave floor, and the panther's roar of triumph blasted across the cave.

The black viper slithered backward with continuous intricate, fluid muscular movements, hissing at the pain. It hadn't gone very far when the panther leaped at it again. The cat's black fur shimmered in the firelight. Its rigid paws grappled with the serpent and flipped it sideways. The viper wrenched violently to free itself and escape. With blinding speed, it glided backward, then stopped as suddenly as it took off, using its tail as an anchor. The viper raised up again to stab and recoil. Its gaze honed in on the cat, and a pair of hollow, venom-injecting fangs unfolded from its upper jaw. The black cat lunged at the snake with full fury, but not fast enough. Using quicksilver contractions, the serpent side-winded out of its way. The panther's claws rasped against bare rock floor, and it tumbled onto its back.

The viper returned at once, only this time, it began a slow, caressing pass over the panther's exposed underbelly. The feline pawed the air softly while the black serpent slithered across it, emitting a long, slow, airy sound, almost of pleasure. In the profound silence of the cave, the cat's soft, whistling breath could be heard everywhere. All of a sudden, the viper's vibrating jaws made a clacking sound, and with a forward sweep of its elongated head, it bit the cat in the throat. An earsplitting shriek ripped through the cave as the serpent's poison surged into the panther. The cat righted itself and crouched for a spring, but the viper was already in retreat. The panther's heavily muscled legs fired forward and back in a chase after its zigzagging prey. Women fled in every direction to get out of the way. The feline quickly bore down on the viper, hooking its sharp, retractable claws into the snake. With one high-powered sweep, the cat slashed the viper's back, ripping off skin and exposing muscle. The viper let out a violent hiss like water poured on fire, then whipped around to face the panther. Firelight glinted in each slit of its reptilian eyes. The panther, whose actions were only increasing the flow of toxicity in its bloodstream, attempted another swipe. It missed and stumbled. The virulent venom of the viper was causing the panther's brain to fail and its lungs to collapse. The black cat stumbled a second time and fell. Its muscles spasmed. It blinked twice in an effort to clear its blurred vision, but the sleek, black-furred animal was in a state of shock.

Abruta surged toward them from a tunnel in the far wall of the cavern. "*CEASE!*" she thundered. Her voice blasted the robed women like a stunning, physical shock wave, and they parted to let her pass. The panther had already begun to change, and soon Sny's human form lay writhing on the cave floor. Her eyes were filled with blood, and bloody threads fell from her gums. The woman was barely breathing.

Huluppu arrived and began to pulse healing power into the huntress's heart, while Abruta raced to do the same for the serpent. Slowly, the viper's rage ebbed away, along with its vibrational pattern, and Colum, too, returned to human form. Half of his chest was shredded. Abruta continued to stream energy into him. Gradually, the youth's breathing slowed, and he fell into a deep, healing sleep. Amorpho, watching at Abruta's side, lifted the youth in her strong arms and carried him back to his hearth.

Colum awoke on his furs, his mother sitting at his side. The blood had been washed from his body, the torn flaps of skin sewn back on, and a healing ointment applied. The crone handed him a cup of stringent fluid, and he drank it without question. A heavy warmth spread through him. "You must rest, my son," crooned his mother.

The youth was asleep before his head reached the furs.

When he woke again later, Bruha was sitting nearby. She looked at Colum with new regard in her eyes. "I came to say, *Long One*, that your strength is formidable. You make a fearsome enemy indeed, and I pity anyone who rises up against you."

The youth struggled to sit up, but a pounding headache stopped him.

"Your wounds were serious, my son," said Hursag. "They are not mended yet."

He fell asleep again, and the next time he woke, the headache was gone. His mother brought him a cup of tea. "How does your chest feel?"

"Sore, but it doesn't hurt nearly as much as it did." He looked at her. "I dreamed Bruha was here and called me 'Long One.'"

Flames flickered on the crone's wrinkled face. "That wasn't a dream. Do you remember what happened?"

Colum struggled to see through the fog in his head, but finally, some hazy memories returned.

"Jack?" he whispered.

"He's dead, my son. We buried him in the forest."

Tears ran down Colum's face, not only for the loss of Jack but for the honor the women had bestowed on him.

"I remember when Sny stabbed Jack," he said weakly. "But then it's cloudy."

"Try to remember. Take your time," said Hursag quietly.

Colum had a vague recollection of being drawn inward, into the formless depths of himself, where he existed as . . . what? A kind of *vibration detector*? "Did I shape-shift, Nana? Is that why Bruha called me 'Long One'?"

"Yes, you did, into a beautiful black viper with a red band around its neck like the one that crawled out on your arm. Close your eyes, my son. See if anything comes back to you." The crone's words were more an induction than a suggestion.

What are these radiant, wavy, red forms I see? This heat I feel in them? So many strange sensations! Something is filling my mouth and spraying out in an orgasmic, exhilarating discharge!

Something sharp is raking my skin. Horrible pain in my side. A smell of fresh blood in the air. My blood!

He opened his eyes, dazed by the vision, and stared at his mother. "Are these my memories?"

"Yes, my son," she said. "It took rage over Jack's death to bring your serpent fully to life. You're remembering what it felt like to be one."

The youth recalled his futile attempts to stop Sny from killing Jack, saw the grimace of horror on Jack's face, felt his own helplessness to save the man. After which came the *rage and transformation.*

"I fought Sny, didn't I?"

"Yes." She took his cup from him. "If you feel well enough to walk, our Mistress wishes to see you." With Hursag's help, Colum managed to stand. She put her arm around his waist to steady him, and they walked slowly to the Queen's throne. Women at every hearth stopped what they were doing to look solemnly at the youth. Many gave him a short nod of respect. At last they arrived before the Queen's throne.

CHAPTER FIFTEEN

Several women had gathered at the Queen's throne by the time Hursag and Colum arrived.

A band of silver, shining in the torchlight, encircled Lillake's blue-black hair. She fixed her emerald eyes on Colum. "There has been a *disturbance* in our realm," she announced. "Son of Hursag, is it true you fought with a sister and nearly killed her?"

"Yes, Mistress." He stared wide-eyed at the Queen. The distant din of a drum could be heard in the background.

"And why did you fight?"

"She killed Jack, Mistress."

Lillake sat forward on her throne. "Would you take the life of a *sister* over the life of a pet?"

"Jack was a man, Mistress. Not a deer or a rabbit. He didn't deserve to die, not that way."

Strix spoke from where she stood with the other women. "The man was an outsider, brother, who overstayed his time with us. If you hadn't taken him for a pet, the fight would never have happened."

Bruha lumbered forward a few steps. "Colum did nothing wrong, sister. Many of our young ones keep pets."

"Children keep pets." Strix frowned. "As a child, if Colum felt aggrieved by Sny, he should have gone to his mother for redress."

"Mistress, we all knew the sap was rising in Hursag's son," said Amorpho. "His snake was ready to burst free at the least provocation. We also know that Sny killed the man in order to provoke him."

Huluppu swayed slightly like a willow tree in a breeze. "Amorpho speaks the truth, Mistress. Our only surprise was the thundering power of Colum's response."

Yaga gave a disarming laugh. "Oh, yes, it took my breath away to see our brother shape-shift into the magnificent viper that he is!" With a huge grin on her face, she added, "And then to see him join in a wild romp with Sny's panther! After all, she's the one who invited him to dance."

"And," intercepted another crone, "since both are still alive, nothing is lost to us."

Lillake nodded gravely and looked at Colum. "It's true you were provoked, and your passion aroused the viper in you. It is also true that it is Sny's nature to hunt men, and once Jack entered our forest, he became fair game. He was never meant to stay here."

Lillake focused intensely on the youth. "You are a serpent, Son of Hursag . . . a column indeed. A column exists to support and uphold." She pulled an obsidian blade from the belt at her waist and pointed it at him. "This dagger has the power to send its human sheath to our lake."

With her words, a memory arose in Colum powerful enough to submerge him into the lake's watery blackness. It was a memory of drowning, and he knew it belonged to the man in the labyrinth. The youth could feel the man's desperate efforts to return to the water's surface as if *he* were the one struggling. Suffocating terror and a desperation to break through the water consumed every cell of his body.

Lillake waved her hand, and the memory disappeared. "Answer me, Son of Hursag: Whose column are you?"

The face of a muscular, thick-necked man now appeared in

his mind's eye. The man sat on an iron chair in a circular stone chamber and seemed to be scowling.

Colum felt a moment of panic. *It must be the king of the laby-rinth. How can the Queen ask me such a question? Does she doubt my loyalty?*

"If I am a column, Mistress, I uphold the life of this cave. I support you and all my sisters."

Lillake leaned close enough to cut the barest scratch across his throat. The youth blanched but didn't move. "You speak truly," she said and resheathed her knife. "Our cave is an ancient artifice, Son of Hursag. It is older than the labyrinth ruled by Nirah. In all these millennia, we've never needed a man to uphold our cavern. *But all things change.*" The Dark Moon stood and, with a shake of her luxurious blue-black hair, announced to the women around her in a loud, clear voice, "Our brother Colum has become a man among us. Spread the word. He is to be celebrated!"

"And Sny?" ventured Strix.

"She and Colum must reconcile," replied the Queen.

Strix shook her head as if Lillake were asking the impossible. "The panther has never made peace with a man before."

The Queen nodded at Hursag. "I leave their reconciliation to you, sister."

Later, Colum sat with his mother, her face hidden under a black cowl, near the warm glow of their fire. The strange new memories were coming all the time now. He could recall with detail the faces of the men who labored in the labyrinth. What's more, whenever a memory flashed of an audience with Uncle, the hardness of the floor pressed against *his* knees, and *his own* heart beat faster.

Hursag broke into his reverie. "You look very thoughtful," she said.

He gave a slight shudder. "I was thinking of the memories I've been having, Nana. Lately, I can feel what the man in them feels."

"And does it bother you?"

The youth grimaced. "Sometimes."

"I'm sure he must see and feel life very differently than you."

"About as differently as my snake!" Colum exclaimed. He stared at the fire for a moment, then asked, "Is he dead now, Nana? Did he die in the cauldron?"

"Not exactly, my son. You wouldn't experience his memories if he didn't reside somewhere within you."

"The way my snake does?"

"They both share your deepest cells." She stroked his hair. "The man's mind has lain dormant in the pith of your blood and is now awakening along with his memories."

"Is he aware of me?"

"It seems so."

The crone turned to him, saying carefully, "Sny approaches. Ready yourself. The Queen has sent her to reconcile with you."

An instinctive reflex to fight the huntress sprang up inside him, a desire coming from his cold-blooded reptile. With his mind, he carefully coaxed the viper back into its sleeping coils just as Sny crossed the boundary to their hearth.

"Greetings, Mammi."

"Welcome, Sny."

The huntress took a deep breath. "I wish to apologize for doing harm to your son."

"Please sit, sister."

Sny sat reluctantly on a flat rock, and the crone placed her blue-veined hand gently on the Panther Woman's shoulder. "You acknowledge, then, that Colum's rage was provoked by your action? That you were the one who triggered his viper to fight you?"

"Yes, Mammi," said Sny, squirming on the rock seat.

Colum tried to imagine how hard it must be for Sny to accept censure, even from someone she loved and admired.

The crone continued. "You nearly killed him."

Sny flushed. "I have no excuse, Mammi. My own rage took over. I never meant to hurt you."

"Rage over what, sister?" pursued the crone. "That my son kept Jack as a pet? Or that Colum lives in the cave as one of us?"

A muscle twitched along Sny's jaw. "Our cave is no place for men, Mammi, and now that Colum has shape-shifted, he is a man. He is no longer a child." The Panther Woman's face darkened. "You know as well as I do that men are an invasive species among us." She seemed to search for the right words. "When I bite into a man's neck, it gives me shivers of delight to see him go all dough-soft and white with fear. I savor the flavor of his fear in my mouth. Nothing else will stop their limitless consumption. You cannot deny that men are not good for our world."

"My son is not such a man, sister. My son is born from the cauldron of our blood. He has been nourished on my milk and raised in our cave as one of us." The crone took a piece of mashed wood out of a basket and dropped it in a pot of simmering water. "Ash for healing," she announced.

A look of concern crossed Sny's face. "What are you doing, Mammi?"

"Our Mistress desires a genuine peace between the two of you, and I am preparing a brew to help make that peace a reality." A chunk of bark followed the ash. "Willow to quell the pain," she intoned.

"Is this really necessary, Mammi?"

"Quite necessary." A third piece of wood plopped into the water. "Hazel to see the wisdom of what is." Next, Hursag threw in a handful of wood shavings. "Rowan to control one's temper."

The crone pulled a small pouch of red toadstools from the basket and sprinkled the fungi into the pot.

"Who sits beside you, sister?" asked Hursag.

Sny's face turned to stone. "My brother."

"Yes, your brother—*my son*. For far too long I searched for someone who could bring in my milk, and in all that time, the only person with the power to make it flow is the one who sits beside you." The crone's voice held a ring of caution. "Would you crush my joy by seeking to harm him?"

"It was never my intention to hurt you, Mammi." She hung her head. "My anger blinded me to your feelings. And yet . . ."

"Yes?"

"I still don't see how any man can belong to our *sisterhood*."

"Colum is not a mere man, sister. Everyone in the cave has witnessed the ferocity of your battle together." The crone's eyes narrowed. "And in the end, who prevailed?"

Sny was silent.

"Without Huluppu's ministrations, my son's venom would certainly have killed you."

Sny spoke in solemn tones. "For your sake, Mammi, I swear I'll never attack him again. I will not harm the one who has brought in your milk."

"That's not good enough, sister."

"What else do you want from me?" asked Sny with a look of shock.

"Your reconciliation must go deeper than that. If not, in some unguarded moment, your spleen will boil again and turn your vow to ash. Then there will be another battle, one neither of you may survive." The Lion Woman stared directly into the Panther Woman's eyes. "You know I speak the truth."

Colum watched Sny's breast heave. His own heart was pounding.

"My son was pulled from the cauldron of our blood, sister," continued Hursag. "He dances on the Queen's web with as much verve as any of us. Can you not see that? He shares *essence* with us!"

Color flooded Sny's cheeks, but she seemed incapable of reply.

Hursag turned her attention to Colum. "Your rage, too, no less than Sny's, threatens to split apart the fabric of our cave."

It was his turn to redden. "Yes, Mother."

The crone dipped a cup into the steaming pot and held it out to him. "Drink, and pass the cup to Sny."

Anxious to have their ordeal over with, the two culprits drank without protest, then waited for the brew to take effect.

"Speak to one another from your hearts," said Hursag after some time. "Sny, you begin."

"I don't know what to say, Mammi."

"Start by telling Colum your true name."

A flash of horror entered the Panther Woman's eyes. "That will give him power over me!"

"You are fortunate to still be alive, sister."

Sny recoiled at the reminder. Colum, feeling her chagrin, looked away. He knew how supremely dangerous she was, and never once had he seen any signs of uncertainty or distress in her.

"I am called Sagacious Huntress," said Sny at last.

The words entered Colum as a deep vibration.

The brew was moving through their bodies like a fever. Hursag placed Colum's hand in Sny's, and soon the youth could no longer tell where Sny's hand began and his own left off. He began to spin with her sensations, stalking the forest on velvet paws, a lone cat on the prowl for meat. Together as a single feline they ripped through prey, using razor-sharp teeth and gorging to satisfaction. The youth looked through the panther's sharp, farsighted, keenly discerning eyes, seeing the forest as a hunter.

He moved through her . . . *as her* . . . until at last he found a petrified, dead place in Sny filled with undigested bitterness. She groaned when Colum touched it, and he quickly withdrew. Now shadows flitted into view. Before long, he could make out that the shadows were of men. Wherever they went, life was stripped from the land and left barren. The youth knew that the deeds of men, who were cut off from their own moistening depths, had created the dry place in the panther. He saw that Sny, as a vital protectress, kept them as far away from the territory of her sisters as possible. If necessary, she would cover her sisters with the shield of herself and gladly die for them. The realization filled him with a profound sadness, and he began to weep. When the huntress saw the tears streaming down Colum's cheeks, her own eyes burned.

Hursag separated their hands. Shaken, Sny stood and staggered away.

"Are we reconciled, Nana?" asked Colum.

"Not yet, my son, but the process has started. If a true spirit of reconciliation is to take root within Sny, she needs some time and space to herself."

Deciding he needed the same, Colum wandered off to the river. He sat next to a gigantic gypsum flower. The floral formation had been shaped by underground water oozing and dripping in the same location for thousands of years through a system of limestone passageways. He watched a colorless centipede crawling across the rocky petals. When he looked up again, he startled. A woman he had seen once before stood on the other side of the gypsum flower. There was no pigment in her skin. Her long fingers stretched toward him like bleached bones.

It was the Rock Woman.

"Your poison is virulent, brother," said the woman, her voice a chalky rasp. It was hard to tell if she spoke with an actual larynx or if her words reverberated in some hollow inside her throat.

"It's been a while since I've seen you, sister," said the youth.

"I spend most of my time asleep in the rock, dreaming." A wry smile formed at the corner of her hard-lined mouth. "I dreamed of you."

"Me?"

"I dreamed your toxic passion for a sister engendered new fruit in our cave." Her eyes blinked glacially slowly. Then the colorless woman leaned her back against the gypsum flower, and her whole body slowly faded into it.

Colum watched, dumbfounded, as she disappeared. *What did she say? Toxic passion?* It made him think of how he'd caressed Sny's underbelly as a viper and the eerie, seductive thrill that accompanied each caress. *No fruit will come of that!* Colum rose to leave the riverbank, thinking of his relationship with the huntress. It might be a fragile one, but after their toadstool ritual, he no longer regarded her a lethal threat.

The youth wandered back to his hearth, still shaken by his

brief encounter with the Rock Woman. On the way, he saw Ayylo walking and called out her name.

The Queen's daughter joined him with a smile. "You're the main topic of conversation in the cave, brother. Everyone is talking about what a fearsome adversary you are. How Hursag's child turned into a serpent strong and clever enough to defeat one of our greatest huntresses!"

Ayylo's luxurious hair rippled over her shoulders like falling water. *How is it that her beauty has the power to startle me each time I see her?*

"I didn't defeat her. We nearly killed one another."

Ayylo's emerald eyes sparkled. "Don't underestimate yourself, brother."

Ayylo stopped at Huluppu's hearth, and Colum continued on. As he passed Abruta's hearth, the ten-eyed woman said warmly, "I see you are well, brother."

"Without your care, Abruta, I would have bled out from my fight with Sny. Thank you."

"You don't have to thank me. We are family, brother." Her bottom row of eyes fixed on him. "You move differently since your metamorphosis."

"Differently? How?"

"Your movements are more serpentine. You flow in a way you didn't before. It's quite beautiful."

He stepped onto her hearth and helped himself to a cup of water. "It's subtle, but I feel different."

"How are you handling your new memories?"

His body tensed slightly. "It depends on the memory."

"I can imagine."

"To tell the truth, Abruta, they make me feel fragmented, as if I'm no longer a single person."

"You're not. A serpent lives in you."

Colum's snake flickered deep within his arteries and cells at its mention. "I know that now."

The woman looked at him sympathetically. "Of course, the snake is part of your physical body, while the other Colum exists in you as memories."

"It's just that there are so many memories of him!"

She nodded. "Filled with emotions, I'm sure." Abruta's upper eyes made a quick sweep of the cave while her lower ones stayed fixed on Colum. "You're aware, are you not, that your anger triggered your transformation into a viper?"

"I am."

"It's nothing to be ashamed of, brother. The power of a fury like yours can explode stars. Such an energy is vital to life. You simply must learn to confront and shape it."

"I will do my best." He took another drink of water. "Can I tell you something else?"

"Anything, brother."

"When I took my mother's red toadstools, I saw a figure. She was made of . . . of a kind of phosphorus light." He found it hard to continue. "She called herself *Dark Dreaming*."

"Go on," said Abruta, lowering her voice as the top row of her eyes swept the cave again.

"The figure said that Sny is afraid I'll bring change to our cave."

"Did she say anything else?"

"Yes. She said, '*The center cannot hold.*'"

All ten of Abruta's eyes blinked as one, and she looked at him with all of them at once.

"What do you see, Abruta?"

"As a serpent, you are a bundle of nervous excitement, brother, always growing beyond yourself. When the papery sheath of your skin becomes too restrictive, too confining, you shed that skin to leave it behind." She paused. "A snake's transformations are not trifling, brother."

"What are you saying?"

"That *Dark Dreaming* may be right, and you, Son of Hursag, may be a catalyst of change for us all." Abruta turned. "Your mother calls."

Colum pondered Abruta's words as he returned to his hearth. As soon as he arrived, his mother stood up and came toward him. "We have work to do! The Raven Women are coming! They're flying in from another star system to celebrate the transformations of you and Iblis into viper and raven." She gave him a radiant smile. "And you and I must prepare a feast worthy of them!"

"Will they take Iblis with them when they go?"

"Indeed they will. But while they are here, we must keep their bellies full of food and beer."

"How many are there?" he asked.

"Three. There's your godmother, Ethliu, who is one of your protectors and was present at your birth. Lagash, Iblis's mother. And Erinye."

"Iblis will be so happy, Nana!"

"Yes," Hursag said, smiling, "she was born to fly with them! Now I must fetch a pig from the forest. Prepare the roasting pit while I'm gone."

CHAPTER SIXTEEN

Hursag returned from the forest with her pig. As she prepared to butcher it, Colum filled the center of the roasting pit with a great amount of kindling wood and set it on fire. While the wood burned down, the crone deftly slit the wild pig's throat and scalded the animal's skin in boiling water to remove its bristles. Together, mother and son took out the pig's organs, cleaned its interior, and placed hot rocks in the empty cavity. After rubbing its outer body with fresh herbs, they propped open the porcine mouth with an apple to let the heat filter through. Colum spread lumps of smoldering wood evenly over the pit's bottom and placed the pig on a grate over them. Before long, the first rich odors of roasting pork wafted into the air.

The two of them left the pig to roast and returned to their hearth, where they began to prepare the rest of the feast. Colum felt a special intimacy cooking with his mother. He enjoyed the harmony between them.

"My hair must be a mess," she laughed and sat down, their work done at last.

Colum rummaged in his mother's personal basket looking

for her bronze-wire hairbrush. He then brushed the crone's silver strands until they shimmered. "Shall I plait them, Nana?"

"Oh, yes."

The youth made two thick braids, interweaving them with red ribbons. When he finished, Hursag pulled a purple silk robe from another basket. Purple was a color of power for the women in the cave, and power flowed naturally from her. As soon as she changed clothes, the crone pulled a sky-blue tunic from the basket.

"This is for you," she said and passed it to him.

He gave her a look of surprise. "When did you make this, Nana?"

"I worked on it while you slept."

Wind sounded overhead, and the two of them looked up. A giant raven was flying in circles around the cave's dome. The bird swooped down close enough for the youth to feel the breeze of her wings. Dust and ash swirled. The glossy bird's talons tightened on his shoulders. The next instant, the raven lifted him into the air with rapid, powerful flaps of her wings. Halfway up, the raven let go of Colum's shoulders. He reached out to grasp one of the bird's legs and, dangling, sailed with her toward the dome. Colum threw up his free hand and tried to grab the raptor's other leg, feeling as if his arm might dislocate. He missed. The youth tried again. This time, with a strong swing of his body and a ragged rush of wind sounding in his ears, his hand connected with the raven's free leg. The bird's wings flapped at full power. It felt dizzying to be swept up in a wide circle under the cave's ceiling. Clinging tighter to the raven's legs, he glanced down at the river that wound through the cave like a dark ribbon. Hundreds of dancing flames spread out in every direction across the cavern's center. The giant bird wheeled majestically before heading for the pit of coals with its roasting pig.

Colum and the raven came ever closer to a clear patch below. The youth released his grip and landed safely in a full-body roll. The raven landed next to him in a rush of air and flying ash. It turned its head to stare at Colum out of one eye. Firelight glistened on her glossy blue-black feathers. The raptor contracted her undulating shoulders and her powerful wings relaxed to fold by her sides.

The raven held her bill high, fluffed her neck, and, in a loud and throaty voice, called out, "CAAAAW!"

Hursag sprinted over. "Ethliu, my dearest sister!"

Human fingers stretched out through the ends of the raptor's wingtips, and where the bird's beak and dark eyes had been, a human face appeared. A few seconds later, an elegant-looking woman stood in the raven's place. Horizontal rows of glistening blue-black raven feathers made up her wide skirt. Her upper body was naked with two rounded breasts jutting out. The woman's breasts were partially covered by the golden ripples of her hair spilling over them.

Ethliu embraced Hursag. "Ah, sister! It seems I saw you last but a moment ago."

"And so it seems to me," said Hursag warmly. "Welcome back!"

Ethliu turned to Colum with a smile. "And you . . ." She took a long look at him. "Why, you are a young man now!" She placed a hand on his shoulder. "I was hoping you'd be quick enough to grab my legs when I dropped you. Did you enjoy the flight?"

"It was exhilarating!" he exclaimed, still out of breath.

Two more ravens squeezed through ventilator shafts in the dome. Instead of circling as Ethliu had done, they flew down with lightning swiftness, one after the other, to land directly. Firelight reflected off their outstretched wings, creating an iridescent sheen on their feathers. The large ravens stood close to the pit, pluming their breast feathers, stamping their feet, and shaking their heads. In a matter of seconds, they, too, morphed into human form. One woman had black hair and ebony skin and wore a crimson tunic.

She must be Iblis's mother, Lagash.

The hair of Lagash's pale-skinned partner was red, and she wore a green tunic. Soon all four women were laughing and hugging each other.

The redheaded woman looked at the youth with glittering

eyes. "Greetings, Colum. I am Erinye. I have flown through more than one solar storm to meet you."

The outer strangeness of the woman sent a shiver through him. "I am honored, noble sister."

"My son and I are both honored that the three of you flew all this way to see us," said Hursag with great affection in her voice.

"Your mother and I fought many battles together," said Erinye to Colum.

The statement threw him. *Battles? His mother? What kind of battles?* Out loud he said, "I'd love to hear stories about your time together, sister."

Lagash spoke next. "I've heard you and my daughter are close friends, Colum."

"We are. We've spent many hours together. Shall I find her for you?"

Lagash laughed. "There's no way Iblis missed our arrival. I'm sure she's already on her way."

"Tell me, Colum, is it true?" asked Erinye.

"Is what true, sister?"

"That Hursag, Great Lion of the High Steppe, rich in cunning—"

"Quite enough adulation, sister," said Hursag, placing a hand on Erinye's arm.

"Not nearly enough!" objected the red-haired woman with a laugh. Her tone turned more somber then. "Is it true, brother, that in giving birth to you, she has birthed a most *bold serpent*?"

Colum nodded, reddening.

"Follow me, sisters," Hursag said, beckoning. "The warmth of a crackling fire awaits you after the cold winds of space."

They strolled from the roasting pit to her hearth, interrupted along the way by women everywhere who came up to greet them.

At last they arrived at Hursag's fire. "How thirsty you must be after such a long journey! Sit and drink your fill!" The crone pointed to a large stone vessel filled with golden beer. "Be assured, my son shall keep the beer bowl overflowing for you!"

Lagash beamed. "Ah! We all know you grow the best barley of anyone here!"

Ethliu sat on one of the flat rocks close to the fire covered now with cream-colored goatskins and arranged in a circle. "Will Abruta join us, sister?"

"She's on her way from the forest," Hursag replied.

Iblis appeared suddenly, bounding across the rock floor half wild with excitement. "Mother! Mother!" she cried and ran into Lagash's open arms. "You've come at last to take me with you!"

Lagash embraced her warmly. "Yes, child. After our feast, we will leave together. Go, say your farewells. Gather what you wish to bring and put it in a bag, but the bag must be small and light enough to tie around your waist."

Iblis's bright eyes shone. "Save me a piece of pig, brother," she said with a look at Colum.

"I will." He already felt a pang at the thought of her leaving.

"And be sure it has lots of crackling on the skin. Who knows when I'll have another bite of anything so good!" With that she skipped away humming a cheerful tune.

Colum left the Raven Women to return to the pit. There he sliced up the glistening pig and filled a platter with its steaming meat. He carried the meat to his mother's hearth and placed the savory offering before their guests. Soon the women were devouring the pork, along with platters of warm cabbage, mashed plantains, and yams, and drawing in Hursag's beer through long reed straws. Roars of laughter interspersed their spirited conversation as they ate and drank in joyful reunion. Each time they drained the vessel of beer, Colum added more.

Ten-eyed Abruta soon joined the circle. The visiting women rose to embrace her, then all five women sat down again, chatting away. Colum pulled the fattened pork apart into manageable pieces and distributed a second helping on their plates. He gladly scorched his fingers on the hot golden crackling for their pleasure, serving side dishes of olives, figs, pomegranates, pears soaked in honey, and his mother's delicious, yeasty bread.

Erinye took a bite of the pig's crunchy tail. "You've outdone yourself this time, sister!"

Lagash tore off a piece of bread and spread a smear of honeyed pears over it. After popping it in her mouth, she turned to Colum, narrowing her amber eyes. "I see you have a snake coiled inside you, brother."

"You can *see* it?" he asked, not sure if she was teasing or not.

"Oh, yes. It is sleeping, and when it yawns, its poisonous fangs are all pink."

Erinye grinned. "Perhaps Colum's snake will grow wings."

The youth shook his head. "Snakes don't have wings, sister."

"You've never heard of flying serpents?"

He flushed. "Well, no."

The red-haired woman stroked her throat as though it were still covered with feathers. "Well, they exist." She paused, then added, "I would venture to say your viper has a certain penchant for stretching beyond limitations."

Black-haired Lagash sucked on her reed straw, taking a long draught of beer. "You look quite healthy, brother. But then, your mother's great swollen breasts no doubt poured her life-giving milk into you with the same gusto she pours her beer into us with." They all laughed.

"It's true, sister, I've wanted for nothing," said the youth, laughing with them. He looked at Lagash. "I will miss Iblis when you go."

"I'm sorry to deprive you of her company, brother, but neither of you are children anymore. You are both shape-shifting adults now." The Raven Woman gave him a compassionate smile. "All things change."

Colum nodded, then asked, "How do you fly in space, Lagash? Is it different than flying in the forest or our cave?"

"Well, we begin by oscillating at a raven's frequencies until we're all on the same wavelength. The next thing is to tune ourselves to the frequency of where it is we wish to go and simply let the vibrations take us there. By shifting our particles to certain octaves, it feels as if we're in motion."

"You mean you aren't really?"

"That's right," replied Iblis' mother, "but it feels as if we are streaming through space interdimensionally. With the proper attunement, one can vibrate coherently with all kinds of places and realities. They all exist simultaneously, you see, but your vibration determines which one you experience in the moment. That is the great gift of a Raven Woman." Her dark brown eyes glistened in the firelight. "With our mastery of frequency, we can go *anywhere, everywhere!*"

"You mean this cave is only one of those frequencies?" he ventured.

"That's right!" laughed Erinye.

"Are you really flying then?"

"Oh, yes, brother, our flights graze many galaxies," answered Ethliu. "And yet, no matter where we are, there are times when we find ourselves compelled to return to the frequency of this cave. It happened when you were about to be reborn in the cauldron of our blood. The power produced by the frequency of all our sisters gathered together for your rebirth penetrated the space I was flying in and drew me back."

"And," added Lagash, "even in our exploration of other spaces, we are attuned at the deepest level to the frequencies of the Dark Moon and dance on *her* web. With a mere pluck of its strings, she can make us tremble or shimmer wherever we are."

The youth stared at the women, entranced and confused.

Ethliu looked tenderly at him. "I can see that the memories of the man-you-were are returning, brother, and he is ill at ease with our fields of knowledge. Shape-shifting. Galaxy-grazing. How to make sense of such things? It was hard enough for him to deal with a king who could read his mind." Without asking Colum's permission, the woman leaned forward and placed her hands on either side of his head. At once the youth in him merged with the man's memories.

Ethliu dropped her hands. "I hope I've done a good thing by healing the split in you, brother."

Colum dissolved into tears of relief and gratitude. He couldn't say conceptually what had happened, but he felt profoundly different. The new memories no longer floated around in his mind as if they belonged to someone else. Man and youth were equally real to one another now with a connection that went deeper than memory.

"What have you done?" asked the youth in awe.

"The Colum forged in the labyrinth wasn't meant to die, brother. But with the Beetle calling to him, he was meant to change radically. That call brought him to our cave and offered him a way to make those changes, a way *equivalent to death*," replied Ethliu. "He accepted by entering the Cauldron of Rebirth of his own accord, and by doing so, he came closer to his true self."

"And what is that, sister?"

"Exactly who you are now." The golden-haired woman flashed him a radiant smile. "Ironsmith. Child of the Cave. Viper."

"Thank you for bringing us together," he said from his heart.

"There's nothing to thank me for. Sooner or later, you would have achieved this inner oneness on your own."

Lagash looked gently at Colum. "When next we fly, brother, your vibration will be part of our valence."

Colum felt the fierce, tensile strength of all three Raven Women. A real change was happening in him. Now that Ethliu's touch had dissipated the fog in his brain, he could feel his own newfound iron discipline merging with his spontaneity and playful curiosity.

Erinye gave a loud belch, her cheeks as red as her hair from drinking too much beer. "Hursag, when I think of the rivers of blood from the men Sny has killed, I'm amazed to learn your young shoot had the power to defeat her."

Hursag threw another log on the fire, her purple robe shimmering in its flames. "Why such surprise, sister? The labyrinth's blue light, along with the pyrite's red fire, flows through my son's veins, does it not? Are a panther's claws and teeth any more lethal than a viper's sting?"

Erinye prized the marrow out of the bone of the pig with her knife and swallowed it down with warm, frothy beer. "As I recall, even our lake spewed him out! And to submerge himself in the cauldron's blood-soaked water required far more heart than will."

The women swayed on the sitting rocks, their stomachs full of food and drink. Lagash tilted back so far she fell off her rock onto the furs. Once there, she stretched out on her side, too inebriated to get back on the rock. "I'm sorry the Lady Kasi wasn't able to stay with us," she said.

Dervor's magnificent wings flashed in Colum's mind. The newly integrated Colum remembered the ardency of her desire to become one of them. "She's not here because of me," he said.

"That's true," agreed Erinye. "She attacked a sister to save your life."

Colum's breath shivered at the memory. The Dervor of Colum's boyish dreams was once more a flesh-and-blood woman to him. The one he had left London and his freedom to be with again. "They all turned on her so fast," he said. "They would have torn her into shreds if the Queen hadn't buried her in the rock vault."

"Yes," Lagash said, nodding, "the Queen intervened to save her."

Abruta spoke. "By sparing Kasi, the Queen saved our sisters from their own instinctive rage, thus restoring peace to our cave."

Hursag's amber eyes narrowed. "Who among us doesn't know the power of violence to rivet our attention, shatter our equilibrium, and produce delirium? Violence creates chaos, which throws us all off-center. Our Queen sacrificed Lady Kasi to break the cycle of violence." The crone's voice lowered. "A cycle unleashed by Kasi, who acted out of love to save my son."

"Our Mistress does what is necessary to maintain peace in the cave," said Erinye.

"At the same time, nothing in the universe has the power to throw *her* off-center, for she dances with it all," Abruta added.

CHAPTER SEVENTEEN

The Raven Women lay like reclining Romans on Hursag's furs as the dancing flames of her fire played on their faces. They sang a few bawdy songs together, but it was obvious the feasting was winding down.

Erinye sucked in a full gulp of beer and beamed at Hursag. "I sing to you, sister, for you have let the good beer be poured out in double measure!"

Amidst all their ribald laughter, Colum had kept the fire stoked and the beer vessel filled. Lagash now patted the furs beside her. "Come sit with us, Colum. You have labored enough."

"Gladly, sister," he said and settled into the furs beside her.

Erinye gazed at him. "When I look into your eyes, brother, I see the element of fire. The red-hot iron at the core of the stars fuels you not only in the labyrinth but also in our cave."

Lagash nodded. "Hence the red band around your viper's neck."

Erinye's own eyes blazed. "I hope you will fly with us someday, Son of Hursag. But for that, your serpent must sprout wings."

"You found your way to this cave against all odds," mused

Ethliu. Her trove of golden-orange hair, glowing in the fire-light, and her eternally youthful radiance made Colum forget how ancient she was.

He shook his head. "What was against all odds, sister, was finding my way into its heart and soul." He spoke for both versions of himself, the man and the youth. Neither of them felt any bewilderment being around these women. Both indulged naturally in the sensuality of Hursag's feast in the most vibrant, intense ways, tasting and appreciating the flavors and textures of the food and feeling the shifting moods of the women's stories.

Lagash turned to Colum. "What was it like to battle Sny?"

Colum answered at once. "Intoxicating. Maddening. This wild exultation ran through me the whole time."

Erinye laughed drunkenly. "Sounds like flying!"

"It's not the first time I've felt that way," he confessed. "Once, my hair turned into leeches and I found myself craving blood." Colum didn't mention swimming with the pyrite, which now was as much his youth's experience as the man's.

"As a leech, what you really craved was to suck in *life itself*," said Erinye. "Tell me, does the Lady Kasi still stir your heart?"

Colum blushed. "She is lost to me. Locked up in Uncle's labyrinth."

Ethliu raised an eyebrow. "She can't be that lost. After all, the labyrinth abuts our cave. Where is your ardor?"

"It has nothing to do with ardor, sister. Her loyalty is to Uncle, not me. You know as well as I do that our realms are separate."

"Oh, but I disagree!" exclaimed Lagash with a shake of her head. "It has everything to do with ardor, brother. You couldn't see a crow in a bowlful of milk if you can't see that."

He tried to change the subject. "What's it like in space?"

Erinye stretched her arms in the air. "The universe is a violent place, Colum, blazing with beauty. Entire galaxies stretch, rip, and swallow their smaller galactic neighbors as voraciously as a vulture eats carrion."

Lagash nodded. "Even though we fly as pure vibration, there are no guarantees on our flights. We careen along our merry way, mere sparks of life rushing through the vast immensity of space. We steer through unknown venues filled with countless wrong turns and dead ends." She smiled a radiant smile. "Much like Nirah's labyrinth."

"There are dead ends in space?"

Erinye jumped in. "Many! Veer too close to an exploding star? Uh-oh, can't go that way! Yet in another direction waits a rogue, storm-racked exoplanet raining molten iron!" Colum could hear the trill of excitement in the Raven Woman's voice. "Why are we even here, if not for the massive violence of a stellar fire jettisoning us into existence? And each of us, brother, must find a way to suffer our own piece of its flames." Her eyes glowed brighter still. "Violence is *life's intensity to be.*"

Colum listened with rapt attention and took Erinye's words in deeply. "I know how fast my own violence can be sparked. And the last thing I want is to upset the harmony of this cave by arousing the anger of another sister and setting off a cycle of vengeance."

Ethliu spoke. "Our sense of control is an illusion. You must let go of the illusion and become one with the resonance playing you in the moment. Isn't that what you did when you swam with the pyrite? You let it take you where it would, brother, on a wild, glorious ride! Just as you do when dancing on Lillake's web. You resonate with her vibrating strings, and they transport you in a flow of ecstatic, instinctual frenzy."

"Oh, yes!"

"The instinct of a snake moves in the marrow of your bones," said Ethliu. "Your viper has no rage, only purpose and the exhilaration of the kill. It kills without blinking an eye. We ravens are scavengers. Without beaks that can tear, we must go after something already torn apart and finish the dance that was started."

"And in space, Ethliu?"

"A raven in space is hardly different." She smiled. "As earthly ravens, our purpose is to eat carrion and transform death. Winged fatal necessities are we! And in our flights among the stars, we carry the same resonance."

They watched the fire together in silence. Soon Colum heard

the women snoring on the furs. He glanced at the embers with their soft orange glow under Hursag's potbellied cauldron.

These Raven Women travel through space on their shimmering black wings, and yet they find delight in an orgy of drinking, belching, and farting. Their outrageous sense of humor is matched only by their appetite for life. Colum got up to stir the fire's embers and put on a fresh log. Then he sat on a rock and thought of Dervor with her large, grey eyes. *She's above me right now, asleep or laboring somewhere in the labyrinth. Was Ethliu right? Can I do something about our separation? Is it true I can't see a crow in a bowl of milk? But what am I supposed to see? Dervor can't return to the cave, and I belong here now. No, better not to think of her. Only pain lies there.*

He watched a black beetle scuttle across the floor toward an inverted iron spoon. A small lump of balled-up pastry lay under the round iron dome. The beetle's chitinous exoskeleton pushed against the spoon, its horn rasping at the metal. The spoon didn't budge. Then the beetle grasped the sides of the cutlery with toothed forearms and, stretching the joints of its back legs as far as they would expand, shoved vigorously against the spoon. The insect pushed hard with the roughened cuticle of its body to get the stubborn piece of iron to move. The small fans of the insect's antennae opened and closed with its effort. Suddenly, to Colum's amazement, the heavy spoon moved aside! The fan of the insect's antennae quickly unfurled again, and it began to taste the double treat of flour soaked in a puddle of fermented beer.

How does a scarab experience the world? And does it have anything in common with the giant beetle that crawls in the Void beneath us? Oh, Bambara, how long has it been since you were sent there? Colum envisioned the huge, notched body of an oversized scarab scooping toward Bambara as if he were a morsel of savory food. *Did the beetle roll you up like a ball of dung? Did it draw you into its mouth as a human pastry and extract your bodily essences? I'm sorry this had to be your end, my friend. You, a great and mighty warrior.*

You deserved so much better.

After a long sleep, the women began to stir. Lagash sat up first and scratched her belly with a contented grunt. Hursag woke up next to sit beside her.

"I'm afraid our time with you has come to an end," said Lagash.

When the others woke, Colum and Hursag accompanied the Raven Women to the Queen to pay their respects, then returned to Hursag's hearth for their final farewells.

Erinye held a wet index finger in the air. "The winds for our departure are good. We must go before they change."

Lagash flung her arms around Colum, smelling of stale beer. "I hope your snake grows wings, brother, so we can fly through the galaxy together!" The Raven Woman made an awkward and unsuccessful attempt to shape-shift. "It does require a certain level of sobriety to transition, and I'm not quite there," she laughed.

Iblis ran over with a small leather bag of precious keepsakes jostling on a cord around her waist. "Mother, wait!"

"Climb onto my back, child!" called Lagash, her feet twisting into claws. The next moment, she turned into a full-blown raven.

The girl gave Colum an almost suffocating hug before Ethliu helped her climb up and position herself on her mother's back. Only then did Lagash begin to flap her blue-black wings.

"Don't forget me!" cried Iblis, still human. Then, in an instant, she sprouted the most beautiful purple breast feathers he had ever seen.

"Never!" he called back. The girl's happiness in joining her mother made Colum's heart glad, but he wondered if he would ever see her again.

Flying unsteadily, Lagash ascended to the top of the dome, where mother and daughter disappeared into the cave's vent shafts.

Erinye hugged Colum tightly. "We fly through multiverses, brother. Who knows when we'll meet again, *but meet we shall!*"

Feathers appeared on the redhead's neck, enlarging and elongating. With her next breath, the transformation was complete and she, too, flew into the air.

Now only Ethliu, his protector, remained. She fastened her eyes on Colum. "The death of the man Jack has not been wasted."

"What do you mean, sister?"

"I mean it drove you into Sny's embrace, and great good may come of that."

"I hope she and I can be friends," he said. "And I'm truly glad I had this time with you, sister."

"I am glad as well." The golden-haired woman morphed into a raven with lustrous black plumage, and in a flurry of feathers, she joined Erinye in the air.

With powerful downbeats of their wings, the two ravens wheeled up to the dome in ever-widening circles. They flew twice around the dome with shrill cries, causing every woman to look up, and then vanished.

After they left, Colum felt restless and went for a stroll. He skirted around fires and tethered animals until his perambulations led him to Sny's hearth. Kle-Ptuza was busily grinding roots with mortar and pestle, while Sny slept at her side.

"What do you want?" snapped the Raptor Woman. Her copper hair was pulled back severely, giving her a forbidding look. "No one invited you to our hearth." The tone in the woman's voice set Colum's teeth on edge. She dumped the ground roots into a simmering pot and stirred them a little too fiercely.

Sny awoke. "Oh, Colum, hello." She sat up and looked at her mate. "The Queen has commanded that we visit each other."

"Then go ahead. I have more important things to do," retorted Kle-Ptuza. The Raptor Woman squared her shoulders and strode off.

"We couldn't help notice the feast your mother gave our raven sisters," said Sny. A draft from the fire blew smoke around and made her squint.

"Yes. That was my first time being with them, and my mother

wanted to make it special." He hesitated, unsure of how to proceed. "Sny, there's a question I've been wanting to ask you."

"Go ahead, ask it."

"You left before we could really talk, and I was wondering what the red toadstools revealed to you about me."

Sny poked at the fire. "They showed me how deep your connection with Mammi is." Her voice dropped. "I saw something else too."

"What?"

"I had a vision of you as a flaming serpent, lifting the cave up toward the surface of the earth. Out of the cave grew a great tree that broke through to the surface."

Colum listened intently, waiting for her to go on.

"I'm not sure exactly what it means, but this I do know: in here we call the labyrinth 'Nirah's Folded Pit.' As the dragon in the heart of the labyrinth, Nirah shields our cave. And even though I hate him, I know our Queen regards him as the cave's protector." Sny paused, as if wondering how to phrase her next words. "I think Nirah must have glimpsed the snake in you. After all, snakes and dragons share the same lineage."

"Do you think that's why he chose me to be his slave?"

Sny shrugged. "In my vision, your snake becomes the column. That is the name Nirah gave you, isn't it?" Sny stared into the fire intently for a long moment. "When you came to our cave, I saw you as an intruder. After you were reborn as Mammi's child, I was able to tolerate you, for a time. But now, I believe you were always meant to be swallowed into the belly of our cave, that it is your destiny. And so it is also ours."

Colum was speechless.

"When we fought," Sny continued, "you streaked across my belly like hissing hot steam and stuck your spurs in me."

"Spurs? What are you talking about?"

"Every snake has spurs, brother," she replied.

Colum stared at her, confused. Then Sny said firmly, "I want you to come to the forest with me."

"I'm forbidden to enter the forest."

"You? Afraid to transgress limits? I don't believe it."

Her offer confounded him. *Is she trying to trick me into entering the forest without the Queen's permission? But that would put her in jeopardy too. Is she trying to create a genuine relationship with me? In that case, a trip to the forest might be worth the risk. Trust has to start somewhere. If she ends up betraying me, I'll deal with that then.*

"Very well, sister, let's go."

"Good." Sny's eyes ranged the cave. Then she handed Colum a hooded robe and pouch of water. "Slip this over your tunic and pull the hood down."

She drew a dark hooded cloak around her, and together they strolled leisurely toward one of the tunnel openings. Sny slid into the dark passageway, followed by Colum. A lamp made of smooth stone rested on a niche in the wall. The huntress lit the lichen-and-juniper wick that rested in the stone's hollow. It gave off just enough light for them to make their way through the shaft.

"Keep your head down, and if we meet anyone, let me do the talking," she cautioned.

A draft from an adjacent tunnel blew Colum's hood back as they passed by. He yanked it up immediately. After what felt like a long walk, he started to breathe fresh air. The air came as a shock after a lifetime in the smoke-filled cave. Shafts of light began to enter the tunnel.

After several more steps, Colum emerged from the tunnel on the top of a cliff to find himself looking out over a forest of old-growth trees. It was dawn and the sky was ablaze with pinks, reds, and oranges. The colors flared in the air's moisture. The forest's deep, luminous green stretched out as far as his eye could see, broken here and there by a meadow or lake. The sheer beauty of the panoramic view filled Colum with a sense of euphoria.

"My head feels so clear!" he cried. Every sinus and cavity had opened dramatically.

"It's the air," Sny told him. "This forest is pristine."

Colum caught the acrid smell of a goat, then, turning his

head in the direction of the scent, saw a distant goat scramble up a cliffside. "I smelled the goat over there," he said in awe, "but it's so far away."

"That's the man in you speaking."

Birds sang everywhere, flitting by on wings of light. A great surge of energy swept through him, and he knew the amazing wilderness was its source.

Sny put her hand on his shoulder. "Stay close to me. It's easy to get lost."

At once the Panther Woman began skidding and sliding down the rocky cliff with Colum close behind. Giant oaks with splendid crowns towered into the sky in front of them. Colum was sliding so fast that toward the bottom he nearly hit a porcupine folding leaves into its mouth.

Sny led her companion into a grove of the huge, mossy oaks, their green boughs tenting over them. The ground was thick with plant humus and rotting timber, and giant spiderwebs shimmered throughout the oaken branches. A flurry of different scents stirred up a heart-wrenching nostalgia in Colum and made him feel he was home at last.

My hunter-gatherer ancestors must have roamed a forest just like this. How can so much life occupy the same space?

"I want to show you something," said Sny.

The huntress led him out of the oak grove and along a river filled with sparkling, clear water. On either side of the river, willow trees trailed several feet of lichen. A stab of joy pierced Colum's heart as he watched the lichen float around the willows like delicate, loosely woven gowns. Red squirrels ran up and down the tree trunks in a world of their own.

Sny smiled at him. "This is Huluppu's grove."

"Everywhere I look, it's all forest."

"There are a few meadows," replied the huntress, "but grasslands never took the forest over. It has existed untouched like this for millennia."

A falcon swooped down not far from them. It hopped up on a huge bole of oak, then cocked its head to gaze sidelong at Colum with one beady eye.

Immediately he wondered, *Is that a bird or a curious sister?*

The falcon flew to a rock on the edge of the sparkling river and drank. As Colum watched the raptor take off, he caught sight of a wolverine drinking farther down the river. Sny saw it too. "That wolverine was prowling where we stand now not very long ago," she said, sniffing. "Its pungent odor is all over these rocks and branches."

"I smell it too, and I'm not a panther."

"You don't have to be. You are a son of this forest, and as such, its secrets are revealed to you."

His face was radiant. "I feel reborn, Sny."

"As do I, brother. The forest opens all our senses. That is what you are feeling now."

They walked on and soon came to another giant tree. Colum climbed atop its large, gnarled root. His feet sank ever so slightly into the tree's spongy, dark-colored wood as he stared up at the luxuriant branches towering over him in every direction. Colum focused on the green foliage, feeling as if the tree's sap flowed not only up the mighty trunk but through him.

Sny watched the youth carefully. "Your skin is pale from being too long in the cave, brother, yet I see a fresh wildness in your blue eyes." She looked away. "I nearly killed you when we fought."

"I'm glad we both survived," he said quietly.

"When I took Mammi's toadstools, I heard a wailing wind," said Sny. "I knew it came from the cries of all the men I've hunted and killed. Their pleas to live affected me no more than air escaping from the nose." She sat on a tree root opposite Colum and put her head in her hands. "Since drinking Mammi's red brew, their deaths have lost their sweetness for me," said the huntress. She looked up again. "I have asked myself, brother, am I still a hunter? And if not, who am I? All these centuries, the blood of my prey has kept the spirit of my panther strong."

"I think I understand what you're feeling," replied Colum. "I, too, have been forced to make changes that left me wondering who I am."

"So you have, brother." After a brief silence, she continued,

"For untold years I've been a huntress. I delighted in seeing the terror that rose in men's faces once I had my claws in them. My whole body quivered in anticipation of the kill." She looked at him. "You must have felt a similar thrill when you struck your poison into me."

"I did."

"I contributed my blood to the cauldron of your rebirth, brother, certain that you would remain stillborn in our cave. I never suspected that you had the power to transmogrify."

A hawk flew over them, then circled back to land on a stump only a short distance away. As Colum watched, it suddenly transformed, and there stood Sny's mate, Kle-Ptuza. The hair stood up on the back of Colum's neck. Shards of sunlight slanted through the tree leaves and lit up the Raptor Woman's sharp, angular face. Black leather pants fit her legs like a second skin. Colum sensed the incessant drumbeat of a barely controlled anger and knew she hungered for a kill.

Kle-Ptuza turned to Sny with a savage scowl. "So it's true. You've brought this *man* into our sacred forest."

"It's his forest too, sister," replied Sny. She moved slowly to place herself between her mate and Colum.

But Colum stepped forward, not wanting to be the source of friction between the two women or to damage the fragile friendship he and Sny were forming. "It was my decision to come to the forest," he said.

The Raptor Woman lashed out at him. "Everyone takes you to be such a bright young *man*, but you don't deceive me. Your days with us are numbered."

Kle-Ptuza's free-floating sense of primal menace had a way of making Colum feel unmoored. When he didn't respond, the huntress let out a screech of frustrated rage. Her form blurred, and the next moment, a hawk stood in front of Colum. The raptor flew into the air and disappeared over the treetops.

"We'd better return to the cave," said Sny in a resigned voice.

CHAPTER EIGHTEEN

Hursag looked up from her weaving when Colum returned. The young man's curling tresses fell like a swarm of snakes over his shoulders. He still had a boyish air, but his eyes held the look of an experienced man. The crone left her weaving to come over and caress his cheek. Her touch filled him with maternal comfort.

"There's something I need to tell you, Mother."

"What is that, my son?"

"I visited the forest with Sny. Ever since I took the toadstools, I've wanted to know her better." He sat down across from her. "She invited me to go to the forest with her, and it seemed a way to earn her trust."

"And was it?" asked Hursag.

"I think so. Only Kle-Ptuza found us there together, and as you might guess, she was furious." He stared at the fire. "I'm sorry. I know I wasn't supposed to go into the forest. I'm worried about how the Queen will feel about it."

"You have to understand, my son, that when you were born, many of the women doubted you would ever fully become one of us. Though they welcomed your birth into the cave, your belonging was granted to you because here you were, a child being raised in our midst, living your life as we live ours. It wasn't until they saw you turn into a viper and battle Sny's panther that they realized you are, in fact, truly the same as us, cut from the same cloth. Your animal nature is as strong as anyone's here. That has changed your standing among your sisters and allows you to enter our forest now as one who belongs. That you were able to do this is a reversal of all they believe."

Colum let his mother's words, and their deeper implications, sink in.

"And how did you experience the forest?"

Colum's eyes lit up. "Oh, Mother, where to start? The sheer *greenness* of the place! The sky was so blue, the sun so bright! The air was so clear and fresh. I felt so alive!" He looked down, and his smile faded.

"What is it, my son?"

He stared at the fire. "I realized how much I *crave* the sunlight, Mother. How wonderful its warmth felt on my face. I have memories of it from my other life, but I had no idea how *good* it would feel." His voice lowered. "It was hard to reenter that dark tunnel and come back."

They were both silent for a while. The flames of their fire crackled, and Hursag patted his hand. "Come," said the crone, standing. "Huluppu has prepared a bath for you."

"A bath?" He smiled and kissed her wrinkled cheek. "Thank you, Mother. A bath is just what I could use right now."

Huluppu's trailing cloak of willow leaves formed a neat circle around her bare feet. On one side of the woman's fire were stacks of clay jars lined up in rows and filled with herbs. She was like a healing forest spirit in the cave.

"Greetings, sister," called Colum as he drew near.

"Greetings, brother."

Colum stripped off his tunic to step into the stone tub. The water smelled of lavender, and Colum let out a deep sigh as he settled into its warmth.

After a long, relaxing soak, he rose dripping wet out of the tub and slipped on his tunic.

"Come, sit by my fire," invited Huluppu. Her voice was high and lilting like a reed pipe whose tunes made him want to dance. "I've prepared you a special tea at your mother's request."

"What kind of tea, Huluppu?"

"It's for dreaming."

He sat beside her. After a few sips of tea, he stared up at the dome ceiling. "Are there people up there, Huluppu?"

"I assume so."

"Do you think they wonder if people exist down here?" he asked wistfully.

"Perhaps they dream of us."

He was starting to feel drowsy. "Perhaps."

"Lie down, Son of Hursag," beckoned the Willow Woman, "and let the dreams take you where they will."

The youth stretched out on her furs and closed his eyes. Almost at once he fell into sleep. The first thing he saw was Bambara's ebony face glistening with sweat. The tall, muscular man walked at his side through Uncle's warren of blue-lit, cheerless, iron tunnels. A woman rounded the corner and came toward them. Her large eyes were as grey as the shirt and pants she wore.

"Dervor!" he cried out joyously.

But when he tried to speak further, all that came out was a hiss. He realized his limbs had disappeared. Black scales covered his long, cylindrical body. The woman, on seeing him change, skidded backward several steps.

Suddenly, he was no longer in the labyrinth but straddled a huge blue-black raven flying through the far reaches of the galaxy. Solar winds blasted past his face, making his temples buzz. Stellar energy shot through his body like needles. He looked over and saw Dervor riding naked next to him on the back of a second raven. Her long tresses billowed out behind her. Colum felt an irrepressible joy coursing through him.

The dream image faded, and he now saw a blue-black beetle

rolling a sheet of shimmering gold into a sphere of blinding light. He heard Uncle's voice boom, "BEETLE!"

Colum awoke on Huluppu's furs, his heart jackhammering. He started to sit up but fell back, disoriented.

"Easy, brother, I'm here with you," said Huluppu gently. She gave him some water and he soon felt strong enough to walk back to his hearth.

On his way, Amorpho called out, "Brother!" Colum turned in her direction. "Come, have a chat with me," she said and pointed to a sitting rock near her fire.

He settled on the rock. "You're looking well, sister."

"As are you," she said.

Colum caught the look of concern on her face. "Is something on your mind, sister?"

Amorpho nodded. "Now that you have shape-shifted, everyone regards you as a man. I'm sure you can feel the difference between who you were before you fought Sny and who you are now."

"Yes, it's unmistakable."

"In this cave, Colum, we are inaccessible to men. Now and then, we might bring one here for our own purposes, but they are never meant to stay." Amorpho stared at the youth, then shook her large head from side to side like a great bull. "But perhaps you've noticed that after Jack's death, no more men have been brought into our cave?"

"No, I hadn't," he said, startled at the realization.

"We stopped bringing men in because of you."

"What do you mean?"

"We love you as a true brother. Your feelings are as important to us as our own." The Bull Woman repositioned her powerful hips on the flat rock and sighed. "When we saw how much pain Jack's suffering and death caused you, we hurt for you."

Colum was taken aback, deeply touched by her words. He stared at her in the firelight, feeling a fierce kinship with the woman. What else did he not know? How deep did their love for him go?

CHAPTER NINETEEN

Colum stood in front of the limestone wall that led to Ayylo's private perch. The rock on her ledge was colored a delicate pink, tinted by iron oxide. A massive stalagmite rose from the cave floor on his left as he began his climb.

A column like me. It supports nothing, yet no one can say it doesn't belong here.

Soon Colum pulled himself up over the edge of the wall. Ayylo extended a welcoming hand to help him. A strong musky fragrance wafted into his nostrils. She offered him some wine, and the two of them gazed out over a panoramic view of the cave. Feral, furred, feathery multiplicities moved everywhere, the rise and fall of their voices forming a musical medley.

A black onyx comb held Ayylo's golden-red hair in place on one side of her face. On the other side, her hair fell in luxurious waves down a bare shoulder. The Queen's daughter rubbed her thigh against Colum's, asking, "Have you noticed?"

"Noticed what?"

"There are signs of new life in the belly of one of our sisters."

"Really?" He was surprised. Pregnancy was a rare and happy event in the cave. "How do you know?"

"I've caught whiffs of it in the air."

Ayylo stretched out her long legs, and Colum's thoughts of pregnant women fled. The woman's physical beauty never ceased to take his breath away. "I could look at you forever," he said.

The Queen's daughter turned to face him. "Everyone in the cave knows you're a man now. Open yourself to my allure, and the whole art of woman shall be yours," said Ayylo, and she kissed him with an open mouth for the first time.

He kissed her back.

"Will you accept the friendship of my lips and thighs, dearest brother?"

Her words jumbled Colum's thoughts, filling him with trepidation and desire. "I . . . I . . ."

Ayylo lifted her garment over her head and cast it aside with a radiant smile. "Look how you swell, brother!"

"How can I not?" Colum stared open-mouthed at the woman's unblemished skin, jutting breasts, and smooth stomach, too drunk on her sensual beauty to be embarrassed. Both man and youth were willing.

Ayylo playfully shoved him onto his back, then crouched over him on all fours like a cat. "We are wild forces of nature, brother! Predator lion and poisonous viper are we!"

She began kissing his mouth, neck, and chest. A hot scent of musk rose in waves from her armpits. The musk was powerful, earthy, sweet, and captivating, like Ayylo herself. The scent unleashed avalanches of primal, shuddering pleasure in Colum. The Queen's daughter, all purring gold and muscle, pressed her body down on her lover and everything in him responded. Ayylo's rich sensory feedback made the youth feel stronger, bolder. His chest rose and fell in blissful, cycling sensations, each one expanding and liberating him. The cavern walls seemed to shake and the river overflow its banks at their lovemaking. In the end, Colum's spirit flared into hers, and he let out a loud *hiss* of prolonged rapture.

The Serpent Man lay on the rocky ledge beside the Queen's daughter and stared up at the dome. His muscles were limp in profound relaxation. Musk saturated his senses, and a riveting aliveness flowed through every cell of his body. He felt supremely happy.

Ayylo slipped her fingers into his, whispering, "Your sweet milk swims in me, my brother. Shall I create a child with it?"

He looked at her, shocked at the question. "Can you do that, Ayylo? Can you just decide?"

"Yes, of course I can," she said softly. "But you are not just any man. You are my brother, and I won't do something so important without your consent."

Colum stared out at the expanse of the cave dotted with a myriad of red fires. Down there, robed figures moved around as if in a choreographed dance. He could hear the flux of their voices, an occasional peal of laughter, and the sound of musical instruments being played. After his lovemaking with Ayylo, the scene filled him with a sense of powerful, palpable solidarity with the women.

The Queen's daughter broke into his reverie. "I can tell this may not be the right time to ask you that question." She smiled gently. "No matter. This won't be the last time we make love. Know this, brother: I keep the names of those dearest to me deep in my heart. And your name is among them."

Tears caught in his throat at her words.

Colum returned afterward to his mother's hearth.

"Your body gives off a glow, my son," said Hursag.

"Well, I am sitting by the fire, Mother."

Hursag laughed. "The Queen's daughter is many times blessed with beauty, is she not?"

"She is indeed." Smoke from his mother's fire billowed upward. Colum stared at the flames.

I was like this burning wood when I made love to Ayylo—smoking, crackling, popping, ablaze with her fiery radiance. He thought of Ayylo's strange statement about creating a child together, but the idea made him restless. *Me? A father? I'm in no way ready for that!*

Colum decided to go for a stroll. He passed K'lifah grinding flour and glimpsed her spittle falling into the white powder.

At that moment, Yaga came over. Strands of stringy grey hair stuck out of her bun. "Effluvium is such a rich, salty ingredient." She winked at him. "K'lifah's saliva imparts a special taste and signature to her bread, does it not?"

Colum laughed. "There's no doubt of that, sister."

The crone placed a thin, veined hand on his arm. "You shine brighter than usual, little brother. Has someone sparked a fire in you?"

"Fire? Why, I don't know what you're talking about, Yaga."

She slapped him on the back, laughing. "Of course you don't! Well, my advice to you is, don't think about it, just enjoy. Too much thinking binds our energy and gives us constipation." The crone hobbled away, laughing even harder.

Colum continued on to the river. He sat down and dangled his feet in the cool water. Feeling someone approaching behind him, he turned and saw Sny in a brown robe.

The Panther Woman sat next to him. "I need to talk to you."

"About what happened in the forest?" They had avoided each other since then, and Colum was afraid his encounter with Kle-Ptuza had put a damper on their newfound goodwill. Perhaps ended it entirely.

"The forest isn't the only unknown territory you've entered recently."

Did she blush? "What do you mean?"

"I carry a life in me."

He stared blankly at her.

"I'm pregnant, Colum."

The news startled him. He'd wondered why she was wearing a robe instead of her usual black leather pants and top. "Congratulations! What wonderful news for the whole cave!"

"The baby is kicking. Do you want to feel?" Without waiting for an answer, Sny took his hand and placed it on her stomach. It felt like a small melon under her robe. "Thank you," she said, smiling.

"For what?"

"For this life you have given me."

His hand leaped from her belly as if he had touched fire. "Me? Impossible!"

"I thought so too, at first. It happened during our battle."

Colum strained to remember the battle, but the shock of her words had turned the whole thing into a blur. Besides, he didn't feel as though his human self was even a part of that battle, as it took place under the direction of a charged reptilian brain.

"We were fighting, Sny! *To the death!*"

"Fighting . . . lovemaking . . . what does it matter?" She shook her head as if it didn't. "Both are acts of passion. What matters is that in the rapture of our combat, you impregnated me."

The muscles of his face went slack at the thought. The man in him trembled with disbelief. "Are you saying I *raped* you?"

"No, brother. We came at each other with equal force." Her eyes shone with happiness. "Panther and snake—what a pair! Your transformation into a viper saved your life and engendered new life in me."

The stunning news rendered him speechless.

"It is in a panther's nature to kill, brother," continued Sny. "I live to kill. The terror of my prey doesn't elicit any mercy in me. But you are not prey, brother. You are the son of Hursag, a man worthy to be the father of my child." She took a deep breath. "I could feel you moving across my underbelly and knew you were pulsing differently. In that moment, it was not my death you sought." Sny patted her stomach, beaming. "It wasn't rape, brother, it was *lovemaking*. The lovemaking of a serpent and panther aroused by one another. How exhilarating!"

"And Kle-Ptuza?" asked Colum, shaking. "What about her? She wants to crush the skull of the red-banded serpent who did this to you." He looked deep into her eyes. "The last thing your mate wants is my blood in her child."

"True. It's different for Kle-Ptuza than it is for me. After all, I am the one who ate your mother's mushrooms and know who you are now." The Panther Woman smiled impishly. "Many of our sisters wish nothing more than to bear a child sired by you and would happily trade places with me."

Ayylo's recent question now returned in full force. Colum stared down at the river as a whirlwind of feelings swirled in him. Anger, trepidation, and confusion vied with anticipation, pride, and excitement.

Sny stood up. "Soon everyone will see I'm wearing a robe, but I wanted to make sure you were the first to know." And with that, she left.

Colum watched her leave. Sny, the predatory panther, once ravenous to hunt men, now seemed so tame, so content. The youth shook his head, utterly bewildered.

When he arrived back at his hearth, Hursag was putting logs on the fire. Colum sat beside her.

"Sny just came to see me."

"And?"

Colum reddened. "She said she's pregnant with my child."

Hursag sat down to face him and took his hands in hers. "I surmised as much when I saw her wearing a robe."

Smoke curled up from their fire. "You didn't suspect I was the father, did you? How could I be? I've never lain with her!"

"What did she say?"

"Sny says the baby was conceived in the heat of our battle."

Hursag squeezed his hand. "And so she was, my son."

"You knew that?"

"It's easy to guess. Sny has never been with a man."

Colum looked down. "I'm not sure I'd be a good father. There are no fathers in the cave; how do I even know what a father looks like?"

The crone's eyes softened. "You know what love is, my son. It doesn't matter whether the parent is a woman or a man. The birth of another child is good news for all of us."

"Not for Kle-Ptuza," he said, frowning.

Hursag patted his knee. "Even she can change."

CHAPTER TWENTY

Colum lay naked next to Ayylo and inhaled her musky odor. How many times had he made his way to the woman's ledge to make love to her? Since that first time, he was drawn over and over by her magnetic presence. Each time he fell more enraptured, and he could feel something inside of him coming more alive, the youth maturing into a man, the man growing into a true lover. "Oh, the sweet *deliciousness* of you," he crooned, kissing her neck from behind.

Flushed, the Queen's daughter turned over to kiss him on the lips. "I find the taste of you equally sweet," she purred, her musk rolling over him in waves.

He drew in a rhapsodized breath. "How many men have you made love to, Ayylo? Hundreds? Thousands? After making love to you, how could they ever be satisfied again?"

"And what about you, my love?" asked Ayylo, pushing aside a few curls that had fallen across his cheek. "You should see yourself. You're like a wild man." She looked at her fresh-faced lover and shivered. "So seductive!"

The fire lit up his glossy hair. "You bring out the wildness in me."

Ayylo sat up. "There's something we must discuss."

Colum shook his head to break out of his love stupor. "What's that?" he asked.

"The child Sny carries."

Caught off guard, Colum sat up too. "It happened while we were fighting, Ayylo. I have no idea how." He frowned briefly. "I don't like to think my daughter was conceived in an act of violence."

"True," said Ayylo softly, "but she'll be raised in love."

"Without me, if Kle-Ptuza has anything to say about it." Colum wrapped his arms defensively around his knees. "Nothing would make her happier than tearing out my heart and grinding my bones for her bread." His brows furrowed. "I have a feeling she doesn't want me anywhere near the baby."

Ayylo idly unfurled one of Colum's curls with her finger. "There's something strange, frightening almost, about you these days. Even your rage carries *life*." She leaned against his lithe, muscular body, and they stared into the fire. "No man has ever defeated Sny or Kle-Ptuza. Your battle with Sny must have humiliated both of them. Kle-Ptuza has chafed at our sisters' decision not to bring men in from the forest anymore. I fear she feels our way of life, one she's known for millennia, has been fundamentally threatened by not just your presence but your status among us." She stroked the back of his hand. "The gift of a daughter is a wondrous thing, but is it enough to wipe out her humiliation? Every time she sees the baby, she will see you as well, and the pain of that will continue to sting. But now she knows you'll do battle if provoked, and that you can be as merciless as she."

"I don't want to provoke a fight with her, Ayylo. That could rupture the whole sisterhood."

"Then maybe it's time to leave the cave," she replied quietly.

"*What?* What are you saying?"

She turned to face him. "I've decided to go to the upper world, and I am asking you to come with me."

Ayylo's offer released tides of emotion in him. He thought immediately of the forest and the beauty of the upper world. A part of him wanted nothing more than to be with the Queen's daughter in that world. Yet another part yearned to stay, to know his unborn child. "Ayylo, I want so badly to go with you, but I can't leave my daughter. I want to figure out what it means to be a father."

"I understand, Colum. You need to be here for the birth to discover how you feel once she's here. But I myself can't stay."

Colum walked back to his hearth, thinking of Ayylo. *She's like a fire, sparking . . . smoldering . . . burning! With her my own flames soar high, exhausting themselves in embers only to flare again! She makes me burn with desires I never even knew I had. Who wouldn't give everything to live with such a goddess in the sunlit world?*

His thoughts shifted to Sny and the baby growing inside her. *No one dare call our battle lovemaking. She tried to rip open my throat and bleed me out. And what did I do? Injected deadly poison into her. Yet between Sny's flying fur and my scales rubbing across her belly, our two worlds collided to create a new one! What is this compelling need I feel to know my daughter? To look after her? It's as if the news of her conception has birthed a father in me. And yet I know nothing of fathering.* He thought of Hursag's primal and unshakable love for him, and his eyes burned with tears. *I want to be present for my child the way my mother was present for me. But I'm not a mother.*

Man and youth together contemplated Colum's status. Ever since Sny took him to the forest and he saw the sun blazing in that blue, blue sky and all those green, living plants . . . he felt restless in the cave's darkness. A part of him yearned to live on the surface of the world again. *What is it I want? Truly want?*

The question felt like a tearing conflict in his soul. He stared out at the great limestone chamber and the fluidity of its moving inhabitants. Wherever he looked, he saw women's shapes morphing and emerging in new and arresting ways. The whole cave brimmed with sensual immediacy. *This is their chrysalis: a world outside of time, where they make their changes in secret.*

And I have been blessed to live here. Some of my sisters are light-years ahead of me, yet they treat me always with gentle respect. Their blood runs in my veins, and it runs in my daughter's veins. I, too, am a shape-shifter. I've danced on Lillake's web and been suckled by a woman too ancient to count her years. And yet, as a man, can I ever truly be one of them?

Grey-ringed stalagmites and stalactites grew throughout the cave, reminding Colum of ribs and making him feel at times like he was inside the body of a whale. He stared in the direction of Lillake's throne. He knew the throne was positioned over a circular iron lid and that under the lid lurked a void. Just then, he heard Bruha's booming voice.

"Colum!" bellowed the Hippo Woman. She was returning from the forest with a heavy load of freshly cut wood on her back. "Carry some of this wood with me to my hearth, brother, and we can drink beer together!"

He sprinted over. A jug of beer would give him a chance to forget his whole dilemma, even if only briefly. It was exactly what he needed.

The two of them deposited the wood at Bruha's hearth, where Colum helped her stack it.

"That's quite a bundle, Bruha. You won't have to go back to the forest anytime soon."

The Hippo Woman rolled back the cover on a basin of beer that she kept in a hole in the ground. Bruha handed Colum a long reed straw and the two of them drank, froth spilling over the rim.

"The forest air gives me such a thirst!" beamed the woman. A few thistles and nettles still clung to her sparse grey hair.

Colum was a little too close to the fire, and its heat was making sweat drip down his face. "Your beer is always good, Bruha," he said, sipping the bitter brew with pleasure.

"It was a good foraging day," Bruha said, smiling. She stood up to drop ramps, wild carrots, and mustard greens into a pot of water. "Oh, I collected a special fungi too," she said, shaking out a cloth bag full of tightly branched clusters of hot pink, yolk-yellow, and dark blue mushrooms into her simmering pot. "You don't often find these blooming in the forest."

Colum contemplated the fire as Bruha tended her soup. She turned to Colum with a wide grin.

"Sneaky of you, brother, to be cavorting when the rest of us thought you were fighting."

"What are you talking about, Bruha?"

"You know very well I'm talking about your battle with Sny. I honestly feared one of you was going to die." The woman's face turned solemn. "The death of either of you would have been an inconsolable loss for the cave." Bruha's face brightened again. "But to our amazement, not only did you both survive; you made new life!" She whacked him on the back in her delight.

Colum coughed. "It's not as if I knew what I was doing, sister."

The large, imposing woman placed a hand on the swell of her hip. "I'm not blind to the fact that you are older now, brother. I've noticed how you've begun to think and act more like a man lately." Bruha sat down and smoothed her robe across her knees. "And that is a good thing."

"That I'm growing up?"

"Yes, Colum, for no sooner did you shape-shift than you became a father!" She let out the guffaw of a hippopotamus, her large belly shaking at the humor of it all.

He looked at Bruha's enormous girth, along with the grey, horny cuticles that passed for her toes, and felt only love and appreciation for her. "The news of Sny's pregnancy caught me by surprise too," he said.

"Well, you will make a good father. Of that I have no doubts."

He frowned. "Not if Kle-Ptuza has her way."

"It's true she hates men and can be quite dangerous," said Bruha with a grave nod, "but you are somewhat nerve-shattering yourself." A huskiness entered the Hippo Woman's voice. "There is a fearsome intensity coiled at your core, brother, and Kle-Ptuza is aware of it now."

Colum's cheeks were already crimson from sitting too close to Bruha's fire and drinking too much of her beer, so his blush at her compliment stayed hidden. "I don't dispute Kle-Ptuza's right to raise my daughter, I simply want to share in her upbringing."

"And so you shall." A sense of power and ease emanated from the Hippo Woman. "It's true there is no precedent for a man to raise a child in our cave, but never discount the one universal law."

"What is that, Bruha?"

Her dark beady eyes twinkled. *"All things change!"* The woman reached for a clay pipe with one hand and, with the other, plucked a fist-size plug of tobacco from a nearby jar. She winked at him. "In a conflict with no solution, brother, one must always go deeper for an answer."

"I don't think I can go deeper than the cave, Bruha."

The woman twisted a chunk of tobacco off her plug, stuck it in the bowl of her pipe, and lit it with a burning stick snatched from the fire. After taking several long puffs, she passed the pipe to Colum. He smoked beside her for a long time, enjoying the strength and quality of the tobacco.

At last the youth stood. "Thank you for the good beer and excellent company, sister."

Bruha rose with him, enfolding him in her arms with genuine affection. Her great warm body comforted Colum. "Remember," she said, "Kle-Ptuza does not have the final say in what happens with your daughter. After all, Hursag is the baby's grandmother, which means the child's well-being is of the greatest importance to her." Bruha sorted through her mushrooms, popped a few in a cloth bag, and handed it to him. "For your mother," she said, smiling.

As Colum meandered in a slow, unwieldy fashion toward his hearth, Yaga approached him.

"Too much beer, brother?" asked the crone, grinning.

"One can never have too much beer, Yaga."

Yaga chuckled. "There is someone waiting for you on the other side of the river."

Colum had sobered by the time he swam across the river to where Sny sat. He was shocked to see the bulge beneath her voluminous robe.

"I sent Yaga for you because Kle-Ptuza is in the forest. Our daughter will be here soon," Sny announced upon his arrival.

Colum had purposely kept his distance so as not to antagonize Kle-Ptuza, but he hadn't realized how much time had actually passed. To his surprise, Sny reached for his hand and placed it on the curve of her belly.

"*She moved!*" he cried, his breath quickening.

"She likes to kick."

Another kick. Then he saw the imprint of a foot and moved his hand on top of it, laughing out loud. "It's like she's doing martial arts in there!" he exclaimed.

"She's communicating with her father," said the Panther Woman. Her face softened on seeing the excitement and tenderness in Colum's eyes.

"You look radiant," said Colum, genuinely happy.

"It turns out I quite enjoy being pregnant," she replied with unbridled delight. "Huluppu brews me special teas, and I've been taking long strolls in the forest."

"You'll make a wonderful mother, Sny."

The Panther Woman smoothed the robe over her stomach and her eyes grew dreamy. "I will indeed."

The two of them listened in silence to water dripping slowly through the cracks and openings in a nearby rock wall.

Finally, Sny broke the silence. "I came here, brother, because I want you to know something."

"Know what?"

"Ever since eating the red toadstools and becoming pregnant, I've felt a strong connection to you."

Colum nodded. "Our lives are bound together in a whole new way now."

"So it seems." Sny shifted her weight, seeking a more comfortable position. "I've never known a man, brother. Not even to conceive a child would I have sullied myself that way. You changed all that." The huntress stared into his blue eyes. "Am I wrong to trust you?"

"No, Sny," he said, slightly taken aback. "You're the mother of my child. I would never betray or harm you in any way." He noticed her face was more rounded, lessening some of its angular intensity. She still gave off a haughty, self-confident air, but the joy in her eyes had a different source now.

"And Kle-Ptuza?" asked Sny.

"I would never try to come between the two of you. All I ask is to be part of my daughter's life."

"I want that as well, brother." Sny lifted her arms high over her head in a long stretch, yawning. "My mate hasn't partaken of your mother's mushrooms or had a new life placed inside her. I'm sure, though, that with time, she'll get used to having you around and will come to know you as I do. After all, you aren't just any man. Not only have you thrown off Nirah's harness; you are Mammi's beloved cub."

Colum knew he must tread carefully. "I'll follow your lead in this, Sny." He glanced at her swollen belly. "I want you to know, sister, that I'm here for you as well as our daughter."

"I do know that, brother." The old hunter's smirk was gone.

As Colum approached his hearth, he felt the man's presence in him intensify. Hursag sat on a rock facing the fire, and he looked at her admiringly.

She's so wise. And her wisdom is somatic, not one that comes from books. Her intimate knowledge of plants and animals is hers because she lived as them. The body of every woman here is porous and complicated and changeable. Up there in the daylight world, space and time are constantly being disrupted and separated. Here, there is no time. The space of this cavern belongs to us all. As a viper, I twine, entangle, strike, eat, climb. Life has no intentionality other than that.

The oval stomach of a goat, stuffed with spiced liver and heart, simmered in her pot.

"Something smells good, Mother."

Hursag stood and dished two portions out of the goat stomach. The two of them ate by the low fire, and Colum savored both the food and his mother's warmth and closeness.

Swallowing the last morsel from his bowl, he announced,

"Ayylo is leaving the cave to go to the upper world. She asked me to go with her."

"What did you tell her?"

"I told her I had to stay here and be a father to my child."

"You know Ayylo loves you, don't you?" queried the crone.

Colum's blue eyes blazed in the crackling firelight. "It would be bliss to be with her, Mother. But something in me yearns to show my daughter the kind of love you showed me."

Hursag's hand caressed his cheek. "Whether you go or stay, your daughter will grow up treasured and happy, drinking milk from a panther's teat." The crone smiled at him. "I know that if you do stay, your love for this babe will prove as ferocious and tender as any mother's."

Colum planted a kiss on his mother's cheek and lay down on the furs. After he fell asleep, a dream came to him. In it, he lay on a straw pallet in a cramped iron cell with his head on Dervor's lap. Colum breathed in the cool blue air, tasting its slight trace of iron dust as he stared up at her haunting grey eyes.

"I miss you more than you know," he confessed.

"Oh, but I do know . . . I've always known."

"I'm so sorry you were sent back here and not to Illinee."

"Do not blame yourself."

"I'm going to be a father."

"What! Who is the mother?"

"Sny."

She gasped.

"Are you jealous?"

No reply.

"I'd like you to be my daughter's friend."

"She's part of you, my darling; how can I not? I already love her with all my heart."

He woke up still feeling the warm imprint of Dervor's lap under the back of his head.

CHAPTER TWENTY-ONE

Colum stared up at Ayylo's hearth, but no warm fire glowed there. He knew the Queen's daughter wasn't out foraging in the forest. She had gone to live on the surface of the world, and the sight of her dark ledge registered as a full-body ache. How he longed to hear the rich caress of her voice, her rippling laughter, or watch her sprint through the cave with a feline athleticism. Without the woman's shining presence, the whole limestone chamber felt emptier.

Oh, my beautiful Ayylo! How I loved drawing out the seashell pins holding your hair in place and watching those red-gold strands whirl down over your shoulders. Making love to you on that ledge was ecstasy. Am I an idiot to stay here?

The youth's knowledge of life in the cave was a web of endless intricate relationships, a web from which the man had been absent. Colum's trysts with Ayylo, however, belonged to both man and youth and helped him feel whole again. The youth was far more relaxed with the man's memories now and, at times, could even access his plutonic intensity and unsparing endurance.

Meanwhile, the man found it easier to shift and flow with life in the cave. He loved the youth's virile, emergent body. It no longer bothered him to smell of fermented beer or change his tunic in front of a myriad of watching eyes. Alive in a hive of humming bees, he discovered that he, too, could hum! And whereas before Colum's two selves had dialogued with each other, now they thought as one.

As Colum stood under Ayylo's ledge, *Dark Dreaming* burst unbidden into his mind. Her intrusion made him shudder. Since their encounter under the influence of his mother's red toadstools, he had thought often of this mysterious figure.

Colum felt a tap on his shoulder and turned to find himself face-to-face with the Queen. Her powerful emanations heightened all his senses.

"Mistress!"

Rows of ash-white cave bats, as thin as glassine paper, dangled upside down to form the cape she wore. Red veins laced their transparent wings. Here and there, a wing fluttered, letting Colum know they were alive.

Lillake's emerald eyes interrogated him. "You seek *Dark Dreaming*?"

Colum startled. "I think it's she who seeks me, Mistress."

"Follow me," she said and strode off, leading him to a remote antechamber not far from the river. It was the Queen's private space and the most secluded area in the cave. The bats on her robe began to chitter as soon as they entered. Inside, burning torches lit up the needle-fine teeth that filled their mouths.

"This is my innermost sanctuary. You may speak freely here," announced Lillake. "Tell me, Son of Hursag, what do you know of *Dark Dreaming*?" The bats on her cape quieted as if awaiting his answer.

"After the battle with Sny, Mistress, my mother gave me some red toadstools to eat. It was under their influence that I saw *Dark Dreaming*. She carried an energy different from anything I'd ever experienced. Different from the labyrinth or the cave."

The Queen's eyes locked on him. "Describe it."

Colum searched for words. "Dark. Ambiguous. *Diaphanous*. Powerful. She seemed to speak from deep inside me."

Lillake nodded. "Your heart beats faster at the memory. Tell me, Son of Hursag, were you attracted or repelled by **Dark Dreaming?**"

"Both, Mistress."

The Queen's green irises glittered in the torchlight. "Our cave is veiled to all but the most determined, yet you found your way here. Not by crossing the bridge into our forest as other men do, but by climbing down our spiraling staircase. Even though with every step you risked a fall into the Void." The Queen gazed at him a moment. "You were born seeking answers, Son of Hursag. And *something* in you knows that the answers you seek are found only in the depths."

He trembled, feeling the truth of her words.

"You possess a fierce drive to go wherever your questions take you. It's why you left London, a free man, to return to Nirah." She smiled. "It's what made you ravenously hungry to eat the fruit of the Tree in Nirah's throne room. And now that drive has led you to my private chamber . . ." Lillake paused. ". . . where you can communicate directly with **Dark Dreaming.**"

A cold panic entered his stomach.

"I've noticed your propensity to fall," said Lillake.

"Fall, Mistress?"

"Did you not fall out of the upper world into the labyrinth?"

"It felt like a fall."

"And in the labyrinth, did you not fall into the lake between Nirah's world and mine?"

He flinched. "Yes, Mistress."

"And did you not plummet with the pyrite into the earth's molten lava?"

His heart raced. "I did."

"And," said the Queen, "you nearly fell off the spiraling staircase on your way to us. In which case you would have spilled past us into *utter darkness.*"

Silence.

"I remind you of this because an encounter with *Dark Dreaming* may precipitate a still-deeper fall."

"Deeper than the core of the planet?" Colum trembled at the implication.

"Yes, my dear man," said Lillake with a short laugh. "So the question is, how deep are you willing to go?"

"I don't know, Mistress."

Lillake gave him an understanding look. "There's no shame if you leave now. Nothing will be lost."

"Nothing will be gained either." He felt like a fluttering insect on the Queen's web.

"Well, Son of Hursag?"

"I'll stay."

"Very well," said Lillake firmly. "Then we must create a more liminal, archaic space for the encounter to happen."

"Isn't this chamber archaic enough?"

The Queen shook her head. "Once *Dark Dreaming* manifests, she tends to disassemble the barrier between her reality and yours, so that your reality begins to blur. To maintain a firm sense of yourself, you must meet her in an in-between place." Lillake smiled. "And what is more liminal than that which lies within you?"

Colum understood at once. "My viper!"

"Can you awaken it?" asked Lillake.

"I'll try."

The dormant snake began to flutter inside Colum, feeling the intensity of Colum's intention to bring it to life. The viper strained to push through the deep, phylogenetic substrate of Colum's body. In response, Colum's immune and nervous systems became more mutable, more improvisational, allowing the viper to take them over. A radical alteration took place as Colum's human form slowly turned into that of a snake. Silky scales covered his powerful muscles. Hinged jaws moved on his triangular face. Cloacal scent glands picked up Lillake's odor. Thermally exquisite nerve endings, embedded in his facial scales, located exactly where her warm body lay. His now supersensitive eyes detected the infrared range of the Queen's antechamber. The transformation was now complete, shifting the ground of Colum's identity profoundly. Only this time, the viper's finely honed sensory data did not erase Colum's cognitive data, allowing his human awareness to remain intact.

The Queen, too, began to morph, her lengthening body stretching slowly and sensuously across the floor of her lair as she transformed into an enormous boa constrictor. Lillake brought her face close to his and communicated telepathically to him.

Once my transformation is complete, I shall swallow you.

Colum found he could respond in kind. *Swallow me?*

*I do this to make the boundaries between you and **Dark Dreaming** more porous.*

Colum grimaced, though the grimace was only in his mind. The viper's somatic awareness made him feel as if he consisted of pure nerves. A thousand different points pricked him. He reared back, away from the Queen's heat image directly in front of him. Colum felt himself as a single sensation of measured readiness.

Lillake spoke again. *I shall now swallow you into the darkness of my belly.*

The Queen's human head morphed into the flattened form of a boa constrictor, a serpent far more ancient than a viper. The boa's lush-textured, soft-scaled skin pulsed over a large muscular body. The larger snake bowed its lower jaw outward, dislocating it to adjust to the viper's shape, and began to swallow the smaller reptile tail first. The constrictor's muscular throat and mouth drew the viper further into its interior, then pushed the serpent's body leisurely along as if it were an item on a conveyor belt. At last only the viper's head remained exposed in the Queen's antechamber. With a final contraction, the boa constrictor's jaws closed around the viper's head. The viper disappeared into the boa's gullet and total darkness. The viper's torso rocked, slid, crimped, rolled, and spasmed toward the constrictor's interior like an ungainly lump of meat.

The movement finally ended, and Colum tried to enter a state of receptivity. Suspended in blackness in the belly of the Dark Moon, Colum felt safe, embraced even. Slowly, he began to discern a faint humanoid figure with two glowing eyes.

The figure spoke. *Dream with me if you wish to see deeper than the cave.*

Colum found himself gazing at a three-dimensional jumble of feathers positioned on a tree branch. The feathers twitched, and an owl's head emerged. The owl tilted its head with a look so comical it filled Colum with delight. His laughter sent waves of happiness through him.

The scene switched to a rowboat on a river. He was in the rowboat, leaning over the side trying to untangle a fishing line. Suddenly, a large pike leaped straight out of the water and body-slammed him, splashing cold water on his face and chest. The pike's prehistoric snout opened to bite off two of Colum's fingers with razor-sharp teeth. Colum's nervous system exploded with amazement and pain!

Surrender to the dream.

Colum made an effort to do so. Once he did, the river scene was replaced by one of Dervor walking through an iron corridor. *Such a great stride she has!* The depth and strength of his love for her rocked him. The mere sight of the woman snapped his nervous system into joy and vitality! The scene faded.

How is it that you can unleash such powerful emotions in me?

I paint with your palette of colors. Dervor, in the labyrinth, is the color of blue for you. If I use the exact shade of blue, you see her with your heart. Her blue stretches from the depths of the sea to the heights of the sky. It shines in the deepest darkness and makes you feel calm.

Colum felt Dervor's blue seeping into the pores of his skin, the cells of his body.

Ayylo is a fiery blend of red and orange. She quickens your heart, warms your blood, and fires your passion. Her orange-red colors grab all your attention.

Colum flashed on a curl of Ayylo's hair like a swirl of firelight, and on the amber flames in her eyes. For him she was love made visible, and his face flushed bright crimson at the mere sight of her.

Dark Dreaming painted a new canvas. In this one he saw an exploding volcano spew blistering molten ash high into the air. The sight held an uncanny, unearthly beauty. The ash billowed down, spreading like a grey blanket over a crowd of people. Asphyxiating heat scorched their lungs, and they began to die suffocating deaths. Ash-covered faces stared at him like grey ghosts. Colum turned away in horror.

Surrender to what is. Do not resist.

With great effort, Colum returned his gaze, only to find himself the sole participant of a new scene painted with grey. He balanced on a slippery rock ledge overlooking a body of dark grey water. With a shock, he realized this was Uncle's lake. He lost his balance and tumbled into the water, splashing and struggling. His spirit was crushed with a disruption so profound his sense of self barely registered. An existential dread filled him, so terrifying that Colum feared the thin veneer of his sanity might shred. Blind panic pounded in his heart.

Bow to the lake's purpose.

His mind screamed. *I cannot!*

The scene ended abruptly and a new one materialized. He stood on a hilltop with a panoramic view of soldiers sweeping over the earth like killer ants, clutching weapons and quivering in their eagerness to loot, rape, and kill.

War, glory, gore. Breathe deep the glorified gore. And color it bloodred.

The dreadful scene vanished, and a sense of profound grief swept through Colum.

For whom do you weep?

All of them. I weep for the slaughtered, and for the soldiers adrift in unrelenting enmity who risk losing their minds and hearts.

Silence.

Why are you showing me this?

So you may experience the full range and quality of your feelings and know your palette of colors.

But what you've shown me is such a sweeping torrent!

A torrent filled with potencies. Fiery excitations. Emotion with the power to move you to action. Without awareness of what sparks these different feelings in you or where they will take you, you'll be blown about by the prevailing winds.

I think I understand. Owl or pike or Dervor. Exploding volcanoes or warring hordes. In the grip of my erupting feelings, I act blindly.

Yes. Laughter, happiness, pain, or despair, each emotion fires your nerves to create a life-altering mood with the power to move you in one direction or another. You must see deeper. You must sacrifice your sun-related eye for an inner one.

A scene arose of him as a man sitting on the lap of a shriveled hag, milk spurting from her sagging teat into his mouth. Colum felt a nauseating repulsion. Then the scene shifted and he found himself a child in the same lap, but now it was the lap of a loving mother, her milk filling him with all that was sweet.

Your perspective determines how you see the world, and that becomes reality for you. The question is, do you have the desire to see more deeply? To see into, through, and around what you are looking at without muddying the colors of your emotions? Seeing all. Feeling all. Ask for your eye to open, Colum, so that you may see the entire spectrum of what life is displaying.

Dark Dreaming's form faded before he could ask more, and the boa constrictor began to move the viper's body out of its open jaws. A rank wetness glistened on the scales of the smaller snake's reticulated skin as it emerged into the rock chamber. Once there, it closed its eyes in exhaustion.

Colum awoke on the limestone floor in human form with no idea how long he had slept. His cheeks were sunken, and his damp, shriveled skin emitted a sour, acrid odor. His muscles made small involuntary jumps and shudders in an effort to shake off a near-total paralysis. He raised himself up, feeling weak and disoriented.

The Queen, too, had resumed her human form and now placed her hands on his shoulders to steady him. Suddenly,

Colum noticed the top halves of the two middle fingers on his right hand were missing. *The leaping pike!* He let out an insane laugh at the memory.

"What makes you laugh?" queried the Queen.

He held up his mutilated hand. "It wasn't a fantasy after all!"

She laughed with him. "Unless all life is fantasy."

Colum tried to get to his feet, but it made him dizzy, and his legs were too wobbly to support him. "I feel so . . . *strange*."

The Queen's emerald eyes flared. "With good reason, Son of Hursag. You have encountered **Dark Dreaming** in the belly of a boa constrictor."

He looked with gratitude at her shining face. "Thank you."

Lillake pressed her fingers against his forehead and he fell into a deep sleep. "Rest now," she whispered.

CHAPTER TWENTY-TWO

Colum sat alone in the Queen's antechamber with his back to the cavern wall. The Queen had left him there to gather himself together. Although his viper's long, sinuous body was gone, he had not yet shed the last of its reptile sentience.

To morph from one form to another is the air I breathe. It's who I am.

When he finally got up to leave, the low, sputtering light of torches on the wall illuminated his way back to the main cavern. It felt strange to return to the immense hall with its vaulting dome. He passed pillars of calcite and alabaster glistening in the firelight. The odors of food were everywhere. After the silence of Lillake's antechamber, the chattering, howling, screeching, tweeting, hissing, growling voices of the shape-shifting women sounded even more wild and inscrutable than before.

Colum had traveled some distance before he realized no one was calling out to him. Whenever he turned to greet someone, she would look the other way. It gave him an eerie, unsettled feeling. He passed Yaga's hearth, close enough to see her face twitch from the smoke of her fire, but when he tried to make eye contact, the crone leaned over her cauldron and stirred as if she didn't see him.

Relief flooded Colum when he finally caught sight of his mother in the distance. The last thing he wanted was to return to an empty hearth.

"Welcome, son," said Hursag with a warm smile. "Look what Abruta brought us from the lake. Fresh pike!"

"Wonderful!" exclaimed Colum.

With quick strokes of her long, blunt knife, she gutted and gilled the fish, then she plopped the fillet in a hot pan and fried it with herbs. The odor of frying fish alerted him to how famished he was. The youth poured himself a cup of water and drank thirstily.

"Sit, my son. It will be ready soon."

Colum sat on a rock to watch the fish fry, and before long his mother, smelling of smoke and fish oil, served him. He tore into the white flesh until only the bones were left.

"I saw you go into the Queen's chamber," she said.

He fixed his blue eyes on her. "I went to meet *Dark Dreaming*."

Hursag stared at the missing tops of his two fingers. With a grunt, she lifted his hand to examine them. "She had you dancing on a knife's edge, I see."

"I—"

Her hand went up to stop him. "You don't have to tell me anything. What transpired in the Queen's chamber is meant for you alone." Her look held more respect than sympathy. "You must go to Huluppu. She will attend to your fingers."

———

On his way to visit the Willow Woman, a wild rabbit zipped in front of him and nearly tripped him. Aneski, a young girl of four or five, went racing after it. The child leaped into the air to catch the rabbit, missed, and began to fall toward a blazing hearth fire. Colum dove across the short distance between them just in time to push Aneski aside, catching his own tunic on fire in the process. He patted out the flames with bare hands.

The next instant, a great horned owl flew down, changing

into human form as it came. By the time it landed, Aneski's mother, not the owl, was standing there. She pulled her trembling daughter into her arms. "You are fast, brother!" she cried. "Are you hurt?"

"I'll be fine."

Mother and daughter took off after the errant rabbit, which had zigzagged its way past several more hearths.

The encounter made him think of his unborn daughter, and of the love that flowed effortlessly from every woman in the cave for all their daughters.

Yet no one here knows the love of a father.

Colum arrived at the Willow Woman's hearth to find Sny visiting. Huluppu pointed to a flat rock by her fire. "Sit, brother. Join us."

He was grateful to feel welcomed. He looked at Sny, startled at how huge her breasts had grown. Suddenly, he saw the impression of tiny toes poking through Sny's tight robe. His utter surprise made the two women laugh.

"Go ahead, touch it," said Sny, still laughing.

Colum placed his hand shyly over the toe prints on Sny's belly. The next instant, they disappeared, followed by a hard kick. "She's always on the move, this little one."

Sny stroked her swollen belly, and Colum saw the wonder in her eyes.

Huluppu noticed Colum's wounds and looked among her jars for what she needed. She lifted his hand to gently smear salve over the area of his missing fingertips and wrapped a clean cloth around them.

"Thank you, Huluppu."

Sny stood up. "Colum, I am inviting you to be present at our daughter's birth."

Astonishment and gratitude spread across his face. "Thank you, Sny. I would like nothing better."

"Good." The huntress smiled and walked away.

Colum lingered with Huluppu, oblivious to the flying ash from her fire that landed in his hair and on his skin. "Will you be helping with the birth, sister?"

"Yes, as will your mother."

Huluppu was renowned as a midwife, but he had never seen his mother assist at a birth before. Nevertheless, he felt relieved to know both women would be there.

The Willow Woman looked at him. "Something bothers you, brother."

"It's just that Kle-Ptuza resents me so much I'm not sure I should be at the birth."

"Give her time. Sny has asked you to be there, and Kle-Ptuza has no choice but to honor her wishes. Once she realizes you aren't trying to usurp her place, she'll come around."

Colum frowned. "You know as well as I do, sister, that that's not likely."

"Perhaps, but each new birth is a wondrous event in our cave. Kle-Ptuza loves Sny and desires her happiness." Huluppu's moss-green eyes glinted in the firelight. "Besides, you have as much right to be present at this birth as any of us."

Colum's curls glittered in the firelight like loosely coiled snakes. "Thank you, sister." Huluppu, like his mother, had a way of making him feel as if his best self were his real self.

"Your mother says that the memories of the man-you-were have returned. Tell me, brother, do they flow naturally in you?"

"They do, sister."

"Does knowledge of your former life cause you conflict?"

"Not since Ethliu brought unity to my two selves. I do feel differently about who I am, though."

"I ask because I sense a new power and maturity in you, brother. Now I know it comes partly from that unity." The Willow Woman smiled at him. "You aren't a child anymore, brother. You're a grown man, and handsome at that. Nor are you just any man. No, brother, you are Hursag's son, born of our blood. A powerful serpent and a fierce fighter. Your battle with Sny and her pregnancy have awakened a new hunger among our sisters. There's a sexual heat crackling in your eyes. Your virility attracts many of them. If you were an ordinary man, they'd think nothing of asking Ayylo to share you with them.

But they've held back their advances because they've noticed the way the Queen's daughter looks at you."

"What are you saying?"

"I've never seen her look at a man quite like *that* before."

"Ayylo asked me to go to the surface with her," he confessed.

"Ah, I see." Huluppu studied him. "But to go with her meant leaving your daughter behind."

"I'm afraid so."

A soloist began to play a flute from somewhere in the cave. At the flute's stunning tones, the words of the poet Arthur Rimbaud burst into Colum's mind:

Stags suckle Diana,

Bacchantes sobs,

The moon burns and howls.

Venus enters the cave of blacksmiths and hermits,

Savages dance ceaselessly the festival of the night.

How many lifetimes ago had he heard those words? He remembered sitting in a concert hall in London during the war, listening to *Les Illuminations* by the composer Benjamin Britten. Through the voice of the soprano singer, he'd received his first whiff of the cavern's fierce, wild forces.

I was so moved that night! Did some part of me know even then that I would leave England for a deeper world? One where my saurian self could thrive? And my savage and civilized parts learn to vibrate as one? Tears ran down Colum's face. *I am living Rimbaud's vision! I know the power of toxic fangs. The sting of a panther's claw. With my own eyes I've seen raven wings sparkle with star-crystals. The bright vortex of fires lights up the festive night of the world I inhabit. I have gazed on the Dark Moon's face, danced on her web, stretched out in her serpentine belly. I have imbibed the milk of an ancient crone, made love to a goddess, writhed in orgasm as a snake myself.*

———

Colum left the Willow Woman to return to his own hearth. The flames of fires flared as he passed. Everywhere birds flew and animals roamed, hissing, buzzing, chirping, snorting, grunting, humming. He listened to the women's chatty, bellowing voices and the music of their homemade drums, flutes, and rattles.

What an acoustical experience this place is!

In the cave's twilight darkness, the dreaming mind and the waking mind were co-constituents of a deeper reality. The endless parade of shape-shifting women was an exultant phantasmagoria, their communal consciousness of self and animal continuous and predominant. Their loving acceptance and emotional tolerance of one another never wavered. Colum walked past a group of Bird Women lighting up their fire with wing gossip. These women were family, and he felt no separation from them. Colum loved their openness, which in no way detracted from the mystery they embodied. To him, the vaulted cave was an ensouled cosmos.

"Come join me, brother!" called out Amorpho, the Bull Woman, as he approached.

"Greetings, Amorpho!" Colum stepped into the circle of her hearth and sank down on one of her sitting rocks. A lark trilled overhead.

Amorpho held a bowl full of cured, dried, toasted tobacco leaves, which she pulverized with a pestle. She sat on a flat rock as she worked, spreading her legs wide to make up for her girth. When the tobacco reached the state of a fine powder, she dropped a straw made of a long, thin animal bone into the bowl. The straw's other end went into her nostril. With a gratified look, the Bull Woman breathed in the fresh tobacco powder. A satisfied smile spread across her broad face.

"Ahh, it is *good!*" Amorpho handed Colum a second straw. "It will be even better with a little age."

They took turns snuffing the tobacco. An antelope leaped past a little too close to their fire. Sparks flew. The frightened animal raced toward another hearth, slamming into its cauldron and spilling hot contents everywhere, then dashed off before it could be caught.

"That's Ishku's daughter," laughed the Bull Woman.

Colum laughed with her. "Looks like she's still new at shape-shifting."

Amorpho returned her large brown eyes to Colum. "I nearly shit myself with fear when I saw you disappear inside the dark recesses of the Queen's antechamber, brother."

"You saw me?"

"Oh, yes. None of our sisters have ever entered that chamber."

A moist breeze sent a whiff of bat guano up Colum's nostrils, where it mingled with the smoky aroma of his tobacco. "So that's why no one looked at me when I came out. They probably thought I was a ghost."

Amorpho gave a somber nod. "It made us feel uneasy. I could not fathom why the Queen would take you to her secret lair, Son of Hursag. She must have had a powerful reason, but that is between the two of you." She took another whiff of tobacco.

Colum drew on his bone straw as they sat together in silence.

After a while, Amorpho spoke again. "We are all fictions, brother. The cave itself is a fiction."

"It seems real enough to me."

"To me as well." The Bull Woman smiled. "And it allows us to play our favorite game."

"What game is that, Amorpho?"

"The game of Let's Pretend."

"You mean the one where we endlessly transmogrify?"

Amorpho slapped her burgeoning paunch and let out a deep belly laugh. "It enlarges our vision of what's possible! So let's have fun while the mirage lasts. Eh, little brother? Let's shoot poison with a snake's fangs and snort like a bull! Let us play while we can, you and I, in this world of illusions. Meeting different versions of ourselves as we go."

Colum had seen firsthand Amorpho's bullish power to charge, rush, trample, and toss aside anything that got in her way.

Did I actually regard this wild, ebullient, bombastic, uninhibited woman as freakish at one time? I love her! I love how natural differences are in this cave! A panther rips its prey apart with its teeth. A viper swallows its prey whole. A bluebird pecks at seeds. A bull grazes quietly on grass.

A current of fresh air blew down from a shaft above, swirling the embers and smoke in their fire. The sudden breeze turned the Bull Woman somber. "You suckled at a lion's teat, Colum, drawing in her wisdom, power, and essence." She paused briefly, then asked, "You don't plan to stay tucked away in our cave forever, do you? Not with Ayylo waiting for you on the planet's surface."

"I'm torn, Amorpho. I want to be with Ayylo *and* with my daughter. I've never known a father's love. Maybe I can change that by being a father myself."

The Bull Woman took another snort of tobacco. "The trajectory of your life is changing, Colum. More and more, I hear you speaking from the perspective of the man from the labyrinth. He came in with you as sleeping fragments in your mind that have now been awakened." She looked at him with tenderness. "What a dilemma, brother. Ayylo desires you for her lover just as you're about to become a father. Only you can decide which way to go."

He shook his head in confusion. "If I join Ayylo, I desert my daughter."

Amorpho nodded. "And if you stay, I fear Kle-Ptuza may come between you and your daughter."

The glow of her fire died down, and Amorpho put aside her straw and laced her fingers across her stomach.

"I had a dream of my daughter, Amorpho."

"Oh? What did you dream?"

His lips quivered. "I was holding her in my arms and could barely stand the joy of it."

"Dearest brother, I feel the love you have for this child. But if you decide to join Ayylo, go knowing your daughter will fold as beautifully into our existence as you did. And that her life will be filled with our love."

"I know that, sister." Tears fell down his cheeks. "I know it deep in my bones."

When he returned to his hearth, he found Hursag stretched out on their furs. He lay down next to her and morphed into a long, smooth-scaled, black viper. At the same time, his mother turned into a golden lion. The viper draped its head across the lion's furry chest, falling asleep to the sound of her heartbeats.

CHAPTER TWENTY-THREE

A pressure on Colum's shoulder roused him out of sleep. He looked up to see Abruta's face staring down at him, luminous and vibrant.

"The baby is about to arrive! Your mother is with Sny now!"

He leaped off his heap of furs, too emotional to speak, and hurried with her to Sny's hearth. Sny squatted naked in the middle of a circle of women gathered around her. Kle-Ptuza supported her on one side, while Egrat, a Bear Woman, supported her on the other side. The huntress grunted and tensed under the ligament-stretching movements of the baby's head coming forward. Her splayed legs wobbled slightly with the end of the powerful contraction, and the two women held her more firmly.

Colum stared in wonder at the scene. *It must feel like an earthquake is opening her up!*

The huntress rested briefly but was soon forced into another vigorous, protracted push. When it was over, she panted in a sweat. Hursag spoke in low tones to Sny. Then the laboring woman placed her elbows inside her knees to pull them wider apart. An excited anticipation filled the air as more women arrived to wait quietly in the background. They had witnessed the fierce violence of the child's conception, and her birth seemed to carry a portent for the entire cave.

Bruha clomped over to Colum with shining eyes. "Sny bears the effort of opening well, brother."

Yaga grinned at him. "Her tilled land is about to bear fruit!"

Hursag knelt in front of Sny to check the baby's position, and her fingers grazed the crowning head. "She descends," announced the crone. She began to massage Sny's perineum to stretch the tissue further. "Soften, sister, soften. It won't be long now," she crooned. "Keep breathing."

The force of the Panther Woman's next push made her whole body heave. It reminded Colum of being in the labyrinth and straining to pull an exceptionally heavy load of iron through an exceptionally long corridor.

"Push!" urged the crone. "*Again!*"

Sny bore down, grunting and pushing at the same time.

Colum looked at her with new admiration. *She does this like the supreme cat she is. Her whole focus is on the prize! Only the baby exists!*

Hursag's voice turned even firmer. "Once more. *Push!*"

This time the newborn slid out from between her mother's thighs and into Hursag's hands. She had entered a world of flickering firelight, warm air, and a swirl of strange sounds and smells. Colum heard the baby cry and stared in spellbound silence while Hursag checked her all over. The slippery infant's eyes and hands were wide open and her skin smooth and unwrinkled. Beaming, Hursag gently placed her granddaughter into the new mother's arms. Sweat and tears rolled down Sny's face. When Sny saw Colum, she smiled. Before long, the infant's rooting reflex kicked in, and she began to suck. Her little hand stretched lightly across her mother's breast. To be part of this amazing event filled Colum with profound reverence.

Huluppu gave Sny some water and wiped the sweat from her brow. Another wave of contractions began. Once the placenta was delivered, Hursag gestured for Kle-Ptuza to step forward.

Hursag took the infant and raised her high. At her side, Kle-Ptuza held up the placenta, and together they moved in a slow circle for all to see.

"BEHOLD OUR NEW SISTER!" announced Hursag.

"BEHOLD THE CHILD'S WOMB TWIN WHO CHAN-NELED THE LIFE FORCES TO HER!" called out Kle-Ptuza.

Exultant hurrahs and shouts went up everywhere.

With a quick slash her knife, Huluppu severed the umbili-cal cord. The cheers of the women continued as Huluppu took the placenta and Hursag tenderly handed the newborn to Kle-Ptuza. When Sny's mate returned the infant, Hursag turned to Colum and laid his daughter in his embrace. Some of the assembled women gave each other questioning looks, as others nodded their approval. Kle-Ptuza's face darkened.

Colum stared in wonder at the newborn with her soft head pressing lightly against his hand. Her facial features were flaw-less except for a vivid red oval birthmark at the hairline of her abundant black hair. Tears of love and gratitude spilled down his cheeks. A powerful sense of *Dark Dreaming*'s presence came over him, and he began to feel his brain and heartbeat mesh with hers in a rhythmic cadence. It seemed to him that she was inscribing his most intense life experiences in the infant: standing alone in his London kitchen . . . waking up in Uncle's corbeled throne room . . . having audiences with the king . . . laboring in the labyrinth . . . talking to Dervor in an iron cell . . . drowning in a lake . . . swimming with the pyrite . . . smelting iron with Sokar . . . sinking into the Cauldron of Rebirth . . . drinking Hursag's milk . . . shape-shifting into a viper . . . mak-ing love to Ayylo . . . dancing on Lillake's web. *Dark Dreaming* was somehow facilitating a profound transmission of all this information into his daughter in a matter of seconds. Just as it ended, Hursag took the baby back from him.

"May the daughter of Sny and Kle-Ptuza forever thrive!" cried Hursag, holding the child up once more. "The vigor of us all lives in her!"

Amorpho, her bosom rising up and down with emotion, came forward to anoint the infant's forehead and belly with a fragrant oil. "The stuff of stars shines in her eyes!" proclaimed the Bull Woman in a husky voice.

"Strong-boned she is, and sleek, spawned from the thighs of Sny!" shouted another with a joyful skip.

Young Aneski, whom Colum had saved from the fire, moved closer with her mother for a better view. "How beautiful is my new sister!" she exclaimed.

As a cacophony of voices called out in jubilation, Colum leaned down and spoke quietly to Sny. "You've given our daughter a wonderful beginning, sister. I am forever grateful."

"And I am glad you were here for her birth," she said, smiling.

He looked up to see Kle-Ptuza glaring at him, and he stepped back into the sea of enraptured women, not wanting to take the spotlight from her.

Abruta, all ten eyes twinkling, came up to him in the milling crowd of women. "I wish to congratulate you on your snake's fecundity, brother. Your daughter's presence graces us all."

He beamed. "She's beautiful, is she not?"

"Indeed she is."

Colum looked around at the multiple generations of women celebrating the birth of his daughter. He listened to their impromptu, ecstatic songs and watched them dance to show their happiness over this new sister. A wild orchestra of whistles, flutes, and drums played. Beer flowed. Women all over brought out raisin cakes, green figs, plums, and honeyed bread. From a distance, he could see Sny, babe in arms, lean lovingly against Kle-Ptuza. He couldn't believe that was his daughter sleeping at Sny's breast. Suddenly, from deep in his past, a line from the poet Auden arose. *"We are lived by powers we pretend to understand."*

Yaga shambled up to him, grinning in a way that widened the wrinkles on her face. "You bring us much happiness, brother," said the crone. Lank, greasy strands of uncombed hair escaped Yaga's cowl. "You are a most wondrous viper. I can only imagine what your daughter will shape-shift into!" The crone stroked Colum's cheek with her scrawny forefinger, and the tenderness of her touch made him quiver. "Such an unusual creature you are with eyes as blue as the morning sky. And so many *unpredictable* changes."

Colum wandered to the river's edge after Yaga left, full of high spirits. He had grown up with an affinity for the cave's snaking canal, cut out of limestone half a million years ago. Instead, he lay on his back, stared up at the dome, and listened to the happy festivities in the main cave.

Why did Auden come to my mind back there? How many lifetimes ago did I call London my home? I left an England shaken by war and mired in rationing and the deferral of pleasure. Austerity wasn't new to me when I arrived in the labyrinth. But "Brian" never liked sleeping on a prickly straw pallet on a cold iron floor. Nor would he have enjoyed lying on a pile of twisted fur next to a smoky fire. And he would have hated the arcane otherness of my utterly untamed sisters.

An image flashed in his mind of Dervor's face with her large, grey eyes, and his chest expanded with warmth. *She was so excited to come with me to the cave. She couldn't wait to call these women her sisters. And those wings she sprouted! I can still see their complex, vivid pattern of bold gold lines covering crimson feathers. Wings of splendor!* A pang of loss seared him at the memory. *You were the one who should have stayed, my love, not me. Yet in the end, you chose me over them. You never hesitated. I'm so sorry for what happened. Sny's baby should have been ours, and now the gulf between us is too large to breech. I can still feel you in my arms, my darling, and it makes me ache.*

Colum got up and went for a long swim. Much later, he returned to his mother's hearth, happy to find her there. Hursag patted the furs in front of her, and he lay down. He fell asleep breathing in the wood smoke.

When he awoke, he said, "I had a dream."

The crone's eyes twinkled. "What did you dream, my darling son?"

Colum sat up on the furs, still caught in the feelings of his dream. "I was in the middle of a thunderstorm. The sky was black. I held up a sword, one I forged myself from meteoric iron. Rain poured down in waves blown by ferocious winds that kept changing direction. All at once lightning hit my sword. The blade sizzled with electricity and the electricity shot into my eye."

Hursag stared at him intently, then stood and poured him some water. "Was that the end?"

He nodded. "After Sny took me to the forest, Mother, I started feeling constricted, even squeezed, being here."

"The cave is a womb, my son. The womb of the Dark Moon, our Queen. It gives us shelter in an eternal night. To be squeezed out of it sounds like a birth to me."

He thought of how daylight vanished in the cave. The only glimmers of light in the dark interior were fires tended by the women. He stared upward to see the smoke from those fires disappear through cracks and fissures in the domed ceiling. He knew the cave belonged to a different order of reality, but was it any less real than the surface world?

His eyes brightened. "Well, Mother, now that I'm free to go into the forest whenever I like and have a daughter to love, I don't feel restricted anymore." Then he frowned. "Kle-Ptuza has been surprisingly conciliatory, don't you think?"

"I would hope so since this birth is as special for her as it is for you."

———

Colum stayed away for a while to give Sny and Kle-Ptuza some time alone with the newborn. Soon, however, his need to see the child became too strong, and he found himself walking in their direction. From a distance, he could see Sny lying on a pile of furs nursing the baby. Huluppu sat by their fire while Kle-Ptuza handed the nursing mother a plate of fried trout and fresh greens.

"Who invited you?" she asked with unconcealed irritation when he arrived.

Colum's senses were as acute as any of his sisters. He could smell the output of Kle-Ptuza's sweat glands and read the level of her upset in the flare of her irises. "I came to see the baby."

"Come, sit, brother," invited Sny, and she gently pulled her breast from the infant's mouth. "Hold her while I eat."

Colum sat cross-legged on the furs and, taking the baby in his arms, stared in wonder at every detail of the infant's face.

Kle-Ptuza glared at him. "You think you're her father? You ejected sperm. *Nothing more.*" The Raptor Woman's eyes fastened on Colum. "Celebrate away, *brother*, but we are her parents, not you."

Colum, knowing it was pointless to respond, got to his feet and handed the infant to Huluppu. The last thing he wanted was to incite more rancor from Sny's mate. He did not want to risk being banished to the background of his daughter's life. Then he heard Bruha's clomping steps coming toward them. Before long, the Hippo Woman stood at Huluppu's side, cooing at the baby. Bruha leaned over to press her great moist mouth against the newborn's forehead in a kiss.

"Have you ever seen anything so beautiful!" The rim of hairs fringing the Hippo Woman's ears fluttered as delicately as eyelashes. "For this joyous occasion, I've brought my own honey cakes!"

Sny reached out her hand and pulled Kle-Ptuza to her side. Her mate yielded reluctantly.

Bruha's small eyes noted the baby's full belly. "I see the nursing is going well."

Colum, using Bruha and Huluppu as a buffer, turned to address Kle-Ptuza. "My only wish is to be part of my daughter's life, sister. I have no intention of displacing you."

"As if you could," Kle-Ptuza retorted acidly.

He cursed himself for his choice of words. "Of course. Forgive me, that's not what I meant."

Kle-Ptuza's face hardened. "As if either of us care what you meant. You nearly killed my mate. How can you be trusted with our child?" A dangerous glint entered her eyes. "Isn't it time you returned to your own kind, Colum? No one will stand in your way if you go back to London."

Sny gently stroked her mate's arm. "There's no reason Colum

should not feel joy at our daughter's birth. And remember, Mammi is not only her grandmother but Colum's mother."

"There is one reason and a very good one," replied her mate. "He *raped* you!" For a brief moment, Kle-Ptuza's eyes pleaded with Sny. "Have you forgotten? *No man* can be trusted!"

"Colum is not any man," intervened Bruha. "He is our brother, born of our blood."

Kle-Ptuza's copper eyes flashed at her. "All men are by nature liars and murderers! I'll say it again: you and the others trust Colum far too much. This is *our* space, our feeding-breeding ground. He's an intruder here and always will be." She turned to Colum and hissed, "Stay, and the time you have left with us will be less than a breath!"

He looked steadily into her eyes. "I don't want you for an enemy, sister."

"Then I suggest you follow Ayylo's lead and leave this cave."

Tension pulsed in the muscles of Colum's neck and shoulders. "I have a right to know my child."

"The *child*, the *child* . . . I wish you had never come to our cave to spawn your wayward whelp in the woman I love."

Sny's eyes flashed anger. "What are you saying? She's our child!"

Kle-Ptuza spun around to face her. "It doesn't look like that to me. You saw Hursag hand her to Colum in front of everyone. I don't like the way this is going. I'm being pushed to the side in favor of a man! And he's not some hapless man we'll never see again who happened to cross our bridge. Don't you understand? Colum lives in our cave, and every time we look at her, we'll see *him*. He will always come between us."

With a shock, Colum realized the huntress's hatred of him now extended to his daughter.

"You must not speak this way, sister," pleaded Huluppu.

Ruthless fury burned in Kle-Ptuza's copper eyes. "Have you, too, forgotten, Huluppu? We are the ones who rape the men! They serve *our* purposes; we don't serve theirs!" Rancor laced her every word. "Colum nearly killed my mate! And have you forgotten so soon that bitch who accompanied him to our cave? She nearly killed one of our sisters! What makes you think Colum's *progeny* won't grow up to stain our cave with our blood? Simply to have him here upsets the order of our lives. Am I the only one who sees him for who he truly is?!"

Bruha stomped her feet, visibly angered by the Raptor Woman's vehemence. "Who he truly is is our brother."

Kle-Ptuza pointed at the infant staring wide-eyed in the Hippo Woman's arms. "I'm telling you, Bruha, that baby may look innocent, but she endangers us all!"

The heat of Kle-Ptuza's anger seared Colum's flesh, and he backed away. The Raptor Woman's hand slipped to the knife sheath on her belt. She drew the blade with lightning speed and hurled it at the newborn. With a panther's quickness, Sny pushed Bruha aside and the knife plunged into the new mother's shoulder instead. Kle-Ptuza yanked the blade out of her mate, then struck Sny's jaw with its hilt hard enough to knock her out. She turned to face Colum.

"You're the mistake!" he cried, venom in his voice. The drive to protect his child spread through every cell of his body.

Kle-Ptuza lunged at him, her glare as sharp as her knife. Filled with rage, Colum's fighting instincts took over and he dodged her. Kle-Ptuza flew past him, skidding to a stop several feet away.

Women came running toward them from every direction. They had witnessed Colum's battle with Sny, and they knew anything could happen between these formidable combatants. Raw excitement hovered in the cave's smoke-filled air.

Kle-Ptuza charged again. This time she flew through the air, the ball of her extended foot aimed at Colum's chest. Once more he was too fast for her. The raptor let out a scream of incredulity and landed with a thud. The two fighters circled one another, each looking for an opening. Kle-Ptuza found hers, and her kick landed square in Colum's chest. Women scattered as he stumbled backward.

For a heart-stopping second, Colum began to vibrate. The women watched breathlessly to see if his coiled viper would explode into form, but Kle-Ptuza came at him too soon and the vibration ended. The copper-haired woman sprang into the air. Colum flung himself at her and their two bodies collided, crashing down on the cave floor together. They sprang to their feet. Before Kle-Ptuza could act, Colum's hands locked into a single fist and slammed up under her chin in a blow so hard it would have killed anyone else. Kle-Ptuza staggered as she got up, the veins in her neck pulsing. The two foes parted with heaving chests, sweat streaming down their faces. They paused as they caught their breath, then Kle-Ptuza rushed Colum. Murder blazed in her eyes and her fingers extended into talons. This time the woman's sharp nails raked Colum's right shoulder, lacerating his muscle tissue. Kle-Ptuza twisted her neck like a bird, then sank her teeth deep into the side of Colum's forearm. He yanked himself away, leaving strips of his torn flesh still in her teeth. Kle-Ptuza shrieked, enraged. Their fight was to the death and everyone knew it.

Colum leaped forward, tackling his rival and pushing her to the ground. Blinded with fury, he grabbed her knife, ready to plunge it into her heart.

As Colum looked down at Kle-Ptuza, suddenly he saw her with new eyes. Her face glowed with a golden light as beautiful as the dawn. It was as if the woman's true presence beamed luminously and diaphanously in front of him. The bedazzling image of her streamed directly from his heart and he recognized her as a Great Spirit. Swept up in the magnificence of his shimmering vision, tears of wonder ran down his face. The profound transformation turned Colum's murderous rage toward Kle-Ptuza into a love bordering on bliss. He felt himself enter a flowing intimacy with her as oceanic as the sea itself, and for one luminous moment, they were no longer rivals. Her spirit washed over him so completely there was no separation between them. To fight her was to fight himself, and his knife fell clattering to his side.

Kle-Ptuza's lips drew back in a snarl. Without hesitation, she reached out, seized the knife, and sliced through Colum's throat. Blood spurted into the air. The raptor's face twisted in a triumphant grin as her prey collapsed to the floor sideways.

Stunned gasps could be heard from all those who watched.

A tall birdlike figure with yellow feathers whispered, "Our brother was winning! Why didn't he kill her?"

Kle-Ptuza, her rage quelled at last, stood up expecting cheers, but there were none. The women stood rooted to the ground, unable to process what had just happened. An ominous silence filled the cave.

Abruta broke through the crowd. "Make way! Make way!" Kneeling next to Colum, she ripped off a piece of her robe and tied it tightly around his nearly severed neck, stemming the spray of blood.

Hursag rushed behind her, and the women parted in waves to allow the crone to pass. She gathered her dying son in her arms, positioning him half upright so he could breathe.

"I have you, my son, don't try to speak."

A loud thrumming sounded in Colum's ears, making it hard to hear. His breath, bubbling through a severed trachea, turned harsh and ragged. He was losing sensation in his fingers and toes. He fought to keep his eyes open, looking up at his mother. But when he tried to speak, only a gurgle came out.

"Shhh, my son, there's nothing you need say." The crone's voice filled with infinite tenderness. "Rest now, exactly where you are . . . safe in my arms."

What are these lights I see, Mother? Galaxies glimmering all around me. Is that the sound of space I hear—stars and planets swirling in their orbits as they blink in and out of existence? He stared down at the earth as if he were floating above it. *Oh, look, Mother! I see Dark Moon's web glittering everywhere! How beautiful it is!*

Colum gazed back at Hursag with dimming sight, his breath a shallow froth. A blanket of cold crept over him. His body slumped in her warm arms, and she cradled him closer. He could hear only the crackling of fires.

Hursag saw her son's face go slack. She gently closed his eyelids. Then she threw back her head to let out a single, high, keening cry. The sound of her cry reverberated throughout the cave, turning his death into a reality for everyone.

Yaga shambled over like an old, tired bear. She knelt by Colum's body to run her trembling fingers through his wild curls one last time. The crone then stood and released her own full-throated howl. Soon the cave's interior roiled with agitated shouts, wails, and moans, like undulating waves in a storm. Bewilderment, frustration, and grief, along with an *unfamiliar discomfort*, filled the cavern with a violent caterwauling.

"There is no breath in our brother's nostrils!"

"He shall dance no more on the web of life!"

"Our brother's eyes are forever darkened!"

"See how pale he is! His life blood is poured out!"

"Nevermore shall the ring of our brother's laughter resound in our cave!"

"His spirit has fled!"

"His light has gone out!"

The Queen shimmered in the air like a hologram. The next instant, her translucent, ephemeral form stood fully enfleshed in front of them. She looked at Hursag with deep compassion. "I felt him expire, sister, and came." The Queen knelt by Colum's body and kissed his pale lips, then spoke in a voice meant only for him. "You did it, didn't you? You saw with a *new eye*."

Silence settled heavily in the cave for an interminably long time. Everywhere, untended fires burned low, some sputtering out completely. Without the light of the women's fires, the cave would only be a black sinkhole in the earth.

Finally, Bruha broke the silence as she stepped next to Hursag with a folded cloth of white linen under her arm. "I thought you could use this to wrap him in, sister, for his burial in the forest," offered the Hippo Woman, tears falling down her cheeks.

"No, Bruha," said Hursag, "we shall wind no sheet around him. My son was never meant for our forest."

Strega, with tears streaming down her own craggy cheeks, approached to look at Colum. "But sister, our brother is worthy to be buried there."

"No, Strega, I fear the depths call to him still," replied Hursag.

The Queen turned to her. "Tell us what you wish to do with your son's body, and it shall be done."

"Deliver it to the Void."

Somewhere in the crowd, a young girl whispered to her mother. "What is the *void*?"

"The *dark unknown*," came the reply.

In the back, behind the crowd that had gathered, Abruta made her way like a robed shadow to Sny's hearth. Silently, she lifted the baby from where she lay on the furs next to her still-unconscious mother. After tucking the sleeping infant under the folds of her robe, Abruta hurried off unseen toward the tunnels.

Women all over the cave fidgeted nervously where they stood. As far as they knew, the lid sealing off the Void had never been moved. About to be exposed, the women felt caught in a spell of stasis, a pause before a prelude. And, they knew in their bones, this prelude harbored a power fundamental enough to change them all.

Colum's mother leaned over his blood-sprayed body and, with her tears falling freely onto his face, kissed his closed eyes and still lips.

Lillake's voice rang out. "Prepare yourselves, sisters! Our brother shall enter the Void!"

Nervous moans and quiet gasps could be heard throughout the cave. The Queen strode to her throne, with its two stalactites hanging down on either side, and pushed the iron chair aside, revealing the heavy circular slab of iron beneath it. She lifted off the iron lid as if it were weightless and set it to one side. Those close enough and brave enough to glance down at the impenetrable, inky darkness below leaped backward at once. Women from every corner of the cave stared breathlessly at the Queen. Huluppu, Strix, and Bruha lifted one side of Colum, while Hursag, Amorpho, and Yaga raised the other. The six women carried him in a quiet procession to the edge of the Void's opening. All the other women moved forward with them.

"Our brother's sojourn with us has ended! Drawn by the Great Beetle, the Self-Existent One, he came to us, and drawn by the Great Beetle, he takes his leave of us!" Lillake paused for her words to register throughout the cave. "Colum is our cherished brother! The only brother our cave has ever known!" She paused again. "He returns to the ground, from which all things rise, to the origination of himself!"

The women who carried his body laid it down by the only aperture in the cave that opened onto endless darkness. Hursag then took hold of her son's shoulders, while Lillake leaned over and lifted his ankles. Together they positioned his feet on the edge of the black hole. Hursag nodded at the Queen, who unloosed her firm hands from around Colum's ankles. At the same moment, the old woman let go of his limp shoulders, and he dropped through the fissure into the black rift of darkness.

Those close enough to see let out a single outward breath, as if the cave itself were expiring. Kle-Ptuza herself reeled when she saw Colum fall into the primordial deep. What dreadful powers lurked there?

Hursag alone caught the fulgent gleam of gold and crimson beetle wings unfolding far below her son, and she whispered into the darkness, "Fly with Bambara, my son. Be the flame you are."

As the Queen slid the iron lid back in place with her strong arms, a grating vibration of loss could be heard, one that played every woman present. With Colum in the Void, the canvas of the cave seemed to fray.

Lillake turned a dark look on Kle-Ptuza. "You have done this deed. How did things go so awry?"

Amorpho shoved the confused yet still defiant Kle-Ptuza closer to the Queen.

"Mistress," answered the Raptor Woman, "we are a *sisterhood*. Everyone knows that men have no place among us. All I did was rid the cave of an enemy. We should be rejoicing, not weeping."

Sparks flashed in the Queen's green eyes. "Are you blind, Kle-Ptuza? You broke our only *column*. Because of *you*, his vital iron has been wrenched out of this cave and plunged into the Void." The timber of her words sent a shimmer of wild fright through everyone, including Kle-Ptuza. "For this I *would* utterly destroy you. Yet how can I end your life when Colum himself refused to?" The Queen was silent a moment, and at her silence, all the flames in the cave turned blue. "No, the fate you wished for him is now your fate. You must leave this cave, never to return."

Kle-Ptuza stiffened in shock.

A stunned silence spread through the cave once more, for no sister had ever been exiled.

All of a sudden, Sny, aware that Colum had been murdered at the hands of her mate, burst through the crowd to stand in front of the Queen.

Tears streamed down her face. "Mistress, I beg you to have mercy. Don't send Kle-Ptuza away!"

"She no longer has a place among us, sister." There was no wavering in the Queen's emerald eyes. Without another word, she waved her arm, and Kle-Ptuza vanished.

Sny staggered and would have fallen if Strix hadn't caught her.

"Ready yourselves," declared the Queen, "for our column has fallen."

"*Our column has fallen!*" repeated a chorus of women.

"And we are in the pause before a new solar dawning."

"*A new solar dawning!*"

Lillake's voice intensified, reverberating throughout the cave. "Our snake slumbers, and *ALL IS IN FLUX!*"

EPILOGUE

Abruta stood at the top of the spiraling staircase, where she had emerged into a small cave, and checked on the infant secure in a sling across her chest.

"Sleep, sweet child, so freshly out of your womb-world," she crooned. "I'm sorry to deprive the cave of a treasure as precious as you."

She walked past the metal lid on the ground, exactly where Colum and Dervor had discarded it so long ago, and strode quickly to the cave with the lake. She skillfully traversed its slippery rock ledge. The water remained placid as she crossed, splashing in calm waves against the limestone cliff. Abruta didn't need a torch to find her way, since no darkness was impenetrable to her eyes.

On the other side of the cave's ledge, she entered the labyrinth. The woman's face was inscrutable under the floppy shell of her hood. She moved like a shadow through the iron corridors, easily evading Uncle's slaves as she navigated the maze. At last Abruta arrived in the hallway containing the men's sleeping cells. She approached one of the cells, giving the door a slight push. It swung open and the hooded woman stepped inside.

Dervor sat cross-legged on a straw pallet. Abruta pushed her hood back to reveal her ten eyes. The woman's robe, frayed and dirty at the hem, still smelled of woodsmoke.

"Abruta!" cried Dervor, scrambling to her feet.

"My dearest Kasi," she said quietly, "it pains me to have to come to you under these circumstances. I know this will be difficult to take in, but there is no time. The Queen has sent me to ask for your help."

"What help could I possibly give the Queen?" she asked incredulously.

All ten of Abruta's eyes glistened in the blue light as she lifted the baby from out of the folds of her robe, holding her up for Dervor to see. "This is Colum's child, Kasi."

A sharp gasp escaped Dervor.

Abruta held the infant out toward her. "Would you like to hold her?"

Dervor looked wary as she allowed Abruta to place the newborn in her arms. "Where is Colum?" asked Dervor. "And why are you bringing his baby to me?"

The multi-eyed woman hesitated for a brief moment. "Colum is dead, Kasi. He was killed in a battle with Kle-Ptuza."

A torrent of grief escaped Dervor as a deep wail.

"I'm sorry, my child," Abruta said softly. "I grieve with you. We all do." Abruta sat in silence for several moments as Dervor sobbed. "The Queen is entrusting Colum's daughter to you. She wants you to raise her on the surface of the earth."

"Me?" Dervor sputtered. "I'm a slave!"

Abruta shifted five of her eyes to the baby. "I'm here on the Queen's behalf to ask Uncle for your freedom."

Dervor looked at the infant, catching a glimpse of Colum in her face. The sight softened her broken heart.

"I know this is difficult, Kasi, but the Dark Moon sees deeper than we do," said Abruta gently. "Come."

―――――――

The two women moved silently through the iron corridors. When they reached the throne room, Meath, the door guard, admitted them without a word. Uncle stood up from his iron throne as they entered.

"Greetings, Nirah," said Abruta. "I think you know why I'm here."

The king nodded. "Lillake has communicated with me. I know that Colum is dead. Such a fall has the power to change all our destinies." Uncle stared somberly at the newborn in Abruta's sling. "I never imagined when Colum went down the spiraling stairs that a daughter would ascend them in his place."

"Nor did I, Nirah," replied Abruta. "We live a profound mystery."

Uncle walked over for a closer view of the infant. "How can one so small carry knowledge as deep as the labyrinth and the cave?" He returned to his throne and sat down. "What does the Dark Moon ask of me?"

"My Mistress wishes for Dervor to raise the child on the surface of the earth."

Uncle held his hand for a moment over tired eyes, then, looking at Dervor, said, "I knew how dangerous it was to send you and Colum to the cave. But I never could have foreseen the story that unfolded in the wake of that decision. Nor the depth of its consequences. I fear his death may have loosened both labyrinth and cave from their moorings." He was silent a few moments, then raised his gaze to Dervor. "Are you willing?"

Hot tears rolled down her face as she looked into the baby's bright eyes. "I am, Master. For Colum's sake . . . and for hers."

"Very well. I will provide for your material needs. I will also assign one of my men to assist you as you build a life for yourself and the child. When you leave the labyrinth, the path forward is yours to decide. I will not interfere." The king stood and walked over to Dervor. "My dearest one, I honor your decision to raise this child. You are now free. There is no guide for what you must do next." He embraced her. "We may not see each other again."

"Don't forget us," Dervor said, fresh tears welling in her eyes.

"That is not possible."

ABOUT THE AUTHOR

Merrilee Beckman earned a BA in religious studies from the University of Iowa. She worked as Assistant Chaplain at the University of Iowa Hospitals, taught in public schools in Iowa and South Dakota, and spent two summers on a lookout tower in Idaho working for the US Forest Service. She later studied the works of Carl Jung, which led her to become a dream analyst.